W9-AMM-149

Someone's
In the Kitchen

Someone's
In the Kitchen

Eric E. Pete

E-fect Publishing
HARVEY, LOUISIANA

© 2000, 2002 Eric E. Pete. Printed and bound in the United States of America. All rights reserved. No part of this book may be reproduced or transmitted in any form or by any means, electronic or mechanical, including photocopying, recording, or by an information storage and retrieval system—except by a reviewer who may quote brief passages in a review to be printed in a magazine, newspaper, or on the Web—without permission in writing from the publisher. For information, please contact E-fect Publishing, PO Box 2425, Harvey, LA 70059-2425.

This novel is a work of fiction. Names, characters, places, and incidents are products of the author's imagination or are used fictitiously. Any reference to real people, events, establishments, organizations, businesses, or locales are intended to give the fiction a sense of reality and authenticity and is entirely coincidental. We assume no responsibility for errors, inaccuracies, omissions, or any inconsistency herein.

Third printing 2002

ISBN 0-9704995-1-5

LCCN 2002090665

ATTENTION CORPORATIONS, UNIVERSITIES, COLLEGES, AND PROFESSIONAL ORGANIZATIONS: Quantity discounts are available on bulk purchases of this book for educational, gift purposes, or as premiums for increasing magazine subscriptions or renewals. Special books or book excerpts can also be created to fit specific needs. For information, please contact E-fect Publishing, PO Box 2425, Harvey, LA 70059-2425; ph. 504-433-1727; www.e-fectpublishing.com.

For Marsha. We did it…again.

—Eric

ACKNOWLEDGMENTS

First of all, thanks to my divine muse, God, creator of my "spark" and who has given me the strength to do this. Much Love.

To my darling wife Marsha and my cutie of a daughter (and future heartbreaker), Chelsea, thanks for being there and putting up with my time on the road and long nights at the computer writing while listening to music you probably hate. I love you both so much.

To my mother, Edna, thanks for getting out there in "the trenches" and telling everyone about your son, the author and his books. If anyone wonders where I get my energy from, they only have to look at you.

To all my fans, both old and new, thanks for the support from all over. It's good to know my work's being felt.

Words cannot express the thanks I have to give to my family and friends who have either bought my first novel—*Real for Me*, offered encouragement and support, given me a place to stay while touring the country or simply have told someone about my work. It is all appreciated. Thanks for believing in me. Special shout-outs to Tommy Lemelle and John Jackson for assisting me during the long hours of my first tour.

To my extraordinary "ghost readers"—Jacqueline Scott, Carmel Johnson (President of the Eric E. Pete fan club), Shontea Smith, Natalie Lumpkin-Brown, Jamie Lemonier, Jackie Simien, Demetrius Mitchel, and Judith "Jaye" Bostic. Thanks for taking the time out of your busy schedules to provide me with feedback.

To my fellow authors and friends who have been so supportive along the way, many times going above and beyond what anyone could hope for: Timmothy J. McCann, Karen E. Quinones Miller, Eric Jerome Dickey, Troy Martin, Robert Fleming, Donna Hill, Earl Sewell and Dackeyia Q. Simmons.

To everyone in the media, thanks for taking the time to hear what I had to say, including but not limited to: Jackie Simien, Monica Pierre, Sheletta Smith, Cynthia Arceneaux, Don Tracy, Shonell Bacon, Vanessa Echols, Kelley L. Jones, Edmund W. Lewis, Michica Guillory, Tavis Smiley, Janine Haydel, and Chezon Jackson.

A very special thanks to my friends, L. Peggy Hicks, publicist extraordinaire, of Tri-com and Lisa Cross of the Sistah Circle Book Club. I also cannot forget Tia Shabazz and the Black Writers Alliance as well as my fellow Nubian Newsers. All of your help and assistance has not been forgotten.

To the book clubs that really keep this going including, but not limited to—RAW Sistaz, The Sistah Circle, Souls of Sisterhood, Voices from the Pages, Pages Reading Group, Sistah Girl, Circle of Friends II, Good Book Club, Sister to Sister, Phenomenal Women, Sister-Friends, Soulus Book Club, You Go Girl, Sistahs On the Reading Edge, Soulfully Speaking, The G.R.I.T.S., Journey's End, Afro Thoughts, SistahFriend, African American Reading Club, The Black Women's Reading Circle, Black Women with Book (BWB), Go On Girl, The Bourbon Street Book Club, Lady Godiva Book Club, and Lucky Sisters.

To all the bookstores and booksellers that make it possible for us storytellers to reach the public, thanks. I have to mention these booksellers in particular who really welcomed me in my first year "on the scene": Black Images Book Bazaar, Afro-American Bookstop, Community Book Center, African American Images, Nu-World of Books, Reflections Bookstore, CushCity.com, Montsho Books, Heritage Bookstore & More, Books for Thought, Karibu Books, TheBlackLibrary.com, Apple Book Center, Culture Plus Books, Shrine of the Black Madonna, Black Classics, Dorothea's African American Books & Gifts, Basic Black Books, Afro Books, Cultural Connections, Smiley's Books, Zahra's Books 'n Things, Medu Bookstore, Nubian Bookstore, Alkebu Lan Images, Janice Doctor, A&B Books, Forest Sales & Distributing, Moore's Cultural Expressions, Afrobooks, Blacknificent Books & More, Black Facts, The Black Bookworm, Out of Africa, Waldenbooks-Louisiana (Lake Charles, Lafayette, Gretna) and Mississippi (Biloxi), Books-A-Million-Louisiana (Gretna, Monroe, and Lake Charles), Barnes & Noble-Louisiana (Baton Rouge), Texas (Houston-Galleria), and Illinois (Bloomington), B. Dalton-Louisiana (Gretna and Baton Rouge), and Borders-Louisiana (Metairie).

I can't leave out all the beauty shops and barbershops that helped spread word of my first novel, *Real for Me*. A special thanks to: Rhonda Mullins, Sean Lewis, Zelika Russell, Sharon Jarvis, and Lisha Vining.

To all my co-workers who have been so supportive and have really made me proud to be a part of the same organization, thanks for believing in me. I can't leave off Joe McGhee (Miami Hurricanes #1 Fan), Yvette Richards, Walter Ennis, Grady Faucheaux, Clarence Bertrand, Jhay Davis, and Bob Finley.

To everyone in Houston, my old stomping grounds, and New Orleans, my current home, thanks for the love.

To anyone else that I may have missed, luv ya! Believe me, any omissions were unintentional. Sorry I couldn't mention everybody individually, but you are not forgotten.

"Can't stop. Won't stop. Believe that."

1 Reggie Collins

I remember that day in April as if it were yesterday. I was eight years old at the time. We were still living in down in Victoria, Texas then. I had received an "A" on my math test that morning and couldn't wait to get home to tell my mother. I wasn't good at math back then, so I was especially proud of myself. It had rained all day at school and they kept us inside for recess. I remember looking out the classroom window at the gray sky and fidgeting in my chair the rest of the day.

When the school bus stopped on my block, I pushed my way past my schoolmates. I wanted to be the first one off the bus so bad. The bus had dropped us off early this time. The rain had passed over and the clouds were parting. Steam was now rising off the pavement as the sun beamed down from above. It was now hotter than it was before the rain fell. My black Chuck Taylors plowed through the remaining puddles next to the ditches that lined my street. The bottoms of my Toughskins were soaked, but I didn't care.

The gate to our chainlink fence was already open so that cut a few seconds off my time into the front yard. We lived in a small, basic white house on raised brick columns back then. It had a set of cement steps at the front, which came up onto a screened porch.

My mother usually kept the screen door locked, but I didn't have to bang on it this time. I figured that she had expected me and left it unlocked. I started opening my backpack on the porch to take out my math paper. The front door was pushed shut, but was unlocked too. I knew a big hug awaited me inside. I called out my mom's name, but there was no answer.

I left my backpack against the wall and walked past my dad's black leather recliner in the living room. I heard dishes clanking and noises coming from the kitchen. My mother must have been finishing up some dishes before my dad came home. My hands proudly gripped my test paper on both sides as I rounded the corner to the kitchen.

"Momma?"

A little boy was not prepared for this. Like a cartoon character, my eyes enlarged and my paper fell to the kitchen floor. My mother was in the kitchen, alright. She even had somebody helping her. Our neighbor, Ray from next door, had her bent over the kitchen sink and her hands were flailing around in the dish strainer. The sounds the two of them were making still play in my head. I felt like my heart was going to burst, as I didn't know how to deal with this. My mother's eyes opened as she let out a scream. The scream was *before* she noticed her little Reggie standing there witnessing her freakfest. She stood up suddenly and knocked Ray down to the floor. He fell onto the cracked tile and started fumbling to pull his pants up while my mother ran toward me. She tried to explain that I didn't see what I saw, but I turned and ran off.

I ran out the door and leapt off the porch past the steps. I hit the ground running and was probably down the street before my mother realized I was out of the house. I zigzagged between a few parked cars and ducked down. I caught my breath and hid until my mother's voice died down. I knew she had to return inside to clean up "things". When the coast was clear, I walked over to my favorite tree and climbed up into the large oak.

My dad found me later that evening and talked me down. I don't know what my mother told him, but I never brought it up. The look in his eyes told me he knew. I never saw much of our neighbor, Ray, after that day either. He would always scurry back inside his house whenever my dad was outside at the same time. At 6'5, my dad could be pretty intimidating although he was usually a quiet, but firm man. My mother ran off a year later with another man. We never heard from her again. I never knew what went wrong in my parents' relationship, but I tried in vain not to blame my mother.

My dad would always tell me, "Life is hard, son. You have to be harder."

Shortly after my mother jumped ship, my dad and I moved one hundred twenty-five miles northeast from Victoria to Houston, Texas. My dad had found a job at the Port of Houston. We moved into a house in the South Park section of town that was better than our previous house. After the move, my dad wandered through relationships with women, most of them very nice, but they never seemed to last. I've been in Houston ever since and have never returned to Victoria. I didn't fully understand what had happened that day in April until I was older, but it scared the shit out of me. I wasn't gay or anything, but I didn't want anything to do with sex until I was in high school. When I got to Jesse H. Jones, my hormones overruled my fractured psyche. Most of the kids in my neighborhood had started a lot earlier than me, but I was quick to make up for lost time.

2 Reggie Collins

"Shit."

My day had been going great up until this point. I had made my one-year anniversary as supervisor with Stratford Circle Insurance. My employees at our Sharpstown claim office even presented me with a cake that morning. My probationary period was over and I was on my way to more money and more problems.

Problems went with the job, but I always seemed to have my own set that followed me. Problems like the key marks all over my Pathfinder as I walked out onto the parking lot. I had begged them to put up a fence, but the company higher-ups gave that a thumbs-down. They didn't want the impression of not being part of the community. As I walked closer, I realized there were words scrawled into the side of my ride. This had nothing to do with the neighborhood; this was sealed and delivered to me personally with a kiss.

The words "LITTLE DICK" were etched into my black paint job in more than one spot. Heh. Trina had an imagination on her; I'll give her that. The words couldn't be further from the truth though. At least the psycho-bitch didn't slit my tires. My amusement was brief as I heard the other employees walking out the side door onto the parking lot behind me. I had planned on asking them out for happy hour, but had to change those plans. I unlocked my ride with my remote and jumped in. I looked back in the rearview mirror as I sped out of the parking lot and onto Bissonnet. Couldn't have people laughing at me even if the words weren't true. I punched the steering wheel out of anger. Trina was always a crazy bitch, but this really pissed me off. Money didn't

4

grow on trees and I wasn't about to report this to my insurance company. Women were always my weakness…but then again, I guess I was their weakness as well.

I met Trina at Club Expressions on the north side last year. It was after the Maxwell concert. I should have known she was trouble when whoever she was with left her ass stranded. She was so damn fine though. If I didn't jump on the poontang, somebody else would have. I hit it that night. Didn't even make it back to her apartment. She told me to pull over on the side of the road before we made it to her apartment and we did it in the back of the ride. Wild. Of course, we did it again when we got to her crib. She told me later that she really wasn't stranded. She had seen me and told her friends to leave. Don't know if she was shittin' me, but that was her story. We had our relationship of convenience, but I always kept her at arms length. Trina had a Jekyll and Hyde thing going on and she was quick to blow up. This past weekend, she had wanted me to come over to hook her up, but I was busy. The NBA playoffs were on and besides, I didn't want her getting too comfortable with me. I'm sure the graffiti had something to do with that. I could have filed a police report, but I didn't need anyone else seeing Trina's work. Besides, I wasn't positive she had done this. I'm sure there were a few other unhappy females in Harris County. If it was Trina, I was going to kick her ass later.

Rush hour was about to peak and I had to find someplace to take care of my ride as soon as possible. Think, man. In my job, I had to be familiar with most of the body shops in H-town. I needed some place that would paint for cheap, but good and some place that didn't know me. I remembered this Mexican shop that sold rims and did repairs over in San Jacinto, but there had to be one closer. A little kid in the car on the side of me had read the words and was asking his mom who was "little dick". I raised my windows, kicked on the A/C, and turned up 97.9 The Box on my radio.

I thought of this shop on Westheimer that had repainted my pal, Me-Me's car when someone had keyed it. They did a great job and it didn't cost her much either. I didn't remember the name of the place, but I had nothing to lose. I made a left and whipped my Pathfinder onto Hillcroft.

It was near closing time, but the shop was still open when I drove through the front gate. The sign on the front read "M. Hernandez & Sons". I quickly exited my ride, wanting to separate myself from the shit keyed into it, and walked toward the structure that served as the "office". I could tell the shop used to be a gas station years ago. The island where the gas pumps used to be was still there. The lot was filled with cars and trucks at various stages of completion. That didn't bother me. I was focusing on the ones that had new paint jobs. Their work was impressive, but I only needed a basic paint job. No metallic flakes or shit like that.

I slowed my walk toward the office and removed my tie and watch. No need having them think I was loaded and ripping me on the price. We had a casual dress policy at work, but I still liked to sport my Antonini Loretta now and then. I did a lot of Happy Hours after work and looking good and dressing good never hurt with the ladies.

As I stuffed my tie and watch into my right pants pocket, a Mexican gentleman roughly my age walked out of one of the garages to my left. He was wearing gray coveralls and a white mask dangled around his neck. He wiped the sweat off his brow as he approached me.

"Yessir."

"I need a paint job on the Pathfinder over there," I answered while pointing, "Someone keyed it."

The guy seemed confused. I realized he wasn't that fluent in English when he walked toward the office to get some assistance. He came out with an older guy in a shirt and slacks. I guessed that he was the business end of the establishment.

"Yessir!" the older Hernandez said in the same manner as his son.

I explained my situation to him as well and the three of us walked over together to give the damage a look-see.

"Hmmm. It's not too bad, my friend. I could have this finished in a week maybe."

The younger Hernandez was smiling and spoke quickly to his father in Spanish.

The elder laughed and looked at me. It didn't take a rocket scientist to figure out what they thought was so funny. I kept the same straight face. It was too late to try to get a rental car, so I made a call to a friend on my cell. I got lucky and reached her before she left her office for the evening. I gave her directions and then went into the office to discuss the price with Mr. Hernandez.

3 Reggie Collins

It was almost an hour later when Lila's red Honda S2000 came screeching into the parking lot from Westheimer. Lila had the top down and her long, jet-black hair was blowing in the wind. It was creeping up into the nineties today and the sun had begun to tan Lila's pale yellow face. If she weren't careful, she was going to wind up with a case of sunburn. The thought of a sister catching sunburn made me chuckle.

Lila Reed was an exceptional woman in every sense of the word. She had the looks, the drive, and the intelligence. She was an attorney with Casey Warner and Associates, one of the more prestigious plaintiff firms in H-town. I first met her when I was just a claim rep with Stratford Circle. I had a claim that involved one of her clients. We argued for days while negotiating and wound up settling over drinks one night. Amidst all the screaming and hair pulling, we found there was an attraction along with a healthy dose of sexual tension. We celebrated that night in just the fashion I liked and had been bed buddies since. We were usually on opposite sides when it came to business, but that made for great sex in our personal life.

As I jogged over to Lila's car, I noticed her eyeing my Pathfinder. She lowered her sunglasses and looked up at me.

"Hello, Champ," Lila said as she blew a kiss at me. She thought of her nickname for me in the bedroom one night.

"Hey. Thanks for picking me up."

"You're lucky you caught me. I was about to tell my secretary to take my calls for the day. So...what did you say was wrong with your car?" She was looking in that direction again and trying to see what was damaged. She would have to get closer to see the marks...or the words.

"Keyed. Somebody keyed it. Ready to roll?" I had put my watch back on and had situated myself inside the small confines of her car.

"Sure." Lila seemed content with my answer and put her sports car into gear. She revved the car up and screeched the tires as we made a circle and roared out onto Westheimer heading east.

I smiled as I watched Lila shifting in the sun. She had a way of concentrating when she was driving. She never took her gaze off the road, even in the middle of a heated conversation. I guess I would concentrate too if I had a car like hers. Nothing escaped her notice though. She even saw me checking her lines out. Lila's navy blue pinstriped suit fit her well. I'm sure her wardrobe gave her an advantage in negotiations with most men and probably some women out here. Sexy, sexy. If I weren't such a player, I would have made a move to make Lila mine and mine alone.

"Stop."

"Stop what?"

"Looking at me like that. It's not like you haven't seen me before."

"Lila, you know I never get tired of looking at you."

"Save it, Champ. Keep that line for those silly little girls in the club that be jocking you."

"What about you?"

"Please. It wasn't any of your weak lines that got me that night. I just thought you were so damn cute. Being good in bed helps too."

"Thanks for the compliment, I guess."

"So, who keyed it?"

"Huh?"

"Who keyed your baby back there?"

"I don't know."

Lila took her eyes off the road and looked at me with a smile. "Don't know?" she asked with a smirk.

"Am I being cross-examined, counselor?"

"*Heh.* Alright. Alright. I'll leave it alone. I know you know who did it though. They say when it'll be ready?"

"About a week. I was going to get a rental, but it was too late when I noticed it."

"Why didn't you just wait until tomorrow to drop it off?"

"…I dunno. Just wanted them to get started right away."

"Put a leash on her before she does it again. At least the bitch is literate."

I covered my face and sank down into the tight little space called the passenger seat. Lila must have read the words when she circled around to leave the shop. Nothing escaped her ass.

While stopped at the red light on the corner of Westheimer and South Gessner, a Vietnamese kid in a yellow Honda Accord challenged Lila to a race. Lila asked him what he had to offer and when he said all he had was his car, she told him it wasn't enough and drove off when the light turned green. We had passed a lot of the strip malls and were now crossing Voss. The neighborhood was becoming drastically upscale and well manicured as we came upon the Galleria area where Lila's townhouse was located. This is also where the ratio of BMWs and Jaguars to Chevys had suddenly increased. She lived right down Westheimer from the paint shop, which was one of the reasons I called her. After passing the Galleria, Lila downshifted and whipped the car into the left turn lane at Post Oak Boulevard. When the green turning arrow came on, we sped off again. We were heading toward Lila's high-rise townhouse in Villa d' Este on Uptown Park Boulevard.

"Umm, I thought you were taking me home."

"I am. I just need to stop in real quick. You okay with that?"

"I guess. I don't really have a choice."

Lila smiled at me again and replied, "Yeah. You don't have a choice."

We passed a posh little shopping complex on the right hand side as I looked up at the golden tower Lila called home across the street from it. The female security guard signaled Lila in as we entered the property and sped past the guardhouse. Lila slowed again and her headlights came on as we descended into the parking garage. Her tires were making that irritating squeaky sound on the garage floor as she turned the wheel. Lila took her shades off, as her eyes adjusted to the darkness, and looked for her parking area. Spot number three twenty-five was waiting there for her as usual. Lila brought her S2000 to a stop on the dime. I helped her latch her top closed once she raised it up.

We walked over to the elevator lobby and Lila inserted her card in the reader slot. Within minutes the ding sounded and the elevator doors parted. The elevator took us straight up. One day, I would be living like this too. Lila jingled her key ring like she had something on her mind, but said nothing.

"You know, we never did it in an elevator," I suggested as I ran my finger against the back of Lila's hand.

"Is that *all* you ever think about? I'm not even about to get thrown out of here and lose my deposit."

"You know I'm just messing with you, Lila."

I moved closer to Lila and began massaging her shoulders after pulling her jacket down slightly. Lila moved her hair out of the way for me. Her moan of approval let me know how bad she needed the rub. God, I loved touching her. The touchy-feely moment was cut short by the ding of the elevator as it stopped. Lila grabbed my hand off her shoulder and led me out of the elevator and down the hallway to her door. She was about to insert her card in the door slot when she turned around and kissed me instead. Her lips tasted like peaches. I was going for her tongue when she turned back around to resume opening her door.

"Make yourself at home. I'll only be a minute," she said as her long yellow legs took her further into the townhouse. The white carpet in Lila's place always intrigued me. Heaven knows I couldn't have a place with white carpet. It would be gray *quickly*. I felt guilty just walking on the stuff. I hadn't noticed, but Lila had slipped out of her heels and left them by the door. Maybe that was her secret to a spotless carpet. I decided to follow suit and kicked my shoes off as well.

Ikea was making some serious money off this sister. She did have good taste though. I walked over to this marble table that had Lila's Florida State and sorority paraphernalia displayed on it.

"Hey, Lila," I hollered, "Are these your line sisters in this picture?"

"The one where I'm squinting with the goofy smile?" Lila replied from out of her kitchen.

"Yeah."

"Yep. That was my line at FSU. How about you? How come you didn't pledge anything while at Texas Southern?"

"It wasn't me. Besides, it's hard to pigeonhole yourself when you're all things to all women. Heh."

"Conceited ass. It's not all about getting the opposite sex and partying, Reggie. It's about service to your community, bonding, and growth....Of course, we did party with the best of them."

"Lila? What are you doing in the kitchen?" I had turned and was walking toward Lila's voice now.

"Come see."

I walked past Lila's window view of Memorial Park and I-610 on my way to her kitchen. The cobalt blue tile felt cool under my feet. Lila was standing over the island with her back to me. As I walked closer, she turned around.

"Surprise!" Lila had just lit a single candle on a cupcake that was sitting on the island.

"What?"

"Thought I didn't know, huh?" Lila had a smile from here to Galveston.

"Huh?" I wasn't sure what Lila was talking about.

"Your anniversary, stupid! *As supervisor? No more probation?*"

"You remembered?"

"Yep. Actually, one of your reps reminded me. I was on the phone today with her when she had to go celebrate. Sorry I didn't have time to do more for you, but you caught me off guard when you called for a ride. I already had cupcakes from last night, but I had to pick up some candles at the store."

"So, that's what took you so long to pick me up! Thank you."

"Are you going to blow out the candle?"

I closed my eyes out of habit and blew out the candle. It wasn't my birthday, but I wished for success in all phases of life. These little things Lila did for me always made my stomach knot up. I knew our relationship came with no strings attached, but the commitment alarm was sounding nonetheless. I was lost in my thoughts.

"Hey."

Lila's voice had a low, sexy tone that brought me immediately out of my daze. The stomach knots left me. I looked up....and down and took in the view. Lila had a devious look on her pointed face as she leaned against the kitchen wall with her arms folded. Her skirt was missing. She was still wearing her pinstriped jacket, but the sight of her perky C-cups heaving up underneath told me there was nothing else up top. I hadn't noticed in the car, but Lila was wearing stockings. The thigh-high stockings were attached to her white silk panties by garters. My hard-on was killing me.

Lila knew how badly I wanted her at that moment, but I still tried to play it cool. I walked toward her with the cupcake in my hand as I took a bite. Lila moved away from the wall and met me in the middle of the kitchen floor. Her eyes trailed downward as she looked at me. I had forgotten about my necktie dangling out of my pocket until I felt it wrapping around my neck. Lila had the tie in both hands and pulled me into her. I felt Lila's breasts pressing against my chest as my hands found their way underneath her jacket and against her smooth back. Fuck the cupcake. I let it drop to the floor. Lila's lips brushed against mine and I closed my eyes. She took my upper lip inside her mouth and began licking the frosting off my moustache with her tongue. The kisses/sucking became heavier as I yanked Lila's jacket off. Lila responded in kind and pulled my shirt open, which sent buttons flying onto the blue tile.

I really wanted to satisfy this beautiful friend before me. I picked Lila up and raised her above me. I bit at Lila's mid-section as I carried her over to the island. I gently lowered her onto the island counter and laid her back as I pounced between her legs. I unsnapped the garters with a "pop" and proceeded to remove her panties. Lila knew what was to follow and whispered an "Oh yes." in anticipation. True to form, I didn't disappoint.

I found my way straight to her spot and went to work with my tongue. I used my hands to fondle Lila's breasts and to keep her spasming body from falling off the counter as I worked her into a fever pitch. I felt her nails digging into my scalp, as my face was pulled deeper and deeper.

Once she was begging for the real deal, I pulled her up off the counter and carried her into her bedroom. Lila's glistening body, nipples erect, bobbed up and down on the waterbed as I stood over her. It was always so damn good with her. I started unbuckling my belt.

"Do you have a condom with you, Champ?"

"Huh?"

"Do you have a condom? I mean, I want the dick, but I don't take chances. You're out there bad at times. You dig?"

I smiled and replied, "Yeah. I dig. I don't have one though."

"Top drawer of my nightstand. I've got ribbed and extra lubricated for you. Surprise me."

Lila never took any mess. That's probably what turned me on about her. I carried my naked ass over to the nightstand as I prepared to do some bodysurfing with Ms. Reed on the waterbed.

"Baby. Baby. Wake up."

"Unnnhhhh."

"Shenita. The alarm went off."

"Unnnhhh! Shit. I heard you." Shenita fidgeted under the covers and pulled them further over her head before sighing.

My wife was definitely not a morning person these days. I remembered how it was when we first married. We used to wake up extra early just to make love. There were now the rare horny occasions when she would wake me from my sleep and would be riding on top of me, but they were as rare as Martin Luther King Day parades in South Carolina. Our mornings spent talking and looking into each other's eyes were reduced to her grunts as she walked into the bathroom while pulling her draws from out of her ass. This morning was no different.

Shenita sat up in the bed five minutes later. It was going to be another mad dash to work.

"Hey, baby."

"Hey. You need the car today?"

"Yeah. I need to check on some locations before work tonight." I knew what her reaction would be.

"Still thinking about the restaurant, huh? Don't you think we have enough debt already?"

"It's not like that. I…"

Slam. Shenita was in the bathroom running the shower. The sound of the door locking made it abundantly clear she didn't want company in the shower.

We had been married for four and a half years and we had

been in our new home on the north side for six months. The house still was only half-furnished and we had to sell one of our cars just to afford the note and property tax, but it was brand new and it was ours. Something to build on.

I got up out of the bed and grabbed my warm-ups from the armoire. I had all day to make myself decent. I was one of the chefs at the Mirage restaurant on Richmond and usually worked evenings. It was only our different work schedules that allowed us to get by with one car. "Getting by" was used loosely. Shenita hated having one car now.

Almost an hour later, our Dodge Stratus was backing out of our driveway in the cul-de-sac. Shenita was driving as she was running late...again. Our neighbor, the minister, was walking his little rat-faced dog and waved at us as we ran the stop sign by Spears Road. Shit. I hated riding with her when she didn't have her morning coffee. Shenita didn't utter a word until we were on I-45 heading south. When she arrived at her job at Questcom, she would be sure to blame her tardiness on the construction work.

Traffic was slow on I-45, but it hadn't stopped completely. The closer we got to town, the worse it was going to get.

"Shit. I hate this traffic." Her hands were squeezing the steering wheel. I turned on Majic 102 to ease the mood and decided to change the subject.

"I'll probably dress for work before I pick you up this evening. That way, you can just drop me off at Mirage."

"That'll work. Neal, are you going to need me to pick you up when you're off?"

"Nah. Get some rest, baby. Reggie will probably stop in tonight. I'll just ask him to bring me home."

"Uh huh. Are we doing something with Reggie soon? Y'know Kelly's birthday is coming up."

"I'll bring it up tonight. I'm sure he'll be down for the trip to New Orleans. Kelly still feenin' for him, huh?"

Reggie was my best friend since our days at TSU. He was from South Park and I was from Brookshire, but we still got along when we first met on the yard. He was even around when I first met

Shenita during Homecoming. Reggie and I were roommates in
Cuney Homes then and he was there when I brought her back to
our place to cook for her. Reggie was always the wild stud back
then and still is. I was more of the one-woman kind of guy.
Funny…when I first met Shenita, I thought Reggie was more her
type, but she proved me wrong. Shenita had been in town visiting
her cousin and we started seeing each other once or twice a month
between here and New Orleans. We were married before the Jus-
tice of the Peace a year after I graduated. Reggie was my best man
and Shenita's sister, Kelly, was her matron of honor.

Thinking about our history together brought back a lot of
fond memories. I smiled at Shenita and hoped that we could re-
capture what we once had. We were approaching the Cross Timbers
exit and Shenita would be turning off up ahead. Shenita worked in
the Questcom Superstore inside Northline Mall as a sales rep and
didn't particularly care for her job. I understood. I knew all about
being in a job that didn't appeal to me. The difference was that I
was one to do something about it. It was my dream to own my
own restaurant and it was a dream I planned on making a reality.

"Hey, do you want me to come by for lunch today or cook
something for you?"

"No, I know you want to check out some property today…I'll
try to be more understanding. I'll just get some fast food in the
mall. Oh! Don't forget to mail the payment on the credit card
today. We'll have enough in the account by the time they receive
it." Shenita had stopped in front of the west mall entrance near the
Magic Johnson theatre and left the car running.

"Give me a kiss, Neal." She was putting forth the effort. I
leaned over and obliged.

Shenita looked at the clock in the car and shuffled off into
work. I crawled over the center console and into the driver's seat.
The Mrs. stopped to wave before disappearing. She was as lovely as
the day I met her.

I was left alone and with the car. I had the whole day free and the
city of Houston's commercial real estate market was calling out to me.

5 Reggie Collins

"You're ready for me to drop you back at your apartment?"

"Damn. I'm all breathless and you're ready to dump a brother off on the curb. Heh. I didn't even finish my cupcake." I was drenched in sweat as I rolled over to the padded edge of the bed next to Lila. She was sitting at the foot in her white terrycloth robe.

"Please! Normally I would say you can stay, but I have a big deposition set for tomorrow and need to prepare. If it wasn't for that, I'd be ready for round two."

"Oh no! You're not killing me on a weekday. I have to be able to work tomorrow, y'know. I'm going in the shower *now*."

"Run away, Champ!" Lila laughed as she swatted at my ass on the way to the shower.

I was always ready for round two with Lila, but I played the scared role to make her feel better. I had things to do at my apartment as well, like finding out if Trina had something to do with keying my shit.

It was almost nine o'clock when Lila dropped me off at my apartment on the southwest side. We shared a long, passionate kiss in her car, before I got out. I combed the bushes before I went up my stairs. I didn't need any more crazy surprises.

I was turning my alarm off when the phone started ringing. I closed the door, locked it, and ran over to the phone stand.

"Hello?" I fumbled to pick up the phone before my answering service came on.

"In the middle of something, bro?"

"Nah, Neal! I just got back, that's all."

"Happy Hour again?"

"Nah. It ain't even like that. Lila just dropped me off. Someone keyed my shit."

"What??!!"

"Yeah, dawg. All over." I didn't bother bringing up the words etched into my ride.

"Damn, bro. Sounds like all that fucking around is catching up with you, Mr. King-Dick."

"Shit ain't funny. At least it wouldn't be my own *wife* keying my shit. Speaking of that, you and Shenita getting along any better?"

"…I guess. She gave me a kiss this morning. She seemed okay when she dropped me off at work too. Hey, you passing by here tonight?"

"No. Can't, dawg. I'm without wheels until tomorrow morning."

"Damn. I need a ride home tonight."

"Check with Me-Me. I'm sure she'd be okay with that. She's working tonight, right?"

"Yeah. I'll check with her."

"How's my girl doing? No problems at work, huh?"

"Melissa? Shit. She's probably the best waitress here. You making me look good by her being hired. Don't worry. I know how protective you are of your 'lil' sis'. Nobody's fucking with her."

"Good. I appreciate your looking out for her."

Neal was right though. I was protective of Me-Me. I had been like that since that night at the park back in high school. I was best friends with Joseph, or Jo-Jo as we used to call him, growing up in South Park. Melissa was his little sister, but everyone called her Me-Me. Me-Me would tag along with us wherever we would go. Yep. She was a regular little tomboy back then. Me-Me was a freshman at Jesse H. Jones and we were juniors when everything changed for all of us. Jo-Jo and I decided to shoot hoops at Edgewood Park one night. It was a school night and getting late, so Jo-Jo sent his little sister home. We had been playing with a couple of smart asses that we wanted to shut up. I had a bad feeling as the night went on, but didn't go with my gut. Jo-Jo had real skill and was planning on a scholarship from U of H. Jo-Jo's last play ever was a slam over both of the smart asses on an alley-oop from me. The guys started talking all kinds of trash and Jo-Jo was the first one to walk off. He turned his back and didn't see one of the fools pulling a gun from his gym bag. I saw the .25 go up in slow motion and froze on the spot. Three shots were already squeezed off when I screamed to Jo-Jo to look out. I don't know if it was shock or fear of being shot myself that caused my throat to lock up. Hell, I was only sixteen. Still, Jo-Jo didn't deserve to go out that way. I took Me-Me under my wing as my lil' sis from that day on. To this day, I don't know if that was more out of guilt or a sense of responsibility. I'd like to think that I was just doing what was right.

"Reggie?" Neal had finished shouting out orders to someone in the kitchen and was continuing the conversation.

"You know who keyed your shit?"

"I'm not sure. I've got an idea of who though."

"Trina?"

"Yep. Did the shit at my job too. If it's her, I'm gonna pay her back."

"Yeah? I been told you to leave that psycho-bitch alone. The pussy ain't worth all that noise."

"I'll handle it, Neal."

"Look, I gotta go. These idiots are about to burn something in here. I'll holler at you later, bro."

I grabbed a Heineken from the fridge and put on my Michael Franks CD. I strolled over to the bedroom while humming and entered into my walk-in closet. I was looking for something to wear for work when I realized it. I hadn't eaten anything today...for dinner that is.

It was another busy night in the kitchen at Mirage. One customer had sent back a steak as being undercooked and sent it back again when I put the burn to it. Some people were just hard to please. I was taking all this in as a learning experience though. If... *When* I owned my own restaurant, I was going to have to deal with this. I was so used to being isolated in the back that I lost touch with what the management was going through up front. Management had to be pleased with the reviews I was helping Mirage get in the Houston Chronicle.

"One of the top five eateries in all of southeast Texas, if not the entire south." That was my favorite review. Hell, it was my first. Mirage served what they called "Texican-Caribbean" cuisine. I don't know what the hell it meant, but it did make for interested customers. I had to laugh at creations like "Jerk Chili", but it actually didn't taste bad. Cooking had always been a knack of mine. I loved to cook since I was a little kid.

If it weren't so pathetic, it would be funny how it started. My pops used to beat my moms on the regular after coming in from selling cars all day. "Just doing what a man's gotta do, boy," he used to say with a sly smile. Pops claimed he learned that shit from his dad who came here from Jamaica. He always felt he had something to prove. Anyway, the only place moms found peace in the house was in the kitchen. She used to shed tears while she chopped up the onions and celery for dinner and I was right there at her side. Pops hated my being in the kitchen, but I guess that was one of my ways to strike back at him. Deep down, I think pops had feelings of inadequacy and expressed them the only way he knew how…but then I only took two psychology courses at TSU. Moms finally had her freedom when she passed away from that aneurysm a few years ago. The bastard.

Reggie wasn't going to be able to give me a ride home so I needed to ask Melissa before I forgot. She had been passing through the kitchen all night. I had stolen a glance or two as she walked by humming to herself. The girl had a voice on her, but I don't know if anybody ever told her. The girl also had a nice body on her too, but that definitely wasn't for me to tell her. I was supposed to be looking out for Reggie's little sister, not gawking at her.

"Neal?"

"Huh?"

"Did you hear what I said?"

"N, no. What'd you say, Melissa?"

"Is this my salad here?" Melissa was standing behind me in her black and white waitress outfit. Her thin glasses were resting on her nose. She was twisting the ends of one of her micro-braids in her left hand. The smile told me she wasn't annoyed by my brain cramp.

"That's it. The one on the left."

Melissa snatched the plate off the counter and was zipping out the doors just that quick.

"Hey. Melissa?" I called out to her. She caught the door in mid-swing and stuck her head back in.

"When you get a second, I need to ask a favor of you."

Melissa paused for a second, then responded with a nod.

It was after midnight when Melissa was driving me home in her old Corolla. Melissa needed some gas when we left Mirage, so I volunteered to fill her tank. It was the least I could do in exchange for her making the long drive to my house. We stopped at a Chevron gas station by the North Loop.

"You need anything else in the store?" I asked her as I walked up to the bulletproof window to pay. Melissa gave her usual cute smile and nodded "No". I surprised her with a bag of chips and a strawberry soda.

"I told you I didn't want anything. Thanks though," she said laughingly.

"You can save it for later, Melissa. I hope you like Sour Cream and Onion."

"Neal?"

"Huh?"

"Do me a favor. Call me 'Me-Me'. You sound like my father with that 'Melissa' shit."

"Okay. That's fair, Me-Me. I'm older than you, but I don't think I'm close to being *that* old."

Me-Me laughed at me and we continued our drive north up I-45. I was sleepy and the drone of the car engine was lulling me even more. As I drifted close to the edge, I heard Me-Me's voice singing softly along with the radio.

I was thinking to myself and blurted out, "Have you ever thought about the Apollo?"

"What??!!"

When I heard Me-Me answer, I realized that I had spoken aloud. I sat up in my seat and blinked my eyes a couple of times.

"Your singing. I hear you at work in the kitchen and when you're on break. You're always singing…like a little angel. You need to get on the Apollo." I felt a little embarrassed by what I had blurted out and my voice dropped off at the end.

Me-Me looked at me in confusion for a full five seconds before bursting out in laughter, "Boy! Get the hell outta here! Humph. I *wish* I could blow like that. I wouldn't be driving this old piece of shit for one." She really didn't know she had a gift.

I left the issue alone and told Me-Me to take the next exit onto Rankin Road. It was as still as a graveyard out here at this time of night on a weekday. Funny how different these roads would look in less than nine hours when Shenita would be on her way to work in bumper to bumper traffic. I wondered if she was sleeping soundly now. My dream was for Shenita not to have to worry about traffic ever again.

We headed west on Rankin until we came to my neighborhood. I instructed Me-Me to make a left turn.

"*This* is where you live?" Me-Me asked in surprise. "All these houses are new. Damn."

"Yeah," I replied shyly "they still have lots for sale. Of course, the prices keep going up."

"I didn't know you were living large like this, Neal." I pointed to our cul-de-sac for Me-Me to turn into.

"Please. Living large is something I'm definitely not doing. You know how many banks we had to go through before we found one that would loan us the money? Heh. We had to sell one of our cars just to be able to make the note. On top of that, we're in debt up to our ears, we're still paying on student loans...."

"Okay! Okay! Enough already! You don't have to convince me. You are definitely *not* living large. Happy now?"

Laughter from both of us filled the car as we arrived in my driveway. The lights were still on in the living room.

"Okay. Can I say you have a nice house without your going off on me?"

"Yes. You can. Thank you. We have Reggie over sometimes. Maybe you can pass by with him one day."

"Cool." Me-Me took her glasses off and was rubbing her eyes.

"Are you okay? I'm not going to hear about you falling asleep behind the wheel am I?"

"No. Just a little eyestrain. I probably need new glasses, but I refuse to go with anything larger than these. At least with these, people think they're for fashion."

"You can probably get new lenses in the same size. Your glasses do fit your face perfectly."

"Aww! Thank you."

"...Well. I guess I should let you go now. You really need to think about what I said about your singing."

"Yeah....whatever. What about you? What do you want to do?"

"You really want to know?" I was about to exit the car, but turned back toward Me-Me and repositioned myself.

"I asked, didn't I?"

"My own restaurant. Something to call my own. I really want to do better for Shenita, my wife. She deserves better than the job she has to put up with now. Hopefully I can give her that freedom."

"You're a good man, Neal. She's lucky to have you."

And with that, the outdoor light came on and Shenita walked out the front door on cue.

7 Neal Wallace

Shenita was barefoot and wearing one of her red silk robes. Under normal conditions, the sight of her looking like that would have turned me on but these were far from normal. It was one in the morning, Shenita was out on the front lawn, and I was sitting in someone's car in the driveway. As Shenita approached the passenger side of the car, I saw it. The look in her eyes. She was drunk...and pissed off.

"Shit," I cursed aloud.

"Is something wrong?"

"My wife. She's trippin'. I gotta go." I grabbed the door handle to let myself out, but it was too late. Shenita was already at the window and peering in. Her hand slapped across the glass. Her ring made a "smack" sound that sounded worse than what it was; still Me-Me and me jumped in response.

"What the fuck is she doing??!!" Me-Me shouted out.

I managed to open my door enough to give me room to get out without hitting Shenita. I gave Me-Me an apologetic look before heading out to the front line.

"...the fuck are you doing out here with this bitch? Nigger, I will kick your ass and her ass too!" Shenita was waving her finger in my face, but was maneuvering around me for a view of Me-Me. This was some embarrassing shit.

"Shenita, go in the house. She works with me. She just gave me a ride."

"A ride huh? I thought Reggie was bringing your ass home. Move outta the way!"

Shenita made it to the car and opened the door. Me-Me shouldn't be in this shit.

"What the fuck are you doing in *my* driveway with *my* man, ho?"

"Baby, c'mon. You're drunk and making a fool out of yourself."

"Shut it, boy! I'm talking to the lady here. She can talk for herself. Cantcha, ho?"

Me-Me was straining to hold her mouth back and spoke. "Mrs. Wallace. I was just giving your husband a ride home. Reggie's car is in the shop and he told Neal to ask me. I work with Neal at Mirage. My name's Melissa and not 'ho' or 'bitch'. Now, I've gotta go, so I would appreciate it if you would close my door...now."

Whoa! Me-Me actually managed to shut Shenita down...and without lifting a finger.

Shenita backed away from the car and I moved in quickly to fix this mess.

Before I closed the car door, I leaned in and said, "I am so sorry, Melissa. Shenita's ..."

"Drunk as a skunk. That's what she is. Look, it's okay. I told you to call me 'Me-Me'."

"Sorry, Me-Me. I'll see you tomorrow."

"Okay. Bye."

Me-Me backed out of the driveway and drove off. I looked around at the other houses to see if any lights had come on. I didn't see any. It would take a few weeks before the neighborhood gossip got back to us to know if anyone saw this go down.

"Shenita, you're drunk. Let's go in the house."

"Damn right I'm drunk. I'm waiting for you to come home so I can make love to you and I find you in the driveway with some ho from work."

"There you go again! I told you nothing was going on."

"Yeah. Yeah. Whatever."

I walked Shenita inside the house and closed the door. Shenita had started that drunken giggle of hers as she followed me to the bedroom. I was pissed off and frustrated as I started undressing. I threw my shirt on the floor when I felt Shenita's hands undoing my belt from behind. That giggle was still there as I felt her kisses on my back. As angry as I was with her at the moment, I still loved her touch, her body, her smell. Our intimate moments were so few and far between now too. I just wished Shenita didn't have to get drunk to make love to me. I should have been stronger and passed. Shenita's robe fell to the floor.

"Neal. Fuck me. Fuck the shit out of me. I'm sorry. Okay?"

"...Okay."

8 Reggie Collins

The next morning, I had one of the rental car companies we deal with pick me up. They gave me a convertible Mustang for the price of an economy car so I got to enjoy the traffic with the top down. I chose to wear my black Antonini Loretta with my mint colored shirt and tie that I had picked out the night before. On my way in, I decided on what story to go with to explain why I was in a rental.

Most of the office was already there when I arrived at nine-thirty. I put the top up on my rental and figured out how to fasten it shut. It looked like we were due for some afternoon showers and I didn't need a bill from the rental company too. I fixed myself a cup of coffee on the way to my office and walked past some of my claim team's desks. Doris was balancing her checkbook at her desk while talking to her daughter on the phone. I gave her a polite smile as I sipped from my cup. Sam had a newly reported claim and gave me a high-five on his way out to an accident in Fondren Park. Sam always stayed on top of his shit and was our resident superhero. Loretta was leaning back in her chair as I passed her. She was wearing a green Stratford Circle golf shirt that was too small for that chest of hers. She gave me that pouty look that was for my eyes-only. Loretta, Loretta. That was someone I was sure to never be in my office alone with. I wasn't about to lose my job by banging someone I was in charge of. Now, once she became a member of management, it would be on. Time to start working on that promotion. Until then, I was content fantasizing about having her bronze body sprawled across my desk.

Loretta Juarez was originally from Brownsville, Texas, but had transferred to our office a year ago from Los Angeles where she had been living.

My faithful secretary, Ruby, was waiting for me at her desk outside my office. The fifty-something grandmother of two was as hip as they come. I could tell she just had her highlights redone. The traces of brown were more pronounced than the day before.

"I like, I like, Ruby," I said while pointing as I approached her desk.

"This? Oh, just a little sumthin' I did just for you, Reggie."

"Tell me anything, dear. Any messages?"

"Yep. Mr. Russell called. There's a meeting for all the supervisors next week. Y'all not tryin' to fire my old ass, huh?"

"Heh. You know you ain't going nowhere, baby."

"Some woman called a few times earlier. She didn't leave a message. She said you'd know who it was and that she'd call you back later." It was probably Lila checking on me. She was a sweetie.

"Yeah. I do. Thanks."

I was walking through the celebratory streamers in my doorway left over from yesterday when Ruby muttered to me matter-of-factly, "Loretta walked by earlier to see if you were in too. Hot ass. Hot ass."

"Behave, Ruby." I looked back half-laughing and rolled my eyes.

"It's not me you gotta worry about, baby. Heh. Heh."

I slipped my jacket onto my hanger and made myself comfortable. I had several files and office bills to review. I pulled up my to-do list on my terminal and began my workday. My plan was to work straight through lunch, but around eleven o'clock, my phone had other plans.

"Reggie, it's that woman," Ruby yelled over the ring of the phone call she had just transferred. I should have called Lila back when I first came in.

"Hello, Lila?"

"Who in the fuck is *Lila*?" It was only a matter of time.

"None of your damn business. What do you want, Trina?"

"I want you, baby. You know I love you."

"You got a funny way of showing it."

"...*What do you mean?*" Bingo. She told on herself and confirmed what I already knew.

"Don't play dumb with me. I just can't believe you have the nerve to call here."

I walked around my desk and pushed my office door shut. Time to play the game.

"I just called because I hadn't heard from you since this weekend."

"You mean, when I told you I wasn't coming over?"

"Y...yeah. Since then. So, what's up?"

"Work. You off today?"

"Yes I am. That's why I've been trying to reach you allll morning. Feel 'up' for some lunchtime lovin'?" She'd just given me the way to get my revenge.

I had a lot of work to do, but I replied, "Sure." It was time for part one of the plan.

9 Neal Wallace

I woke up to the smell of sex and Shenita's Alizé all over me. Shenita was snoring as she slept off her buzz and our night of "love-making". She had some time left before work so I slid out from under her naked body and got in the shower. I had stuff to think about. I turned on the water and waited for everything to steam up. My red eyes looked back at me in the mirror as I brushed my teeth. "Sleep!" they screamed out to me, but I ignored them.

While showering, I took a sniff of my bar of soap on advice from the morning commercials. Nothing happened. I didn't know how I was going to apologize to Mel...Me-Me. Hopefully she would forgive me for putting her in that position last night. I guess the bigger issue that needed to be addressed was the relationship between me and my wife. I loved my woman with all my heart and would fight to make the marriage work. The question was going to be if Shenita would work with me. I decided I had been in the shower long enough and dried off.

All was quiet in the house still. I picked up one of the empty bottles off the bedroom floor. How long had she been drinking last night? Right after she dropped me off? I decided to take a stroll through our half-empty house. We had sacrificed and scrapped so much for something to call our own, but still had bare rooms. The lottery would have been right on time. I walked down to our living room and peeked out the curtains. I could see our neighbor, the minister, talking with another neighbor while walking his dog again. I cringed to think that they were discussing our "Springer Moment" from late last night. Oh well. At least I wasn't sleeping with members of my congregation or indicted on racketeering charges like them, so it was still all-good.

I awakened the Mrs. to the smell of food. Nothing like a big ass omelet in bed with orange juice to say "I love you". Before I became a chef, I used to cook for Shenita and the women that came before her all the time. That was my calling card of sorts. Reggie was the big time womanizer and I was the cook. Yep, he would fuck em' and I would stuff em'.

Shenita groaned, but smiled as she sat up in the bed. She was groggy, but grateful.

I knew she had a hell of a hangover.

"Neal, we got any tomato juice in the fridge?"

"No. I looked. Want some aspirin?"

"Yeah. In a little bit. What time is it?"

"You still got time before work. I got up extra early."

"Huh? Extra early? I woulda thought I'd worn your big ass out last night."

"So you remember it, huh? I don't want to go there, but you need to cut back on the drinking."

"Um, um, I'm alright," she said clearing her throat, "I remember *everything* from last night. I may have been a little out of place out front, but I was caught off guard by that girl." Shenita had pulled the sheet up over her chest as she started feeling the chill from the air conditioner kicking on.

"Yeah. You made an ass out of yourself."

"Scuse me?" She stopped the fork halfway up to her mouth.

"I said you made an ass out of yourself. I've gotta apologize to Me-Me."

"Me-Me? Who in the hell is 'Me-Me'?"

"Melissa…my coworker from last night."

"You ain't gotta do shit, but be black and die, nigga. You had nothin' to do with that. That was all on me. And what you doing calling her 'Me-Me'?"

"That's her nickname from back in the day."

"So, you been knowing her from back in the day?"

"No. Reggie has. See, she's like his little sister…"

"Save it. My head is killing me. I don't want to talk about the bitch anymore."

I started to protest the name-calling, but decided to leave well enough alone.

"Shenita. One more thing and I'm going to leave you alone."

"What?"

"How come you only want to make love to me when you're drunk?"

"Aww, Neal. That's not true. I wanted to make love to my teddy bear last night and alcohol had nothing to do with it. I wasn't even drunk. Just a little tipsy."

Just a little tipsy? After drinking two bottles of Alizé? She wasn't going to deal with that issue so I let her enjoy her breakfast. No need stirring up another argument. Had something about me changed over the years? I didn't think I looked much different from when we first tied the knot.

Shenita finished her breakfast and gave me a kiss before heading for the shower.

"Hey, Neal. Want to join me?" Normally, the door would have been locked. I was guessing it was guilt from what I had just brought up.

I looked at the time and answered, "Nah. I showered earlier and you have to be to work in a little bit."

"…Suit yourself."

I put up the breakfast cart in the kitchen and walked back to the bedroom. Shenita was still showering. The door was still unlocked so I walked in.

"Shenita?"

"Yeah?"

"Would it be easier on you, I mean 'us', if I worked days instead?"

"I don't know. Maybe. But you know you can't do that. Mirage doesn't open until the afternoon. You make all your money at night. Look, let's just focus on getting these bills taken care of, okay? Baby, hand me the towel."

"Here you go. You want to do lunch today?"

"I'll pass. We'll probably be swamped today. Might not even take lunch. Oh, I hate that job. Do you need the car? Any property to look at or old restaurants to find?"

"…No. Take the car. I think I'll just sleep."

10 Reggie Collins

"That was quick." Trina was standing before me in her doorway while blowing on her nails she had just painted. Trina's front door had a view of the parking lot and she stole a glance behind me. She was probably looking for my ride to see her handiwork. She didn't know I had a rental and I didn't say anything.

"I took the toll way. Didn't feel like putting up with the construction work and lunch hour traffic." With that said, I walked by Trina and into her place.

Trina was wearing a white sleeveless top and blue jeans. She was barefoot and her always-pretty toes were showing. Everything was always in place on her fine ass. Even her weave was looking as flawless as ever. I'm sure most women probably had to take a double take when looking at it. The only way I found out was up close and personal. Just looking at her made me momentarily forget the key-job on my shit as well as my plan, but I took a deep breath and concentrated.

I could have picked the sofa, but I chose to sit in the chair across from it.

"You know where the room is," Trina said with a confused smile on her face.

"Damn. You in a hurry or something? Can't a brother relax for a spell?"

"Sorry, Reg. You know I haven't had it in a while."

"You don't want to talk for a little while. Besides…don't you have to let your nails dry?"

Trina threw a pillow at me off her sofa before plopping down in frustration. I was pushing her buttons, but had to be careful not to have her go off.

"Why don't you come sit over here? I don't bite."

"Don't bite? Now you're lying. I didn't finish telling you earlier…Someone keyed my shit all up yesterday. Came by my job. That's got me in a down mood."

Trina gave a great impression of somebody in shock. "What?" she cried out as she sat up and leaned forward in concern. "Did you catch them?"

"Nope. I thought it was you earlier, but I know you wouldn't do something like that."

"No. Not to my baby. Here, let me take your mind off that stuff."

With that said, Trina sprang up and walked slowly over to my chair. She kneeled over and took my hand in hers before placing my hand on her left breast. She had been waiting for my touch. As I gently squeezed, Trina closed her eyes and let out a slow, deep breath causing her chest to push closer toward me. I reached out with my free hand and began to unzip her jeans. I slid the hand down inside past her curly hairs until I reached her moistness. Trina's breathing was becoming more shallow and quick now. I was in control. Time for payback to start.

"Who's is this?" I asked in a low voice.

"Y…yours. All yours, Reggie. Please."

"Please what?"

"Now. No more. I can't take no more."

"You know, I might not be able to do this, Trina," I whispered while kissing her neck.

"What? What are y…you talking about?"

"My feelings. I'm getting confused. I know we're just having fun, but I think I'm starting to have some feelings." On cue, I started working both hands feverishly for added effect.

"Aw…aww. Don't worry about that, baby." Trina had pulled her jeans all the way down and the panties were following. "I don't mind if you start having feelings. Let's go in the bedroom and…and talk."

I let out a big smile and said, "You don't mind? For real?"

"I…I said so, didn't I?" Trina replied as she was struggling to undo my belt. I decided to help her out.

"C'mon. Let's go take care of you then." With that said, I stood up and led Trina to her bedroom. I was going to be a little late returning from lunch.

11 Reggie Collins

On the way back to work from topping Trina off, I stopped on Fannin to order two dozen roses for Lila. Had to keep my priorities in order when in the game. Once back at work, I called the shop to see how things were coming along. Mr. Hernandez told me that the paint job would probably be done by next Monday.

Most of my calls wound up being personal rather than business as I rang Neal at home next.

"Hello?"

"Say, bro."

"Reg. What's up with you, dawg?"

"Taking care of shit at work as usual. You working tonight?"

"Yeah. Shenita's bringing me when she gets back from work."

"I got a rental, bro. A drop-top 'Stang! I'll roll by tonight. You need a ride?"

"Yeah. Last night was a disaster. I still gotta apologize to Me-Me."

"Huh?"

"I'll fill you in tonight."

I rolled up on Mirage around ten. I had gone home, cleaned up, and changed clothes. I was wearing my Polo Sport gear now. I revved the engine one last time before I let the valet drive it off. Enough of the showing off. I guess I was still a kid at heart.

It was a weeknight, but the restaurant was still busy, so I chose to make myself scarce at the bar. Might as well cop a seat until things died down. I would have been here last night hanging out with my people if I had wheels then. Trina was still going to get hers for that. I chuckled as I thought about part one being sprung on her.

I caught a glimpse of Me-Me as she passed behind one of the palm trees in the place. They let Neal have some say in the décor. When he had his own place up and running, it was going to be da bomb! That was…if Shenita let him. An expensive undertaking. I wished I had the money to invest to help him out.

Me-Me walked back into view with a tray full of food. She noticed me and smiled from behind her glasses. I pointed toward the bar to let her know where I would be.

Man, Me-Me had grown up into quite a lady. It was hard to see the skinny little tomboy that used to hang with Jo-Jo and me back in the day. I'm sure her brother up in heaven was looking down on the lovely woman she had become. I hoped that I was doing my part to look out for her too.

Me-Me was a 5'8 sculpture of a woman who hid behind these little spectacles she liked to wear on the end of her nose. Her head was full of black micro-braids that flowed down and opened at the ends just past her cappuccino shoulders. Me-Me was the innocent sort, but was also streetwise, if there was such a combination. She was still unsure of herself and of what she wanted to do in life. Just the type of person someone would find a challenge to manipulate. I was going to ensure that didn't happen to my 'lil' sis'. I even helped her get this job a few months earlier with Neal's help after she walked out on her last job. The guy who owned the tax prepa-ration service she worked at was trying to service her as well.

I took a seat at the bar and ordered my usual, Absolut on the rocks. While waiting on my drink, I decided to people watch. A Mariah wannabe was sitting across the bar from me with her old sugar daddy. Her man was wearing his best catalog blazer. Lord, she was going to kill that old man when she got him back to his retirement home. That was probably the plan. He seemed happy though, so I couldn't completely hate on him. Damn, she was fine.

A thick country sister who stuck a tray in front of my face interrupted my libido.

"Melissa said Neal sent these appetizers for you. You must be *Reggie*." Yeah. I'm that muthafucker.

"Yes. That's me. Thanks." I extended my hand and shook hers gently.

"I'm Tookie. I work with your girl on the floor. If you need anything else, let me know. I'll be here all night."

"I'll remember that, Tookie. Thank you again," I replied as I gave her a wink that almost caused her to trip when stepping down from the bar area. I held back a laugh. Sweet girl. What was between her legs was probably sweeter. A thick sister like that could put a serious hurting on you in the bedroom. I was still cool from Trina's workout earlier so I chose to spare Tookie…this time.

I turned my attention to my drink that had just been served and the tray of wings, chips and dip that was before me. It was about an hour and three drinks later when Neal came from in back.

"Sir. We had a report of a roach in the dip. Have you found anything crunchy in yours?" Neal was wearing his chef's hat and looking all professional while giving me a hard time.

"Why no. I have not discovered any foreign matter in my dip, sir."

"Hmm. Perhaps I should add more next time."

I laughed and gave Neal a pound. "You're sick, bro. I should leave your ass here tonight."

"No! I'll stop, Reggie. Last night was wild enough."

"So, what's up with that? Something happen with Me-Me?"

Neal sat down at a nearby table and motioned for me to grab my stuff and join him.

"Yeah?" I asked as I pulled the chair out.

"Man, Shenita was trippin' last night."

"*And?* She's always doing that."

"Me-Me gave me a ride home last night and Shenita came outside. Drunk."

"Oh shit. What are you going to do about her?"

"I don't know. I talked to her about it this morning, but she blew it off."

"Did she say something to Me-Me?"

Neal gave me a stupid look that answered my question. "She

didn't take a swing at her or anything. I've been too busy to tell Me-Me that I'm sorry. She's a special one there. You ever noticed her singing?"

"*Uh huh*. You're sounding all warm and fuzzy. You're not falling in love or something?"

Neal almost choked on that one. He blurted out, "What?! With Melissa? What kind of crazy shit is that?"

"Relax, dawg. I'm just fuckin' with you."

"That wasn't cool. Look, before I forget. Shenita told me to ask you. Can you come with us to New Orleans week after next? It's Kelly's birthday and she wanted to see you again."

"What?! I'll have to use some of my vacation time, but I'm there."

"Yeah. I thought you would be. You and Kelly didn't get a chance to get together after our wedding."

"She's still single?"

"That's what she's saying. At least for her birthday, she will be. Heh."

"Alright. I'll have my ride back by then. You want me to drive? I've got the room. You and the Mrs. can snuggle in back."

"Might be just what we need, bro. It seems like nothing I do works these days. Shenita seems like such a moody, unhappy soul."

"Sounds like somebody's not getting it done in the bedroom. Haha!"

"I'm serious, man. Not everything revolves around sex...except for with you. You've got some issues of your own. All that sleeping around gonna have you wind up with AIDS or something."

"Hey! Watch that shit. I protect myself."

"Every time? C'mon man! I used to live with you in Cuney! You can't shit me!"

"Are you done hating on me? You happy? I'm trying to have a good time, but you killin' the mood, bro."

"Just looking out for you, Reg. Y'know I gotta keep Mr. King-Dick grounded. All these women out here are quick to pump your head up."

"I know, bro. Don't I know. What's up with the thickness who brought the tray out?"

"Who? Tookie? Leave that alone, bro. I'm not having you fuckin' with anybody's head at my job. That shit'll blow up and she'll be bringing food to the wrong tables."

"Must be talking about Tookie," we heard Me-Me say as she interrupted our bullshit session. She must have gotten a break.

"Hey, girl!" I said to my lil' sis as I stood up and gave her a hug and kiss on the cheek, "About time you joined us." Neal stayed in his chair and gave Me-Me a smile.

"I'm on my last break before I get out of here. See, I can't just hang out with the customers like this man here," she said while pointing at a slightly embarrassed Neal who adjusted his chef's hat.

"I hear you met Shenita last night."

"Yeah," Me-Me answered me as if not sure how to respond in front of Neal.

"Look," Neal said, "I'm sorry about how that went down. My wife told me to tell you she's sorry about that." Neal's big ass was lying. Shenita was not one to apologize for shit. I gave Neal a smile that let him know I knew. He felt bad enough about what happened, so I didn't bust his chops.

Me-Me answered Neal, "It's okay. I understand that people have problems sometimes. As long as she understood I wasn't doing anything with you in the car, then I'm cool."

I added, "Shit. Shenita would have cut his shit off right there on the front lawn if you were! Haha!"

"Well, I've got to get back to work, Reg. I'll let you boys finish talking about Tookie. Heh."

"Alright. I'll talk to you later, Me-Me. By the way, Neal set me straight on Tookie."

"Yeah. Sure," Me-Me laughed as she walked off while massaging her neck with her hands.

12 Neal Wallace

I returned to the kitchen to wrap things up, while Reggie downed a few more drinks at the bar. I knew Reggie had to work first thing in the morning, so I had my second-in-charge close up in back. As I cleared the kitchen doors, I heard the sound of Me-Me's voice. She was back at her humming. I paused in the doorway, which was a big restaurant no-no, to listen. If she had known I was listening, she would have clammed up. I waited for Me-Me to walk further away before continuing on toward the bar.

"You ready, bro?"

"Yeah. I think you might need to drive. I'm…tired."

"Tired, huh? Gimme your keys."

"Yeah. Wait. I don't have them."

"Do you know where you saw them last? I'll start looking." I started looking on the floor near Reggie.

"Oops. Oh yeah. I valet parked. Hee. Here's the ticket."

"Drunk ass."

I walked my tipsy friend out to the front of Mirage and waited for Ernest, the valet, to bring the car around. I had forgotten that Reggie was in a rental and was still looking for his Pathfinder when the gold Mustang pulled up. Nice. Back in school, I used to want one of those so bad. This being a convertible made it even better. I gave Ernest a tip with my money and we were off…once I put the top down.

I normally didn't take the Sam Houston Parkway and traffic wasn't that heavy, but I wanted to have a little fun on the way home. My passenger, Reggie, was taking a nap so he didn't complain. I took the car up to one hundred ten miles per hour before backing off it. There were no Department of Public Safety cruisers around, but I didn't need to get thrown under the jail. When we pulled up in my driveway, Reggie was coming around.

"Neal. You mind if I sleep this off on your couch? Just an hour or two before I head out."

"What's mine is yours, dawg. You can use one of the guest bedrooms if you want. Stay the night, even."

"Nah. I need to get home before the morning traffic. Just a couple of hours on the couch and I'll be fine."

"C'mon in the house. I'll leave your keys on the table. I don't like hanging outside at night much these days."

We walked into the house through the side door and came in through the kitchen. I heard the TV on in the living room. Midnight Love was playing on BET. Shenita was still up.

"Hey, baby. Hey, Reggie. You guys been hanging out, huh?"

"Just at work for a little while."

"Oh," said Shenita as she stood up, put her arms around me, and gave me a kiss. She was in her favorite sleep shirt and had her red scarf tied around her head.

"Sup, Nita," Reggie said as he walked from behind us.

"Hey, Reg. You look a little wiped out."

"Gee, thanks. I just need to crash on ya'll's couch 'til around three, if that's okay."

"Sure, Reg. Knock yourself out. I was just about to go upstairs to bed. Coming Neal?" First the kiss, now Shenita was being cheerful. What was up?

"Hey, man. You need us to wake you up?" I asked Reggie as he made himself comfortable on the couch and started closing his eyes.

"…Um. Nah. I should be alright."

"You can leave out the side door. I'll leave the alarm off then. Goodnight."

"Later, bro…and thanks."

"No. Thank you. I got to drive that Stang out there. Heh."

I dimmed the lights downstairs, turned the TV off and headed up to the bedroom. Shenita had already left for the room.

"Close the door," Shenita mentioned as I walked in. She was sitting on the bed and rubbing lotion on her legs. It was some of that pear stuff from Victoria's Secret and its smell was filling the room. "Does Reggie need someone to wake him up?"

"No. He's supposed to get up on his own around three. I thought you'd be asleep by now."

"I know I need to be. Work in the morning as usual."

"Did you check about the transfer?" Shenita was interested in moving to Questcom's main headquarters behind the Greenspoint Mall. It was much closer to our house and would be a step up for her.

"Shit. They're still giving me lip service. They don't want any sisters in corporate. They want to keep us fighting over the scraps…the pagers and shit. Keepin' all the corporate accounts to themselves."

"It'll get better. I just wish it was going to be sooner than later, Shenita."

"I know. You like the lotion I put on?"

"Mmm. You know I do. What's up?" Shenita was being playful and definitely wasn't drinking.

"I got my legs already, but I'm not finished. Want to put some on me?"

"Huh?"

"You heard me."

"Shenita, I know we got company, but you don't have to pretend. Like with the kiss earlier and stuff."

"Company's got nothing to do with this. Reggie's down there asleep and you're up here with your wife behind closed doors."

"You got a point there. Give me the bottle."

Shenita handed me the bottle and raised her sleep shirt over her head with a smile. She was sitting up on her knees naked in the bed as I let the sweet-smelling lotion flow out onto my hand. Maybe there was hope for our love life.

13 Reggie Collins

The world had ended its slow spin and I was at peace. I had taken my tennis shoes off and was curled up on Neal and Shenita's couch. When I turned over once in the night, I realized that I was going to have trouble waking up at three. I was more tired than I thought and drifted back into the dream world. My dreams took me to Lila's arms.

We were in a field under a tree. The wind blew across the top of the grass as I felt Lila's hand across my chest. Lila had plucked some fruit off the tree and was feeding it to me with her other hand. It looked like an apple, but all I smelled was pears everywhere. I didn't remember smelling anything in a dream before, but this was sooo real.

"Reggie?" I heard Lila say as her hand rubbed all over me.

"Huh?"

"Wake up."

"..."

Everything started coming into focus as I realized where I was. A hand was on me, but it wasn't Lila's. Damn. It was Shenita and she was shaking me. I hoped I wasn't saying shit in my sleep. My jeans covered my hard-on, thus sparing me some embarrassment.

"Ooh. What time is it?"

"Three-fifteen," Shenita answered. She was leaning over me in a skimpy red silk robe. I tried not to notice, but it was loosely tied so I had a clear view of everything underneath. Everything. I closed my eyes to give her time to stand up all the way, but that didn't stop the smell of pears from continuing to hit my nose. Damn, she smelled good. It was hard to believe this was the same bitchy woman who had been riding my boy lately. Of course, Shenita used to be cool as hell up until just a few years ago.

"Where's Neal?" I awkwardly asked her as I rubbed my eyes and sat up. I guess I was feeling guilty for the sneak peek I got of the goods.

"Sleeping like a log. I got up to get some water and saw you still on the sofa. You had wanted to leave around three, huh?" In the dim light, I noticed Shenita's robe was still slightly open. I could see in a straight line from her neck down between her breasts and all the way to her belly button. Heh. She had a cute little "in-ey"

"Yeah. *Yawn.* I was more exhausted than I thought. Thanks."

Shenita stepped forward with a smile and said, "Y'know, you're still welcome to spend the night…either here on the sofa or up in the guest bedroom."

"No. I've gotta get a move-on. I appreciate it though," I said as I struggled to get my shoes on. "You can go ahead and lock the door behind me now."

"Okay."

"I didn't say anything in my sleep, did I?"

"Heh. No."

I fished for my keys until I remembered that Neal had put them on the kitchen table. Shenita followed me to the side door and patted me on the back as I walked out.

"Nita?"

"Yeah?"

"This is none of my business and you can curse me out if you want, but you need to give Neal a break. That boy loves you more now than the day he married you. He just wants nothing but the best for you."

Shenita cut her eyes at me and started to say something. She then caught herself and smiled instead before letting out an "I know".

I was speechless, so I simply returned the smile and shuffled off into the night. I still had my head on my shoulders and wasn't about to tempt fate any further.

14 Neal Wallace

The clicking sound of our bedroom door closing brought me out of my sleep briefly. I was drained from the intense lovemaking earlier in the night. Two nights in the same week was incredible, even if she was sober only one of the times. It was Shenita coming back into the room. Her tightly closed silk robe clung to her in the dark.

"Huh?"

"Shhh. Go back to sleep," she said as she worked on loosening her sash.

"Reggie still here?" I asked while squinting at the clock.

"No. He just left. He was still asleep when I went downstairs," Shenita answered as she let her robe slide off her beautiful golden brown body. "I woke him up when I went down to get some water. The door's locked and the alarm's on too."

"That was thoughtful of you, baby."

"I can be nice at times," she shot back as I felt her bare skin come to rest on mine. I pulled the covers over us and we resumed our slumber. My last thought was of Shenita's cold feet rubbing against the hair on my legs.

It felt like I had just closed my eyes again when the alarm went off. Same old routine. The Mrs. was sleeping so soundly. She was still resting on top of me and hadn't moved. I reached out with my hand and strained to get a finger on the clock. I flipped the alarm button off and caused the clock to fall onto the carpet all in one move. Questcom would just have to deal with Shenita coming in a little late today. I smiled and rubbed my wife's back. An hour later brought another story.

"Hey! What time is it??!!" Uh oh.

"I dunno."

"Damn. You let me sleep? What happened to the alarm?"

"I turned it off. You looked so tired."

"Shit," was muttered as she cut her eyes at me before rising up. The bathroom door slammed shut with its usual-for-these-days charm.

I followed Shenita into the bathroom. The glass around the shower was beginning to steam up as she scrubbed at a frantic pace. I sat down on the edge of the bath.

"Sorry, baby. You're not going to be that late."

"Yeah…You forgot I had a meeting first thing this morning, huh?"

"Oh."

"I don't really like my job, but I want to keep it for now. Lord knows we can barely pay the bills as it is." Shenita quickly turned the shower off and was reaching for her towel. I pulled it off the brass rack and handed it to her.

Shenita dried off and ran to the hall closet to get the ironing board. She had forgotten to iron her clothes the night before and was cursing with each push of the spray starch nozzle. I knew to leave her alone right then. The Uptown New Orleans in her was quick to come out when she was stirred.

Thirty minutes later, the car was backing out the driveway like a bat out of hell before shooting down the street. One day, the constable was going to pull Shenita over. I let her take the car without a fuss. There was enough around the house to keep me busy.

I caught a couple of Z's to start off my day. No need being wasted at work later in the evening. It was a nervous sleep, as I felt guilty for letting Shenita sleep late. I would call her around lunch to see if everything went alright. The house was in need of straightening and I started outside. I jogged down the street to check on the mail first. Only bills and credit card offers. Our house didn't come with much yard space, so it only took an hour to knock out the lawn, both front and back. The edging would keep until next week. I finished off with the sprinkler and left it on while I went inside to clean up.

Everything was clean in the kitchen. The marble counter tops were bare and everything was in its place. I assumed the Mrs. had already loaded the dishes in the dishwasher last night. We definitely had laundry to wash so I knew what I had to do. I pulled the sheets off our bed and crammed them in the dirty clothes bag for the long haul down the stairs to the washroom. The married life finally succeeded in convincing me to separate whites from colors. When I was single, I used to go to the laundromat and cram the washer full. Money was tight and as long as my whites didn't come out pink I was alright.

With the first load washing, I decided to carry my dirty carcass back upstairs to the shower. With no one home, I got out of my sweaty T-shirt and shorts right in the washroom and ran upstairs naked. I thought about getting in the whirlpool tub to ease the sore muscles in my back, but was afraid of falling back asleep and drowning.

On the bathroom counter, I noticed Shenita's birth control pills. She was always one to keep up with that. Funny. I never thought to discuss children with Shenita before we were married. I just assumed she would want a kid as much as me. I knew what I got whenever I assumed anything, but love made me foolish. I came from a family that thought of birth control as sacrilege, but I appreciated the hell out of it while knockin' boots with Shenita almost every night before we tied the knot. Oh yeah. The premarital sex was a no-no too. Heh. It was amazing how convenience made some people willing to overlook what were supposed to be strong beliefs. Upon further thought, it was strange that I was an only child...especially with no birth control being practiced in my family. Made me think that my moms kept a few secrets to herself. I didn't blame her for not wanting to create another child with a monster like pops. God rest her soul.

As I showered, my thoughts stayed on children.

Yeah, a boy. A little boy. That would be nice.

15 Reggie Collins

I didn't feel like dressing up for work this morning. I wore one of our standard green and white golf shirts with some khakis. I didn't know what I was thinking when I drank that much at Mirage. If Shenita hadn't woke me up, I probably would still have been on their couch.

"Good morning, Ruby," I said as I strolled into my office.

"Well, well, well. You're in here kind of early, Reggie. Took it easy last night, huh?"

"Heh. Just the opposite. My head's still ringing. Too much unfinished work to take off today."

"I'll try to keep people from bothering you today then."

"Aww. That's why I love you, Ruby."

"Ha! I'll bet your young ass says that to all the girls."

"And you know what? You're right!"

I logged on to my computer terminal and began to go through the complaint call messages that were on my desk. Funny, one of the messages was a complaint on Loretta.

Ms. Juarez almost never had anyone complain about her claim handling. It was probably nothing major. I would follow up with her about it before returning the call. I was about to call Loretta into my office when my phone rang.

"Stratford Circle, this is Reggie."

"I loved the roses, Champ. They are gorgeous! You've got me feeling like a schoolgirl up in here. Thank you."

"Hey, Lila. I'm glad you like them. It was the least I could do. When did they deliver them?"

"Yesterday afternoon. I was on a conference call with one of our partners when my secretary brought them in. I couldn't help but giggle. Did you get your rental?"

"Yep. I got the hook up on a convertible Mustang."

"Convertible, huh? Trying to copy me?"

"You're in a league of your own, Ms. Reed. Believe me, I definitely prefer seeing you drop your top."

"Aww. That's a bad one, Reggie. You sent roses, so I'll forgive that awful crack. What are you doing for lunch?"

"No real plans. You have time in your schedule for me?"

"Not really...but I'll fit you in anyway."

"That is sooo generous of you, Lila. Where do you want to go?"

"How about Copeland's on Richmond."

"Sounds good. Call in ahead of time?"

"Yep."

"Say...around noon?"

"I'll see you there. Hey, where were you last night? I tried to call you to thank you for the roses then, but couldn't catch up with you."

"I was at Mirage hanging with Neal. I was supposed to bring him home last night."

"Oh. I called you late also...to see if you wanted some company."

"A booty call? Maybe I need to send you roses everyday. Hee. Hee. I was drunk and wound up sleeping on Neal and Shenita's couch. I didn't get in until after four."

"*Yeah.* Tell me anything. You don't have to explain where you've been to me."

"No. For real. I was at Neal's. You can ask him...and Shenita if you want."

"Relax. I believe you. Hey, when are we going to go out with them again? I had a good time when we all went to that comedy club."

"Yeah. That sounds good. We'll have to do that soon. I'm going to New Orleans with them in a couple of weeks." *Oops.* I didn't mean to blurt that out. I really would have loved for Lila to go with us, but I'm sure she didn't fit into Kelly's birthday plans for me.

"New Orleans? Shenita's from there, huh?"

"Yeah." *And her sister's having a birthday out there and wants to jump my bones.* Don't volunteer too much, dude.

"Oh." I could hear Lila's gears turning. "Well, I guess I'll see you at noon."

"It's a date. Bye, boo."

I hung up the phone and asked Ruby to call Loretta to my office. I still needed to follow up on the complaint calls and decided to deal with Loretta's first. Loretta walked in moments later looking hot as usual. The Latina was wearing her brown hair down this day with a little gold clip on the side. Her bronze complexion was accented by a gold colored sleeveless blouse and olive slacks, which hugged her rear just right. She always had this look on her face that proclaimed, "I know what you're thinking". Today was no different even though I was calling her in to discuss business only. I offered Loretta a seat and was about to get down to business when my phone rang again.

"Hey, baby." *Shit.* It was Trina. Loretta's eyes were digging into me while her lips were revealing nothing but a smile. I returned the smile.

"Hello."

"Lunch was great yesterday."

"Why, thank you," I replied in a businesslike manner.

"Can you come by my apartment tonight?"

"I don't know. I'll have to call you back." Part one of the plan was a success yesterday so I had to play it careful.

"I'm at work in the shoe store. You promise you'll call me?"

"Yes. I have to go."

I hung up the phone to give Loretta my undivided attention. Loretta leaned over in her chair and asked, "A friend?"

"Yeah. Something like that." *Actually it was the nutcase who keyed my shit.*

"A girlfriend?" I flinched in response to Loretta's forwardness. Apparently she wasn't intimidated or inhibited by my being her supervisor.

"No. I don't have a girlfriend," I answered with my "Billy Dee" voice.

"Good," she replied before switching gears on the dime. "You wanted to see me about something?"

"Uh…yeah. I got a message here from a Mrs. Stein on one of your files. Know anything about this? Something happen?"

Loretta let out a little giggle. "Heh. No. She said she'd call you. She was pleased with how quickly I handled her claim and wanted to let my supervisor know."

"Oh. A good call. It's nice to have those calls to return. I thought it was kind of odd to get a complaint on one of your files; you do such a great job."

"Thanks, boss."

"Hey, stop that 'boss' stuff."

"Well, you are in charge aren't you?"

I didn't answer. I just shook my head and smiled. Loretta got up to excuse herself. I began to pick up the phone to return Mrs. Stein's call, but my eyes were locked on Loretta's ass as it headed out the door. The ass stopped, so I looked up to see Loretta looking back over her shoulder at me.

"Reggie, would you like to do lunch…today?"

"Sure. I mean…I would, but I can't. I already have lunch plans. Sorry."

"You can't change them?" Loretta was running one hand along the door moulding of my office.

"…No." Lila was always tops on my priority list of ladies, but I would never tell Lila that. One of the cardinal rules of Reggie: Never let them know exactly where they stand.

I didn't know what Loretta had in mind for lunch or whether or not it was harmless, but my ignorance would have to suffice for now.

"*Sigh*. Okay then. I'll go check with the rest of the gang."

"Raincheck, alright?"

16 Reggie Collins

I spotted Lila's car as soon as I turned into the restaurant parking lot. There could have been several cars like hers in Houston, but the sorority frame around the license plate confirmed it was my baby's.

When I entered, the hostess showed me to where Lila was seated. I could see Lila's smile in the distance. The aroma of spicy fried seafood filled the air as I walked through the crowded place to our table. Lila stood up to greet me and we shared a short, gentle smooch. She was wearing a turquoise dress and had her hair pinned up this day.

"You're drinking for lunch today?" Lila asked as she twirled the stick in her Bloody Mary.

"Oh no. That's a big no-no. Besides, I don't need anything to remind me of last night."

"I know. Just messing with you, Champ. Ooo," Lila said while eyeing my shirt logo, "You really must be recovering. I can't believe you're wearing a company shirt, Mr. Snappy Dresser."

"Yep. Slumming today. I'll come correct tomorrow."

Our overly perky waitress approached the table and introduced herself. Lila ordered the popcorn shrimp salad and I had red beans and rice. Contrary to Lila's joking request earlier, I simply had a root beer for my drink.

"I like that dress, counselor."

"Thank you. Your eyes told me when you walked up."

"Damn. Do I give everything away with my eyes?"

"Sometimes…No. *All* the time. Maybe I'm just aware because of my job. I know what to look for. There's nothing bad about it though," Lila answered.

"*Yeah.* Try to make me feel better now."

"Okay. How's this?" Lila asked as I felt her leg rub against mine below the table.

"Cute. So, what's up at work? Found somebody else to sue?"

"Found anybody else to cheat out of what you owe them?"

"Aww. That's low. Truce?" I stuck my hand out across the table.

"Truce." Lila returned the favor and we shook on it. She continued, "Going to New Orleans, huh?" I should have known she wouldn't let it go.

"Yep."

"Special occasion?"

"Not really." I remembered what Lila said about my eyes and looked around at my surroundings. I nonchalantly added, "Shenita's going for her sister's birthday or something."

"Oh. I see," Lila said as she crunched on a piece of ice. Her look begged for me to continue.

"And I'm going to drive them out there. Her sister knows me from Neal's wedding and invited me as well."

Our waitress returning with our food interrupted my unspoken interrogation. Service was pretty speedy and much appreciated at this time. I was about to continue talking when a more unfortunate interruption occurred.

"Hey, Reggie!" was heard right as I opened my mouth.

I turned to look down the row of seats and saw the hostess walking toward us with a group of patrons in tow. It was some of my fellow employees; specifically it was Loretta with Sam and Doris bringing up the rear. In a town as big as this, they had to pick the same restaurant for lunch. The hostess continued walking past us, but Loretta slowed to talk. Oh joy.

"Loretta Juarez," she said as she switched her gaze from smiling at me to eyeing Lila.

"Hi, Loretta. I'm Lila Reed."

"*Lila Reed? The* Lila Reed?"

"That's what my parents named me." It was time for me to interrupt.

"Lila, Loretta is a member of my claim group as well as Sam and Doris here."

Sam and Doris waved, but Lila and Loretta never took their eyes off each other.

Lila broke the duel for a second to smile and wave back at the rest of the group.

"Well, I guess we better go to our booth. Enjoy your lunch," Loretta said as she led the eclectic mix of claim reps to the other end of the restaurant.

Loretta then slowed again to adjust the waistband on her slacks. Sam and Doris walked past her while talking to each other. She looked back and gave me a final wave and wink. I simply nodded.

I began stirring my red beans and rice, but Lila hadn't started on her salad. She was smirking.

"The 'hot tamale' likes you," she said with a roll of her tongue.

"Loretta?" I asked as if suddenly naïve.

"Have you fucked her too?"

"Awww…you're all wrong." I didn't know I could turn red with embarrassment until then.

"No. You haven't. She would have been a lot more upset seeing you here with me. When you do 'do' her she's going to be climbing the walls." Lila started chomping on her salad as if she hadn't said anything shocking.

"Lila, please. I'm Loretta's boss. It's not even like that. Why do you have to assume the worst with me and other women?"

"I have a better question for you. When are you going to slow down, Reggie?"

"I don't know. Honestly…Do you have a reason for asking?"

"…Once upon a time, I did."

17 Neal Wallace

I managed to get another nap in before Shenita returned with the car. She had it all day so I got to take it to work. I didn't want to bother Reggie again, especially after him getting drunk last night. I figured I'd wait a few days before bugging him for a ride.

On my way to work, I exited early off the freeway and headed downtown. There were some older vacant buildings near the bus station on Main that I wanted to look at. I passed down McKinney with City Hall on my left and the public library on my right. A family of foreign tourists was crossing the street with their Umbro sportswear on; looking for the museum no doubt. The Wells Fargo Plaza building on Louisiana shot up above the landscape of other glass temples. Reggie's girl, Lila the attorney, had her office up in there. *Sigh*. Incredible place. The building took up a whole damn block. I *knew* I couldn't afford the space in there even if Lila put in a good word for me. I was going to have to set my sights on cheaper restaurant sites...for now. I cursed to myself about the construction work on the streets as I slowed for all the bumps and broken pavement.

I looked at my watch as I made my way to Main and took a right. I found the vacant brown buildings I was looking for, but I had to be to work. I found a pen and piece of paper in the armrest compartment and took them out. I slowed as I looked for the phone number of the commercial realtor on the signs in the windows. I could always come back tomorrow. Even though this wasn't the high end of town, I was sure the space commanded a hefty price. As the colors of the street signs changed and began displaying the

Vietnamese version of the street names just below, I continued south.

My lollygagging caught up with me as I worked my way down to Richmond and zoomed through a few yellow lights, as they turned red. I passed the club, Jamaica Jamaica, on my left and my old memories brought a smile to my face. Reggie and me used to raise hell up in there, but we shied away from that crowd these days…well, at least I did.

I relaxed when I saw Greenway Plaza up ahead with the lighted Mirage sign near the street. I still had minutes to spare. I stopped at the red light and made my turn onto Timmons when the light changed. I saw Melissa…oops…Me-Me's Corolla around back and decided to park next to it. Funny, I thought she was going to be off this day…not that I was checking the schedule or anything. I grabbed my apron from off the back seat and walked into the usual madhouse that I felt perfectly at home in.

This Wednesday started off on a quiet note. Small turnout meant that I was going home early tonight. I was going to be off this weekend too when the crowd was sure to pick up. I did notice Me-Me scurrying around by the hostess area. I managed to holler at her when she passed through the kitchen to place an order.

"What are you doing working today?"

"Tookie took off to visit her mom in Beaumont, so I decided to make some extra cash for the week. If I ever want to get out of my shitty apartment, I'm going to need a lot more hours."

"It's none of my business, but did you ever go to college?"

"Heh. No. No college for me, Neal. I was glad to be out of high school…especially after my brother died. Well…um…I have a break coming up. Want to join me?"

"Sure. I'd be happy to."

Me-Me came around about half an hour later for her break. Things were still relatively slow, so I bailed out on the kitchen and left my hat on the counter. There was a small reserved seating area near the kitchen that most of the employees used. We picked one of the tables there and I pulled the chair out for her before seating myself.

I had palmed some carrot sticks from the back and offered one to Me-Me.

"No thanks," she said while I put one in my mouth like a cigarette.

"I was asking you about college earlier because I know you could be doing better than this. I wasn't trying to upset you or anything. Reggie told me a little bit about your brother and stuff." I looked apologetically across the table.

"No offense taken. I'm okay with that now. Trust me," she said as she lifted her glasses off the end of her nose. She was looking at a smudge on one of the lenses. "Did Reggie make it home okay last night?"

"Yeah. He slept most of it off on our couch last night. I should have called him today just to make sure."

"That boy there," Me-Me said with a giggle.

"Yeah. You always gotta watch Reggie; he's always into something. I love him like a brother though."

"I think we got that in common, Neal," Me-Me uttered with a distant look on her face.

"For as much as Reg has going for him in life, I'd hate to see his fondness for the ladies cause that to all come crashing down."

"Reggie will be alright. He always comes out on top," Me-Me said admiringly in his defense. Her smile made me wonder what was going through her lovely head.

"I didn't hear you singing today."

"Sheesh. I don't do it all the time. You trying to embarrass me again? I only do that when I want to take my mind off things. You not gonna stop, huh?"

"Alright! Alright!"

"How are things going with your wife?"

"Better…I think. She wasn't drunk last night when I came home with Reg, if that's what you mean." I wasn't getting any more personal than that, although she was extremely easy to talk to.

"Heh. Actually, I just meant how are you two getting along. Sobriety's good, I guess."

"Yeah. It's good."

"You said the other night that you wanted your own restaurant." She remembered??!!

"Yeah. I'm surprised you remembered."

"Why wouldn't I? Just because I don't have a college degree like *some people* doesn't mean I don't listen. Haha!"

"Cute. Want to know something?"

"What?"

"I looked at some buildings downtown on my way here. I need to call on the prices."

"Oh? You're serious with this. You know what you want to name it?"

"Not really. I'm open to suggestions." Me-Me closed her eyes and thought.

"How about 'Lullaby'?" The name rolled off Me-Me's tongue as if meant to be.

"What made you think of that?"

"I don't know. It just seemed right. You're always talking about my singing and stuff. Why not?"

"I *like* it." That name had a lot of meaning for me. It made me think of Me-Me's wonderful singing, but also something more...Like what you would sing to a little child. With just one word, my dream burned brighter.

18 Reggie Collins

"I didn't know you were friends with Lila Reed," Loretta gushed out as she came rushing into my office the next day. She was wearing the usual khaki slacks, but had a lace denim shirt, which faintly revealed her shoulders underneath. She was no Salma Hayek, but then Salma was no Loretta Juarez either.

"Yes. Well, now you know." What are you getting at? Spit it out. "Need something?"

"Matter of fact, yes. Want to do lunch today? It's the *least* you could do since you were occupied yesterday."

"You don't quit, do you?" I asked as I gave Loretta a tired smile.

"Am I supposed to? Just let me know, boss."

"…Okay. But it'll have to be somewhere fast. I've got a lot of work to catch up on."

"Wherever you want to take me…Reggie." Oh shit. She started it again. I wish I could tell what was going on in her head, but I was coming up blank. I'm sure I could find out, but my means would be inappropriate for the workplace.

"Alright. Wherever I want to go, huh?"

"Yep."

"Let me clear up a few things on my desk. I'll be ready to go in a few."

Loretta left out and I just sat there for a few minutes, thinking. I looked over at my plaques on the wall before taking a deep breath and walking out on the floor.

Loretta was standing by Sam's cubicle, talking it up with him. She began to wrap up the conversation and excuse herself as I approached.

"Ready?"

"Yes."

"Good." I turned away and looked down at a seated Sam. "Sam, we're going to lunch. Want to come?" It was almost a demand rather than a request. Sam paused before nodding in agreement.

I looked back at Ruby. She was sitting behind her desk outside my office and was shaking her head while silently laughing. I gave her a wink. I never made eye contact with Loretta out of fear of being turned to stone. I sensed her displeasure though. Oh well.

We were walking over to the Mustang when I realized that this was the first time anyone at work had noticed my ride was missing.

Sam whistled and said, "I was wondering who this was for. Nice. You traded in your Pathfinder, Reggie?" Sam was big on cars. The tall, gangly white boy had an old souped-up Chevelle that was his pride and joy.

"No. Uh…it's in the shop. This is just a rental. I have to return it next week."

"Oh. You're going to let me smoke the tires before you bring it back."

"Okay. Just don't wreck it, Sam." Loretta was still silent.

I unlocked the car and dropped the top. It was sunny, but surprisingly mild today.

Sam crawled into the space that doubled for a backseat. Loretta then seated herself in the front. I turned the radio on low as we exited our parking lot onto Bissonnet with a screech. It was such a nice day that I felt like eating outside and I knew just the place. I passed under 59 and turned onto South Braeswood. Yep, Little Frenchie's Fried Chicken was just the ticket today.

I drove up into the shopping center parking lot on the corner of South Braeswood and South Gessner. I backed the car into a parking spot right in front of Frenchie's. I left the top down as we were going to be sitting right outside.

The three of us walked up onto the wooden deck and into the small building. From the looks on their faces, I could tell the two of them had never been here, let alone knew it existed. Loretta cut her eyes at me when I smiled in her direction. Sam simply stared up at the menu on the wall behind the counter. I knew what I wanted, so I ordered first followed by Loretta. I walked out to one of the cement tables and sat down with my two piece and biscuit. Loretta and Sam were still inside, but Loretta followed shortly with her lunch.

"I *should* sit at another table," Loretta said with a smile and a raised eyebrow.

"*What did I do*?" I asked innocently.

"You know what you did. This lunch 'thing' with Sam."

"Loretta...what do you think you're doing? Seriously."

"You're a grown man; a good looking one too. I would think you could figure it out."

"Loretta, I'm your boss. You're playing a dangerous game and I'm sorry, but I can't play. I'm flattered, but I'm sure you'd have no problem finding some other man. *Whew*. You look good and I'm sure you know it. I'm not the one though."

"Because of that attorney? I'm not worrying about her, Reggie. Just give me a little bit of your time...to convince you." Damn. It was hard being me.

"It has nothing to do with my friend. It's just inappropriate, that's all."

Loretta laughed and replied with just a trace of an accent, "You want me. I can see it all over your face. I'll be patient though." What was this shit with women being able to read me all of a sudden? I was doing my best Boy Scout routine and actually behaving for a change, but Loretta was making it hard on a brother.

I was saved when Sam came out with his tray. I couldn't tell if he noticed the abrupt silence as he sat down.

Sam said, "What? Is something hanging from my nose?"

19 Reggie Collins

I knew that my ride wasn't promised until Monday, but I called the shop anyway just before I got off work Friday. The older Hernandez wasn't available, so I had to try to communicate with his son again. I was tempted to ask Loretta to translate, but I needed to avoid any situations with her. She might ask me to return the favor. I managed to get a "Monday, Monday, Monday" out of him, so I assumed I needed to check back Monday.

I had called Neal earlier and we had decided to hit the gym after I got off work. Neal's lucky ass was off already for the whole weekend. I arrived at the 24-hour Body Systems USA ahead of Neal. Traffic from the north had probably slowed him. I hadn't been to the gym in about a month, so I knew I would be sore the entire weekend. Neal probably needed to be in here more than me. Neal was around six feet three and weighed about two twenty-eight, while I was a leaner six feet one and one hundred eighty-five pounds.

I showed my ID card to the attendant at the front desk. He noticed that my membership was almost up and tried to give me a quick renewal sales pitch. I was going to renew, but didn't feel like the bother today. They really made their money with this gym. No matter what time I came in, it always had a crowd. I scanned the place for familiar faces before heading to the locker room with my gym bag. It had been a while. The only face I knew was this older bald brother who was in better shape than I was. Heh. He always had his white sweatband on. There were a lot of unfamiliar faces (and bodies) that I wouldn't mind getting to know though.

In the locker room, I changed into my gray sweat bottoms and black muscle shirt. I laced up my new cross-trainers that hadn't been broken in yet and locked up my clothes.

I saw Neal walking past the turnstile as I stepped out ready to go. Neal was wearing his workout gear. He had already started sweating from the heat outside. His white T-shirt was looking like he had just finished working out and his red shorts were wrinkled.

"Whatchasay, bro."

"Alright, Reg."

"You feel like jogging upstairs?"

"Yeah. Look, Shenita came along."

I looked toward the front desk and saw Shenita coming into view. She was wearing a dark blue sports bra with black stretch pants. For a brief second, my mind took me back to the view I had of what was underneath those clothes when she woke me up on the couch. I quickly put that image out of my head.

"Uh huh. She came to make sure none of these women in here took her big ol' teddy bear away from her at the gym. See, there's hope for you two lovebirds after all," I said jokingly to Neal as I elbowed him. Neal laughed and told me to hush as the Mrs. approached us.

"Hey Nita. What's up?"

"Nothin'. How about with you, Reg?"

"Work, work, work. Lila wanted me to check with you two about going out this weekend."

"That sounds good," Shenita replied. Neal was caught off guard by her response.

"Good. I'll call her tonight and let her know."

Neal added, "Yeah. That time we went to the comedy club was the best."

"Any wedding bells in the future, Reg?" Shenita asked.

"Please. You know me. Besides, if that was the case, I wouldn't be going to New Orleans with you guys."

"So no cold feet about going out there for Kelly's birthday, huh?"

"Nope. I said I'd go. I plan on having a good time."

"Just don't be freaking my sister, ya understand? She's a grown woman and can…and will do what she wants. Just don't mess with her head."

"Damn. Between you and your husband here, you two give me too much credit. Besides…she might blow my mind."

"Uh huh," she said as she cut her eyes and looked at me up and down. Funny. I never saw her look at me that way. She continued, "Well. On that note, I guess I'll let you two gentlemen try to get buff. I'm going right over to this treadmill. I need to work on this fat ass."

Neal responded, "Baby, you don't need any work on your ass. It's perfect just the way it is." And you know what? Upon further review, he was right too.

"Ready to do a few laps?" I asked Neal. He shrugged and we headed upstairs.

The indoor track made up the bulk of the second level and circled the perimeter of the gym below. There were two sets of joggers on the track already. One group was passing as we walked out onto the track from the stairway. It was made up of two older white men who looked like they belonged on the golf course instead. One was checking his pulse while the other was jabbering about a patient of his. The other group, which was on the other side of the building, consisted of a sister and a blonde white girl. They both looked like they were wannabe models. They were probably getting in shape to purge after a good meal later on. Heh.

After stretching, we started off at a moderate pace.

"You still got your speed from college, Neal?" Neal played football for TSU his sophomore year and was a terror in the backfield.

"Hell naw. The only thing I've chased recently was my neighbor's dog when he took our paper. He got away."

"I hear ya, bro. I need to make it in here consistently, but it's hard."

"Your women keepin' you too busy?"

"…Sometimes."

"How do you keep Lila around? I mean, I know you and her have that understanding, but…damn. She just seems different."

"Yeah. Lila's special. She's free to do what she wants too, but why go anywhere else when you got 'The Reg'. I think our relationship works because it fits her schedule too."

"So what would you do if she suddenly gave you an ultimatum one day?"

"I don't know. I try not to give that kind of stuff much thought. I've got another problem lately," I said as I eyed the two female joggers that were overtaking us.

"That mess with Trina?"

"Nah. I'm working on that problem now. No, this one's at work. Sexy ass Mexican chick named Loretta. She's a member of my claim group."

"So you're in charge of her. Damn. That's nothing but trouble."

"I know. Believe me, I know. I'm not touching that, but she's making it hard."

"Now how come I never had your kind of problems? What is it? What kind of cologne you wearin', bro? *Tell me.*"

"You so crazy. C'mon…let's finish another lap before those girls pass us again."

20 Neal Wallace

We had planned on meeting somewhere before the club, but Lila was running late. Shenita and I went on ahead and had a light dinner at the Seacourt Bar and Grill before going over to Club N-Sane for a night of dancing and partying. We heard 97.9 broadcasting live from there the week before and Shenita thought it might be a great idea to check it out. Shenita had me speechless. She was wearing this tight, black sleeveless bodysuit with black sandals. It had a V neckline with these two metal snaps that matched her belt. This was my first time seeing her in this. She had her hair combed over to one side, just the way I like it too. I wore a white silk shirt that was my birthday present from last year along with a pair of black slacks.

We were just in time to get a good table near the dance floor. Reggie had called on our cell phone to let us know they were on their way. While we waited, Shenita ordered a glass of wine and I ordered a Crown and Coke. The deejay was beginning to pick up the pace of the music as more people began to flow in. I had just looked at my watch and was about to order another round when Shenita spotted Lila and Reg.

The two of them made one hell of a good-looking couple and were aware of it. Both of them gave off an air of confidence that I wished I had. Lila was wearing black like Shenita, but had a different look. She wore a simple black dress; a *short* simple black dress that contrasted with her skin tone. Lila was wearing her long black hair straight down this night. Her statement said, "less is best". My boy, Reggie, was stylin' as usual. He was wearing one of his black Italian numbers with a red shirt. I noticed the handholding that was going down between the two of them and smiled. Reggie may have been too stubborn or cocky to admit it, but he was in love.

"Sorry we're running late, y'all," Reggie said as he pulled out Lila's chair for her.

"It's all my fault. Reggie was ready to go, but I had to listen to a client bitch and moan for an hour."

"On a Saturday?" Shenita blurted out.

"Yes. It happens from time to time. Especially when there's a lot of money on the line," Lila answered politely.

I said, "Well, I'm glad you two made it. We don't get to go out much with our work schedules and stuff."

"And with our bills," Shenita huffed. I cringed in embarrassment.

"Anybody ready to dance?" Reggie asked to loosen the mood. He gave me a smile that said, "You're welcome".

Shenita and I were ready and Reggie coerced Lila out on the floor. We found a spot where we couples could dance next to each other. Reggie was always a natural on the floor and this time was no different. Lila was a little more reserved, but that may have had more to do with the length of her dress. Shenita was grinding up against me and giving me memories of our last lovemaking session. I was always a little bit of a klutz when it came to dancing except for when doing the electric slide. I did my usual number where I held my arms up and clapped while trying to look cool. Most eyes would be on Shenita so I would be okay. I didn't know if Shenita's upbringing in New Orleans had anything to do with it, but she was so free, uninhibited, and *happy* when she danced. It was like being with a different woman. Yep, my baby was a sexy muther.

We danced most of the night with a few breaks in between and even got a Soul Train dance line started up in the club. At one point, the deejay went Old School and the four of us started doing the wop. Later on, Shenita would holler "switch!" and she and Lila would swap dance partners. I felt a little awkward dancing with Lila and kept my distance out of fear of stepping on her toes. The other couple of Reggie and Shenita had no such problems. The two of them were getting off as if they had been dancing together for years. A slight twinge of jealousy crept up as I looked on. I knew I couldn't dance like that, but I wished I were able to do something on Nita's level to bring joy to her. We switched a few more times and each time, Shenita would have to switch gears when coming back to me; Lila too. I was becoming a little too obsessed with my inadequacies when the deejay came to my rescue.

Donell Jones' *Where I Wanna Be* came on. Shenita was still dancing with Reggie and got caught in an awkward moment of her own until Reggie motioned for Lila to dance with him. I was tired, so Shenita and I left the two of them on the floor and went back to our table. I ordered another round for the two of us.

"Look at the two of them out there. I think my boy's falling in love."

"You think? Reggie's always going to be Reggie, Neal. I think he likes Lila a lot, but that's as far as it goes."

"You sound a little bit catty with that remark, baby. You're not trying to hate on Ms. Reed out there, huh?"

"Heh. Hell no. I'm just saying what I think. You know I'm saving all my hate for you, my big teddy bear."

"If I didn't know better, I'd swear you want my boy for yourself."

"Ha! *Please*. I want Reggie as much as you want his little friend that works with you,…what's her name? Fee-Fee?"

"Cute. Don't forget I got the keys to the car tonight."

"Don't forget I would have no problem getting a ride home either."

I took a look at Shenita and said, "Yeah, but to *whose* home?" I was just playing around, but I may have crossed the line.

"That was some rude shit, Neal." Shenita's eyes were giving me those "hate rays".

"*What*?! I thought we were just playing around."

"Uh huh. Whatever. I don't want to talk about it anymore."

"…So I guess this means no slow dance, huh?"

21 Reggie Collins

A night of fun at Lila's side made all my problems and issues seem inconsequential.

The smell of her Gucci Rush perfume was intoxicating as I held her tightly in my arms on the dance floor. Donell Jones' song said it all. I was surprised that Neal and Shenita weren't out on the floor too. It looked like they were having a great time as well. The deejay kept the mood going and went to *Adore* by Prince next. I guess he really wanted some babies made tonight.

Lila's head was resting on my shoulder as her hair brushed across my lips. I started to blow it away, but left it there. I was in Club N-Sane with the most beautiful woman in the place and she was all mine...just as I was hers, for the time we were together. I was having all kinds of dangerous thoughts this night.

We were slow dancing for what seemed an eternity before the music changed and brought us back down to Earth.

Lila looked up at me and said, "Let's go." No further words were needed. Her eyes said it all.

I led Lila off the dance floor by the hand and over to our table. Neal and Shenita were sitting there. Both were finishing off their drinks and weren't saying much.

"Um...we're about to go, y'all. We both had a great time tonight."

"Alright, Reggie. Me and the Mrs. are calling it a night too. I'll holler at you later."

Shenita flashed a polite smile at us as she adjusted her bodysuit before standing up. It seemed like her breasts need some rearranging up in there. I was sure Neal was going to set them free when they got home. Haha!

We all walked out together and said a final goodbye before going our separate ways. Lila was feeling chilly in the late night breeze, so I draped my jacket over her.

"Can you keep the top up?" she asked of me as I started the car.

"Anything for you."

"Don't say what you can't deliver," she said as she wrapped her arm around mine. I didn't reply and simply drove instead.

I headed north up Hillcroft toward Westheimer with Lila's townhouse as my destination in mind. When the red light caught us at Richmond, Lila spoke up.

"I want to go to your apartment tonight."

I looked at her. "You know…you're spending the night if we go there."

Spending the night was something we had agreed not to do as part of our "relationship".

"I know," she replied.

I made a right onto Richmond and then looped back to take Hillcroft south to 59…and then home.

Less than thirty minutes later, we were at my door. Lila left my jacket in the car. I was unlocking the door, but kept stopping to kiss her neck and chest. Lila wasn't helping as she had me sandwiched in the doorway with her body. I succeeded in unlocking my door and when I turned the knob, the both of us fell into my apartment and onto the floor. Lila landed on top of me with a laugh and began removing my shirt. She straddled me and her already short dress came all the way up revealing a black thong. I could feel Lila's warmth through my pants as she repositioned herself on top of my waist. We kissed passionately again as I squeezed her tight bare ass.

"Lila?"

"*Mmmm.* Hmmm?"

"My alarm. I gotta turn my alarm off before it goes off." Our heavy breathing and kissing had distracted me from the alarm tone going off by my still-open door.

Lila rolled off me and pulled her dress back down. I jumped up and punched in my code before the chime stopped. I didn't need my alarm service calling me for my password and shit. This was not the time for answering calls. I turned around expecting to see Lila still on the living room floor, but she was standing before me. I pushed the door closed and locked it without taking my eyes off her. It was different this night, as I never saw her look vulnerable before.

My shirt was halfway off, so I let it fall to the floor. I took Lila's hand and she walked over to me and began digging her nails into the back of my neck as she nipped at the front of my neck and kissed my chest. I reached behind her and pulled her zipper down. Lila then slowed to let the dress drop to her ankles before resuming. I felt Lila's bare breasts against my chest as our sweat mixed. Her perfume and the feel of her skin were beginning to work me up and I began unbuckling my belt.

"*Reggie. Take me,*" she whispered amidst the silence of the room. I reached under Lila's arms and hoisted her up. Lila responded by wrapping her legs around me and pushing my head in between her breasts. I carried her across the dimly lit apartment and to my bedroom as I left a passion mark on her chest. Lila hated those, especially since she was so bright, but I heard no complaints from her this time.

I reached over and turned the ceiling fan on before lowering her onto the bed. Lila let her shoes fall to the floor and arched her back to remove her thong. She then flipped it off her foot and in my general vicinity. I approached the bed and Lila crawled over like a cat and finished removing my belt and pants. She grabbed my boxers with one hand and with a *yank* they were down on the floor. Lila then pulled me down onto the bed and we resumed kissing. I grabbed her breasts in both hands and began working her nipples and running my tongue across them. We were positioned on our sides and Lila had put me between her legs. I could feel her wetness all over it and rubbed the head against her clitoris. Lila began to grind against it in response.

Lila's breathing had gotten louder and she suddenly rolled onto her back.

"Give it to me," she begged.

I began to get up to get a condom from out the bathroom, but Lila had a different idea.

"No," she said as she grabbed my arm.

"No?" I asked back in disbelief. "Are you sure?"

"I want all of you this time. I love you, Reg."

"I...I know."

"*Make love to me, Champ.*"

Lila slid back further in the bed and spread her legs to welcome me inside her. As I entered Lila and went deeper, I heard a tearful "*Yes*" come out of her mouth.

22 Neal Wallace

Upon our return from Club N-Sane, there was no action for this brother. It was straight to bed for us in our house on Manboro Court. On Sunday, I was still feeling the aftermath of last night's joking that had gone too far.

We both woke up on time to make it to the ten-fifteen service at New Light. I pulled my suit out of the closet, so I could change quickly once out of the shower. As I was fixing a quick breakfast in the kitchen, Shenita's sister, Kelly, called collect from New Orleans. She probably was checking up with Shenita about our upcoming trip. I hung up the phone when I heard Shenita pick up the other line. Kelly lived in a shotgun-style house in the Uptown area of New Orleans with her grandmother. Shenita and Kelly's grandmother was senile and generally stayed in her bedroom, so Kelly had run of the whole house.

Shenita stayed on the phone upstairs until I reminded her of the time. She was still pissed off from my comments last night, so she stayed pretty tight-lipped. Needless to say, we made it to the service late. I used to attend Sunday services at a smaller church down in Third Ward, but New Light was much closer to our house. Besides that, Shenita was used to the larger surroundings from her time back home when she attended one of the more popular full-gospel Baptist churches.

When service ended around noon, I thought we were going home, but Shenita had something she needed to do. She had brought a plastic Dillard's bag in the car with us when we left for church, but I was too busy to really notice until now.

"I need to go to Dillard's by the Galleria," she said as she leaned into the backseat and retrieved her bag.

"Okay." I entered onto I-45 as instructed and stole a glance at what Shenita was fumbling with in the bag.

"Hey! That's your outfit from last night. Something wrong with it?"

"Nope. Unless you count costing too much as something wrong."

"But, you wore that."

"*Whew*. You catch on fast. Now I know why I married you."

"You're bringing it back?"

"*Yes*. You didn't see me fumbling with the price tag in the club? It kept rubbing against one of my breasts."

"Why don't you keep it? It looked great on you."

"Because we can't afford it! You know how much trouble we're having with our bills now. *Humph*. I wasn't going in the club and be outdressed by Lila Moneybags."

"Oh," was all I could say in response to Shenita's bitter tone.

I didn't say much during the rest of the trip to the store. I hated to say it, but I was finding a lot more to dislike about my wife.

When we arrived at Dillard's, I felt embarrassment in Shenita's having to return the outfit. Maybe I could swing a second job during the day. We danced so much that I was sure the cashier could smell the sweat and/or the perfume all over it. It made me feel worse that the cashier was an older white woman. I was sure this encounter was going to enforce whatever stereotypes were running through her mind.

"I am the head chef at Mirage! Do you know that?" I wanted to walk up to her and scream, but remained in the distance. The cashier's knowing that would only have made things worse and done me no good. Pride was one thing, but being broke was another. Just then, I began to realize where maybe some of Shenita's animosity toward me was coming from; I was failing her as a husband and as the chief provider. How could I expect Shenita to want to have a kid when I couldn't even handle my responsibilities as a husband?

Was this where my pops' rage came from?

"You ready?" Shenita had successfully returned the outfit. The cashier was shaking her head in a *tisk, tisk, tisk* manner behind Shenita's back. I started to say something, but bit my tongue and walked away with my wife.

23 Reggie Collins

I woke up briefly and confirmed it wasn't a dream. Lila's warm body was still in my bed and sleeping soundly. Her outstretched leg was hanging out from under the sheet. I even think I heard a little snore. We had made intense, passionate love through the night. Love. A funny feeling came along with that word; it was a good feeling though. Last night was a very different moment in our relationship. I curled up behind Ms. Reed and kissed her behind her ear. Lila let out a gentle moan as I went back to sleep.

I thought someone in my apartment complex was hammering until I realized it was a knock at my door. We had slept almost the entire morning and Lila was still in a coma. Heh, I wasn't mad at her. I thought that it might have been Neal, so I searched for my boxers on the floor. I put my boxers on and wiped the cold from my eyes. I took one more look at Lila before closing the bedroom door and pumping my fist with an emphatic "yes!"

I should have noticed the knocking being too light to be Neal's, but I wasn't fully awake yet.

"Whoo! Look at that body!" Me-Me shouted as she walked in and gave me a kiss on the cheek. She was wearing short blue shorts and a white Meoshe half-shirt that made my memories of her as a tomboy blur. Me-Me got in a quick squeeze of my right bicep as she strolled by and made herself at home.

"Hey, girl. Do you know what time it is?" I asked as I closed the door.

"Yeah. It's eleven o'clock." Me-Me was in my kitchen and digging in the cabinet.

"*Oh yeah.* I forgot for a second."

"Man, you need to go to H-E-B. You ain't got shit in here."

"You know I lead a bachelor's life, Me-Me. I'll probably go by the store once I get dressed and wake up a little more."

"Out acting wild, huh? You still fucking crazy ass Trina…"

Just then, Me-Me stopped in mid-sentence as she heard the squeak of my bedroom door as it opened. Lila came out wearing my red dress shirt from the night before. The sound of voices must have awakened her. I silently shuddered at thinking Lila heard Me-Me's comments about Trina.

Me-Me's eyes expanded behind her specs at the sight of Lila walking out of my bedroom. I shared almost everything with my lil' sis, so she knew about the "sleeping over" issue with Lila and me. Me-Me cut a quick look at me before regaining her composure and picking her mouth up off the floor.

"Hey, Lila. Did I wake you with my loud mouth, girl?"

"Hey. No. I missed Reggie in the bed beside me and woke up."

I smiled and shrugged my shoulders at Me-Me. We would talk later. Lila wrapped her arms around me and we kissed.

"Sorry about disturbing you two."

"It's alright, Me-Me. We went out with Neal and Shenita last night and just decided to sleep-in this morning."

"You need to go out with us next time. We had a blast," Lila added.

"Nah. I would have to pass on that. I don't think Neal's wife wants to be my buddy any time soon," Me-Me said with a laugh. "Besides, I'm between significant others right now and would just be a fifth wheel."

"Nonsense. You are always welcome, lil' sis."

"Aww. That's what I like about you, Reggie. You're always looking out for me," Me-Me bubbly replied. "Lila, you need to tie this one down."

"Thanks, Me-Me," Lila responded. "I need to leave to buy some rope for him now."

Lila's and my eyes met right then. Our relationship had taken a change and we were both trying to find our way now. The feeling of being on cloud nine earlier this morning was now replaced by an uneasiness on my part. I was so used to the game and the thrill of the chase. Lila was always someone so strong and independent that I would walk on coals for her. Now, in giving me her heart, had she lost mine? Her giving of herself last night was a sign of her great strength, but why was I reacting now as if it were a weakness? Had the rules we laid down changed now? Maybe I was just scared at taking the chance of being hurt and this was my defense mechanism.

"Well, I'm going back in the room to clean up. Nice seeing you again, Me-Me."

Lila sauntered back to my bedroom with her usual confidence. My eyes followed her as I longed to be with her again. I had company though and I'm sure Me-Me had questions.

Me-Me walked out of the kitchen and whispered to me, "Boy, looks like you're finally hanging it up. You are getting kind of old for all that playing around."

Just then, I heard my bathroom shower come on.

"Girl, please," I answered with a huff and a macho thump of my chest. "I'm only thirty years old and have several years left. I can't have a woman spend the night?"

"Shit. You and I know that Lila isn't just *any* woman. Something changed, huh?"

"No…Maybe. I don't know."

"Damn. I'm going to have to start calling first before showing up over here."

"You know you're always welcome without calling. You're my *girl*, remember?" I said as I gave Me-Me a hug. "Remember that time when I let you crash in my bed and you threw up all over it?"

"Heh," Me-Me laughed, "and you rolled me onto the floor while you cleaned it up."

"Yep. I'll always be here for you."

"I know, Reg." I felt Me-Me's hands oddly grip into my back then release.

We ended our embrace and Me-Me smiled before winking and leaving out the door while humming to herself.

I stood there for a second then turned my attention to the closed bedroom door. I could hear the shower still running. My red shirt was hanging by the towels in the bathroom and I could see Lila's silhouette behind the shower curtain. My hormones started kicking into overdrive again as I lusted for more of Lila. I yanked the shower curtain back, startling Lila and sending water splashing onto the bathroom floor. She was standing there wet with a bar of soap in her hand and her hair slicked back. Lila's shock was replaced by a look of desire on her face as well.

"Me-Me's gone?"

"Yep."

She looked down at my boxers and saw my hard-on striving for daylight. She then motioned with one finger for me to join her.

I removed my boxers and stepped into the shower face-to-face with her. The spray from the shower nozzle behind her was flying off her back and causing drops to roll down the front of her body. I leaned over and licked up a bead of water that was resting on one of her hard nipples. Lila stepped up onto the bathtub edge to help with the height difference and grabbed my shoulders to brace herself as her body trembled with anticipation. I slowly moved Lila around so her back was to the wall, then lowered her onto me. We still had a lot to talk about, but now was not the time.

24 Neal Wallace

The embarrassing scene at Dillard's was concluded. Shenita had passed on a walk through the Galleria across the street.

"Do you do this often?" I asked as we walked to our parked car.

"With the clothes? No. It's really nothing out of the ordinary. I can't believe you *never* heard of that."

"I guess it's a woman thing. I only bring stuff back when it doesn't fit."

I opened my car door and unlocked Shenita's.

"I guess you haven't been really poor then," Shenita shot back as she plopped down in the passenger seat.

"I thought about getting a second job."

"You can't do that with your work schedule. They could have you working days at any time."

"Yeah. I thought about that too. Once I get my own place…"

"That restaurant shit again, huh?"

"…Yeah. That restaurant *shit* again." I hated it when she dismissed my thoughts like that. "I found a couple of places downtown. Want to see?"

"…Sure." Surprise, surprise.

When we exited off the freeway downtown, Shenita showed more interest.

"You're looking at putting your restaurant down *here?*" she asked while looking up at the shining skyscrapers.

"Sort of."

We drove past the gleaming towers of capitalism and continued toward the vacant space on Main near the bus station.

"Hey! Where are you going?"

"Just a little further."

"But all the nice stuff is back there," she said while pointing back at the tall stuff.

"There's no way in hell we could afford any space by that 'nice stuff'. It's doubtful I could swing the stuff up ahead, but I'm going to check on it."

We started slowing by the vacant property I had spotted Wednesday.

"Hey! This is by the bus station! *Eeeewww.* Mirage is in a much nicer area."

"Yeah, but I can't afford anything near the Compaq Center. C'mon, this isn't that bad. You have to start somewhere."

I slowed the car and parked next to the sidewalk right across the street.

"Are you coming to look?"

"No. I'll stay in the car."

I started to say something, but held back. I left the car running to keep Shenita cool under the AC. As I ran across the street, a few drops of cold rain landed on me. The clouds overhead were a dark gray while just down the street, they were a fluffy white. We were about to have an afternoon storm from the heat.

I used my hands to see through the glare of the windows. Both places were in relatively good condition, just old. One place looked like it was a former law office and the other one could have been a travel agency. The square footage appeared okay, but neither one had kitchen facilities already. Damn. It would cost a pretty penny to upgrade the facilities and I didn't know if the owner would let me do that. I would also have to check the local business codes and zoning. That was all pending my ability to afford the lease and to secure a business loan.

Just then, the skies opened up and I was caught in a downpour. I still had my suit coat on, so I quickly removed it and threw it over my head. I waited for a truck to pass before I darted across the street to the car.

I was drenched from the waist down when I jumped in. Shenita had slightly reclined her seat and was resting her head in the palm of her hand. As I wiped the water off and turned the AC vents on me, I started relaying what I saw to Shenita. She didn't say anything the whole time, but simply nodded her head. When I stopped talking, she waited for a second and just looked at me.

"You finished?"

"Yeah."

"Neal, if you think I'm going to co-sign for a loan on *that*, you are truly smoking crack. Take me home. I'm supposed to be doing something with our neighbor, Ramona, today."

25 Reggie Collins

"What are you doing here?"

Trina was caught off guard by my showing up on her doorstep late Sunday night. After what had occurred between Lila and me, I really did not want to be here. I started to let this whole thing rest, but I had a job that was unfinished and I hated leaving unfinished work. Besides, being here with Trina told me that I was still single and still the same man.

"I was in the neighborhood, so I figured I'd check you out. I've been thinking about you."

"Come in! Come in!" She bought it…hook, line, and sinker.

"Were you about to go to bed?" I already knew the answer which is why I came by so late. It put her in a more susceptible mood and left me not having to bother with the small talk.

"Yeah. I have to open the store in the morning."

Trina was an assistant manager at Connie Shoes in Northwest Mall. After first meeting her, I had gone by her job and she tried to freak me in the storeroom. When I turned her down back there was when I got my first taste of her Jekyll and Hyde personality. She cursed me out and pushed me out of her store before calling me back an hour later to apologize.

"I can go if you want me to…"

"No, you can sit on my bed while I fall asleep." I was supposed to have called her back the other day and had forgotten all about it. She was playing "distant", but she was an "up close" girl if anything.

I followed Trina down the skinny hallway to her bedroom. Her bedroom smelled of fresh incense. I knew Trina liked to hit the herb from time to time and I had probably disturbed her. Trina was wearing her weave curly now and I got a good view of the faded beauty college logo on her T-shirt when she got into bed.

"Why don't you slip those warm-ups off and come join me?" Trina tried to strike a sexy pose across her bed, but was yawning. I took a seat next to her.

"Sounds good, but I still don't know if I should. Remember when I said I was having these feelings?"

"Yeah. The last time you were over here. So?"

"Ever since I got my Pathfinder keyed, I've been finding myself thinking more and more about you." That wasn't really a lie.

"I told you I had nothing to do with that…" Trina suddenly sprang to life.

"Just hear me out. What I've been thinking about is that…maybe I've been taking you for granted. That's something I don't want to do, Trina. I want more out of this relationship, but I need you to come clean first. It would be hard to move on without honesty." I impressed myself with that.

"…You think you might want to go out with me sometimes?"

"Yeah. That would be nice."

"Marc Anthony's going to be at the Pavilion later this month." Trina mentioned with starry eyes.

"We could do that," I replied. "I'll check on the tickets. You want seats up front or on the hill?"

"The hill would be nice. We could *snuggle* while we watch."

"What do you feel like doing now though?"

"I suddenly feel like celebrating," Trina said with newfound energy as she got out of the bed.

"You know I don't smoke that shit, Trina."

"Haha! I wasn't talking about that, silly." With that said, Trina walked over to her radio/CD player that was plugged in on the floor. She put on some smooth instrumental jazz to help with the mood. I smiled at her as she walked to the light switch and flipped it off.

The lighting from outdoors and the display on her radio kept the room from being pitch black. I could make out Trina's silhouette as my eyes adjusted. She removed her T-shirt and approached me on the bed. I responded by taking off my shirt. Her soft hands ran back and forth along my shoulders as I held her small waist.

"C'mere," I said as I yanked her down onto the bed. I began kissing her gently on the lips at first until I felt her tongue probing out. I then responded in kind. The kissing got more intense as Trina began pulling my warm-up bottoms off. Once we were both fully naked and ready to get down to business, I had her sit on my lap with her back to me. That luscious booty could do some damage. I took a deep breath as her hot, moist confines began enveloping me. Trina then began to gyrate her hips as she dropped it down, sending me into fits. She was always sooo good. I was going to miss this, but had to move on with the plan. I fought getting lost in the moment and regained my composure.

"Trina?" I called out as I held Trina's shoulders from behind and forced her downward onto me as I thrust upward.

"Y, yes?"

"Is it good?"

"*Oooh! Yes!*"

"You know what I want?"

"N, no. Anything. It doesn't matter," she grunted. "Just…Don't…Stop."

She had started squeezing and groping her own breasts. I could feel the warm sweat off Trina's back on my chest.

"I need the truth. Did you do it, baby?"

"Y, your truck?"

"Yes, did you do it?"

"Oh, oh, oh, oh yes!" Trina was climaxing. "I, I did it. Don't, don't stop."

Success.

I had what I needed to know. Part two of my plan was out of the way, but this was getting good so I decided to stay and enjoy the ride.

"Oh, don't worry. I won't stop. Not until I'm through with you."

26 Neal Wallace

Shenita was outside in the driveway with our nosey neighbor, Ramona. I could hear them laughing from inside the house along with an occasional "yeah, girl" or "Whaat??!!" that I could make out. Shenita would fill me in later on what scandals our neighbors with too much time on their hands were involved in. Me? I was content to relax on the couch with a dose of HGTV. I didn't have the money for any of the projects they were showing, but it sure was relaxing. I had changed out of my wet clothes from earlier and had put on some jeans and one of my favorite weekend shirts.

The incident with Shenita returning the outfit had me thinking about my father. I tried not to think about him often. He still lived in the old house in Brookshire, but I never went back after my moms passed away. I had last spoken to him a year ago and Shenita had to twist my arm that time. She had been curious as to how he was doing then. I never shared all the horror stories with her, as I didn't want to drag up the past.

I dragged myself off the couch and went up the stairs to our bedroom. A lot of people had those electronic planners and organizers, but I still liked the old paper address books. My book was looking pretty ratty with several numbers crossed out and/or written over. I still remembered the number, but wanted to check to be sure.

Yep. I had it right.

The phone rang for a while. I was hanging up when I heard his voice.

"Hullo."

"What's up, pops?"

"Well, well, well. I thought you was dead, boy. I tried to call your number a while back and they said it was disconnected."

"Yeah. We moved. How you been?"

"I'm happy to be alive. You forgot where the house is, boy?"

"No. I've just been busy."

"You still married to that Baptiste girl?"

"Yeah. I'm still married to Shenita."

"I used to work with a Baptiste at the car dealership."

"Yeah. You've told me before…several times. She's from New Orleans, so I doubt they're any relation."

"That's a nice girl there. You need to bring her around sometime. You guys got any kids on the way?"

"Nope. Just trying to get everything else in order first."

"You not shootin' blanks are ya, boy?"

"No. Why do you have to be so rude?"

"I'm just wondering if Imma have a grandchild before I pass away."

"Look, I was just calling to check up on you…"

"I know. I know. I ain't cut ya outta my will or anything, boy. You still cookin' for them white folks?"

"I'm a chef. And I cook for everyone."

"Well, at least one of us rubbed off on you."

I began to see red just then. My hands were trembling and I felt the rage that I had fought so hard not to inherit from my pops.

"You lous—"

"Neal, who's that?" Shenita had walked into the bedroom and saw me on the phone with the crazed look on my face.

"Is that your wife?" my pops asked on the other end of the phone in response to hearing Shenita's voice.

"Yeah. It's Shenita."

"Let me talk to her, boy." I closed my eyes and took a deep breath before handing the phone to Shenita. I mumbled to her that it was my pops.

Shenita got into a bright and cheery conversation with my pops as she usually did. I was really wishing I hadn't made that call now. They carried on for several minutes until I went down to the kitchen to get something to drink.

After pouring myself some orange juice, I decided to vegetate on the couch again. I wasn't able to unwind anymore; not after trying to be civil to that son of a bitch. It was going to be another two years before I talked to him again. God forgive me, hopefully he would be dead by then.

"He wanted to say 'bye'. I looked around for you upstairs, but you had disappeared on me."

"Fuck him."

"Damn. You really have issues with him, huh? You need to cut that sweet old man some slack."

"You don't know what you're talking about. He's a miserable son of a bitch."

"That 'miserable son of a bitch' wants to see his son's house."

"What?! You told him where we live?"

"Yeah. I invited him over too. Maybe sometime after we get back from New Orleans."

"Great. *Fuckin'* great. I gotta get out of here before I punch a hole in the wall."

I finished my orange juice in one gulp and grabbed the car keys off the counter. I had ruined what was left of my Sunday with one stupid call.

"Where are you going?" Shenita asked in surprise.

"Out." was the last thing she heard before I slammed the side door.

27 Neal Wallace

"What are you doing here, Neal?"

"I'm just passing by, Tookie. I needed to check the kitchen schedule."

"Damn, you sho' is dedicated. I would have just called in."

"I had nothing else to do tonight. You guys look busy."

"Hell yeah. Now if you'll excuse me, I've got two orders to bring out."

Tookie was right about my being dedicated, but that had nothing to do with it tonight.

I had come by Mirage because I didn't want to return home. I had passed by Reggie's apartment first, but he wasn't there. If he wasn't with Lila, he was out creepin'. The way he and Lila were acting last night, I would bet they were probably together right now.

I had already reviewed the kitchen schedule because of my upcoming trip to New Orleans, so I gave it a pretend look-over this time. I happened to look over at the floor schedule while killing time. Me-Me was working tonight. I really needed someone to talk to, but still didn't feel completely comfortable with her. Sure, she was easy to talk to, but I had to know someone for a while to completely trust them.

I had made up my mind to go for a drive to Galveston and back when I was busted in the kitchen. I heard the familiar humming coming from behind me. The songbird stopped suddenly.

"Neal, what are you doing here?"

"Damn. You're sounding like Tookie. I just came in to check the schedule."

"Oh. I heard you and your wife went out last night with Reggie and Lila. Had a good time?"

"Yeah. It was okay. I was trying to reach Reggie before I came here. He wasn't at home though."

"Probably with Lila. She spent the night at his apartment. You try to call him on his cell?"

"Nah. Reggie always keeps his phone off. He only turns it on when he uses it. That way he doesn't get busted."

"Heh. He's always got everything figured out. You okay? You look like something's wrong," Me-Me said as she adjusted her glasses.

"…Just some stupid shit. I was looking for my dawg to talk to."

"I'm a good listener. Besides, I'm going to need someone else to hang with soon. It looks like Reggie might be getting serious with Lila and might not have much time for me and my stupid problems."

"I don't want to bother you. Besides, you've got work to do."

"Actually, I'll be off work in twenty minutes. I worked the early shift today. Wait up?"

"…What the hell. Sure."

Me-Me convinced me to follow her after she clocked out. We wound up at Casa Taco about a mile down Richmond from Mirage. When I walked in, I suddenly realized that I was starving and ordered a *numero tres* platter. Me-Me ordered a mega-nacho platter and a pitcher of frozen margaritas.

"You didn't have to order a pitcher, Me-Me. I didn't plan on drinking," I said as we carried our food out the outdoor eating area.

"S'okay. I can finish it on my own. I'm off tomorrow anyway."

"Maybe I'll have a little bit. I don't want to have to carry you out of here." The thought of Shenita's drinking episodes had made me change my mind.

We found one empty table facing the traffic on Richmond and put our stuff down.

"Something wrong with your food?" Me-Me asked as she tore into her nachos. I was slowly chewing my food with a look of concentration on my face.

"Heh. No. It's a habit of mine. I always try to figure out what's in someone else's cooking. One of my quirks from being in the business, I guess."

"So, what's on your mind?"

"A lot. Y'know, I was about to drive to Galveston when you caught me in the kitchen."

"One of those drives, huh? I've done that a couple of times. You just get in the car and go wherever it takes you. I did that when I broke up with my last boyfriend. Wound up in San Antonio and almost ran out of gas. Stupid. I called Reggie and he helped me out."

I took the pitcher and filled both our glasses. "Yeah. Reggie may be many things, but he's a loyal friend."

"Yep. He's one of the best things in my screwy life. Enough about me though. Are you gonna tell me why you're so damn glum?"

I took a big sip of my drink. "Things aren't going too good at home."

"If I had to guess, I'd say problems with the Mrs."

"Yep. You'd be right. We're just not getting along like we should. Haven't been for some time. Our money problems aren't helping. I'm hoping our trip to New Orleans will do us some good. It's like we hit some smooth areas, but then we run right into a pothole. Bam!"

"Bam?"

"Bam." We both broke out laughing on that one and toasted each other.

"Y'all thought about counseling?"

"Yeah. I don't think she'd go though. I'm the one with the problem, she'd say."

Me-Me asked, "How's 'Lullaby' coming along?"

"You still haven't forgotten about that. Well, I went back to those places today that I had talked to you about. I got soaked in the rain and my wife wouldn't get out of the car to look at them. Not necessarily in that order."

"Haha!" Me-Me laughed, "I'm sorry, but I couldn't help but laugh. Hee. Hee. I'm just...just picturing you in the rain with your wife in the car."

Our conversation continued on from our thoughts on life to who was our favorite comedian on the Kings of Comedy Tour. We finished off the first pitcher of margaritas and had moved on to number two. As we talked more, I found out that we had a lot in common, but a lot of differences as well which made things even more interesting. When I first met Shenita, I never thought I would find another woman as fascinating. I was wrong. *Whoa.* Something in the margaritas must have been talking. Time to ease up.

The drinks had Me-Me loosening up as well. She was now humming along with the instrumental music that was playing over the outdoor loudspeaker.

"You know what?" I asked of her.

"Nooooo," she answered in a silly manner.

"I want to hear you sing. Right here. Right now."

"And how much are you paying me?"

"I can't pay you anything, but I do have some stroke with your boss at the restaurant. An easier schedule maybe? C'mon!"

"You can't fix that! Boy, I'm getting tired of your harping on my singing. I only did a little singing in the choir when I was a kid, but that's it. Why don't you sing?"

"I'll sing if you sing. I'll even go first, Me-Me." I stood up and started moaning like a dog. The other restaurant goers were just noticing when Me-Me's long arms reached across the table and pulled me back into my chair.

"Boooy, you are crazy. No more drinks for you."

"So are you gonna sing now?"

Me-Me scowled at me from behind her specs before taking them off and laying them on the table. She paused for a second, then undid her top two buttons on her work shirt. I was sort of confused by what she was doing, and then I heard it.

Me-Me closed her eyes and started out slowly, quietly. I couldn't make out what she was singing at first, but as her voice rose I did. I hadn't heard *How Can I Ease the Pain* in a long time. This was a different Melissa Bonds. Shit, she was sultry. Me-Me had her eyes closed and didn't notice the restaurant crowd begin to take notice. I was as caught up as they were, so I didn't interrupt.

When Me-Me hit the a cappella, solo part of the Lisa Fisher song, her voice erupted in a fit of emotion that paralyzed me in my seat. Tears were beginning to stream down Me-Me's face as her voice subsided. I opened my mouth to say something, but the sound of clapping interrupted me. It came gradually at first, then got louder and louder. Me-Me was startled out of her zone by the applause. The restaurant crowd and some of the Casa Taco staff started cheering and whistling. Me-Me's singing was more beautiful than I ever imagined.

"Oh…my…God," was all Me-Me could say as she looked around and wiped the tears from her face. "Why didn't you stop me??"

"I couldn't. It would have cheated everyone here out of hearing your voice."

"I have to get out of here. I am *so* embarrassed."

"Ready to go home, *Ms. Houston*?"

"Yeah. I will get you back for this. I am going home and hide under the covers, but first I want to see the places you found for your restaurant."

"The locations downtown? You want to see them? Tonight?"

"I asked, didn't I?" she said as she twisted one of her braids. "Somebody has to see them with you. That's what buddies are for."

I tried to reach Lila at her office first thing Monday morning and they patched me through to her cell phone. I got back later than expected from Trina's last night and went straight to bed. The trip to New Orleans was coming up this weekend, so I needed to start getting some sleep before then. I hated going out of town on low batteries.

"Hey, Champ," Lila said in a broken tone as the transfer came through from her office.

"Good morning, Ms. Reed. You in traffic?"

"How did you ever guess?" she answered sarcastically, "Luckily, I don't have that far to go. You at work already?"

"Yeah, I'm at the office. I just wanted to tell you how incredible you are."

"Why, thank you, Reggie. Smooches to you too. I tried to call you last night to talk about 'things' between us, but you weren't home and your cell phone wasn't on."

"Yeah, I forgot to turn it-"

"Save it, loverboy. It's none of my business anyway. Look, I'm honestly not trying to pressure you with what I said at your apartment after the club. I know we have our understanding, but I was just being honest and upfront with you. That's all."

"Lila…what made you…"

"Decide?"

"Yeah…What made you decide?"

"I decided at the club that night. Actually, I thought about it when we were having lunch at Copeland's. Remember the stuff I said about you and that little 'hot tamale' at your office?"

"Loretta? How could I forget?"

"Well, I meant what I said about your probably doing her in the future. I'll admit that was pretty harsh of me though. The things I didn't say…were that I didn't want you to sleep with her and that I actually cared about whether or not you did. *That* was most important."

"Damn. You can still surprise me." I was hearing some deep shit.

"One more thing. Remember when I told you that I could read your eyes?"

"Yes."

"I can read them for good as well as bad. Reggie…I know how you feel about me without your saying it. I saw it most of all in your eyes at Club N-Sane. I just figured I'd come out and tell you my feelings that night…and show you."

I took a deep breath and collected my thoughts before speaking. "Lila, I…"

"Don't say anything yet. Look…I have to go see my parents up in Dallas for a couple of weeks. When I say that I don't want to pressure you, I mean it. Just think about what I said and we'll talk when I get back. Okay?"

"…Okay."

"Look, I'm just arriving at work now, baby. I'll talk to you later. I promise."

"Hey!"

"What?"

"…I've got tickets for us at the Pavilion later this month; Marc Anthony. Hillside."

"Oh! That sounds great, Champ. Look, the phone's about to cut off. I'm entering the garage. Bye. I love you."

"Bye, Lila."

Now it was definite. The rules of our relationship had changed, but at least Lila was woman enough to fill me in.

Lila's words rang in my head to the point that I had Ruby hold all calls for the next hour. I sat at my desk with the door closed and doodled on a notepad like I used to do in school when I had something on my mind.

I was getting up to open my office door again when I remembered that my ride was supposed to be ready today. I called the shop and got the elder Hernandez on the line this time. The paint job was finished and my ride was ready to be picked up. The bill wasn't pretty either. Shit. I didn't have that kind of money so I was going to have to use the ol' plastic. Trina was still going to pay for this and it was about to end…soon.

I looked up Trina's work number in the phone book and called her.

"Hey."

"Hey, Reggie. You really worked me over last night. I was an hour late for work."

"Would you rather I hadn't gone over there last night?"

"No. I didn't say that. You know I can't get enough of what you got, boy. You passin' by tonight?"

"…Yeah." I was still thinking of Lila. "I want to make tonight special."

"You're makin' me hot all over, boy."

"Just keep it cool for me until later." Part three coming up.

I hung up the phone and started typing on my computer. I pulled up the computer program we used at Stratford Circle to determine the value of different cars and trucks. The gears were turning in my head as I looked for a specific year, make, and model.

Around three o'clock, I arrived at M. Hernandez & Sons in my rental. I was going to miss putting the top down and squealing the tires, but there was nothing like having my own ride back. The Pathfinder's paint job looked like a mirror in the hot Texas sun. I didn't realize how dull my original paint job was until now.

"You like?" I heard the son say as he walked out of the garage in his coveralls. He had white overspray on his face and moustache and was covered in sweat.

"*Si, mi amigo,*" I answered. "*Hermoso. Hermoso.*"

I looked over my ride up and down before shaking his paint-covered hand and heading into the office to pay up with his dad.

29 Reggie Collins

I went home first before going to Trina's apartment. I was sweaty from being out in the heat at the shop and needed to freshen up anyway. I was still half-hearted about what I was going to do and needed to get my nerve up. I was a player, but not a full-time schemer. When I entered my apartment, I turned my alarm off then pushed my door shut and locked it. I had been having a problem with my front door and needed to call management about it. You could push the door shut without locking it and it would wind up popping open a minute later.

I walked into my closet and found my khaki jacket and put it out on my bed with a pair of my dark blue FUBU denims and one of my plain white T-shirts; something Trina would approve of. While showering, I reflected once again on what Lila had said earlier. She hadn't given me an ultimatum, but it might as well have been. I knew what I felt for her, but was still scared. I closed my eyes and let the shower spray hit me in the face.

It was almost nine o'clock when I knocked on Trina's door. She knew I was coming so I could only imagine what awaited me on the other side of her door. I checked my Boss cologne and took one last look at the piece of paper in my pocket before knocking.

"Come in," she said as she opened the door and stepped to the side. I caught half a view of what she was wearing; a white babydoll top with a matching G-string. It was from Victoria's Secret, I think. It paid for a brother to know his lingerie. It was certainly something I liked on her...or taking off her. I wanted to take her right in the walkway, but stuck with the plan.

"This is for you," I said as I handed the single red rose to her. She took the rose in her manicured hand and smelled it.

"Mmmm. This is different. I like this side of you, Reggie. I don't want you going soft on me though."

"You'll never have to worry about me going 'soft' on you, my dear." I pulled Trina toward me and tasted her lips. "I just felt I should treat you better…especially with our new relationship and all."

Trina gripped onto my ass with her free hand. "I just need to get used to this, that's all," she said with a devilish smile.

"You'll have all the time in the world, Trina." I walked into the living room and continued on to her kitchen. There were lit purple scented candles on Trina's iron and glass coffee table and black throw pillows all over the floor that I had to step over.

"You have any wine?" I asked Trina as I opened her fridge. I hadn't looked back at her since arriving, in order to control my urges.

"I bought a bottle on the way home," she said from her living room. I could hear her reshuffling the pillows on the floor and messing with her stereo system. "It's one of those new wines mixed with the fruit. Is it okay?"

"Good. I've been wanting to try some of this." Actually I hated the fake-jake shit.

I found some glasses in her cabinet and was unscrewing the cap when Trina's stereo kicked on. Gil Scott-Heron's song, *Spirits*, came on. I shook my head and chuckled as I poured the wine into our glasses. The *Spirits* album was playing the night I got dehydrated from sexin' her so much and almost passed out. It appeared dear Trina had a sentimental streak in her…of sorts.

I checked my pocket once more before walking out with the glasses of wine. She was lying on her stomach on top of one of the pillows with her hands supporting her head under her chin. Trina's feet dangled daintily back and forth in the air to the beat of the music.

"You miss me?"

"Nah. I just made myself comfortable while you poured. Why don't you get comfortable too?"

"Always trying to get me out of my clothes," I replied as I kneeled down by her and handed her glass to her.

"You know me," she said as she sat up to take a sip of her drink. Some of the wine rolled off the corner of her mouth. I caught it with my finger and wiped it away. I then tasted it off my finger.

"I'd like to get to know you better, Trina," I said as I took a drink. "I mean, more than just what we've been doing up until now."

"What are you talking about doing, baby?" Trina put down her drink and had moved next to me. She was removing my khaki jacket while gently kissing on my neck. I could feel the tickle of her tongue as it flicked about.

"I'm saying that…maybe we need to move in together."

"*For true?*" she whispered in my ear giving me chills.

"For true," I answered as I reached out and set my glass next to hers. Trina's hands were rubbing on the muscles in my arms. I reached around, grabbed her by the back of her neck and started massaging with my fingertips. Trina closed her eyes and arched her head back. Her body went limp with relaxation and then began to spasm as I bit at her neck. It was time to finish this off.

"Baby?"

"*Hmmm?*"

"You want me?"

"*Yesss.*"

I raised her top up, exposing her tight little breasts, then began sucking on them. Trina fell back onto the pillows, pulling me with her. I felt my T-shirt being pulled up as she tugged on it. I continued ravaging her body and she continued giggling with delight. Trina's foot managed to get between my legs and I felt it rubbing vigorously up against my hard-on in my pants. It wouldn't have surprised me if she tried to use those toes to unbutton my jeans, but I went ahead and assisted her instead. Her hands found their way inside my boxers and had a firm grip on me. I had to take care of things now before I gave in to the moment.

"Trina, I need something from you."

"Alright. I know just how you like it, baby."

"No. Not that." I grabbed on the straps on her G-string and slid it off down her legs.

"Whatever you need. Just name it."

I had kicked my boots off and my jeans were down by my ankles now. I reached into my pocket for the piece of paper before discarding the jeans totally.

"Here," I said as I held the paper out in front of her face.

"Huh?" Trina opened her eyes, interrupting her ecstasy. She looked at me as if I was crazy, but then released her grip on me. "What is this?"

"Read it," I said as I started to penetrate her in order to keep her off guard. She was straining to focus on the paper as I began work slowly, rhythmically on her.

"What...*oooh*...is this? Eight, eight, eighteen hundred dollars?"

"It's my bill, baby. That's how much it cost me to repaint the Pathfinder."

Trina momentarily was shuddering from her first orgasm and her arms flew out to her sides, the repair bill still clenched in her left hand.

"That's what I need from you, Trina," I said as I deepened my stroke and increased my pace. "I need you to pay me back. I need to see that I can trust you before we go any further."

"*Nnnnn*. You can trust me, baby. H...how do you want me to pay you back?"

"Cash." I stopped on the dime in mid-stroke. "I want my money back."

I had stopped, but Trina was still working and refused to stop. She flipped me over and was on top now. She threw one of the pillows that was in her way onto the sofa.

"I...I don't have that kind of money, Reggie. *Mmm*. Where am I going to find eighteen hundred dollars?" Time for the pitch.

"Your car. It's worth at least that." Actually it was worth exactly twenty five hundred, but she probably couldn't get that for it.

"I can't sell my car!" Trina had stopped grinding down on me. "I need it," she said in disbelief.

"Of course. You need it to get around, but we have my ride."

"What do you mean 'we'?"

"Exactly what I said. If we're going to be living together then it won't matter, right?"

"...I guess."

"Good. I really need my money back." I had Trina get off me and then had her bend over doggie-style across a couple of pillows.

"I need my money before Friday," I said as I resumed our 'relations' with a slap of my hand on her ass. "Can you do it?"

"Y...*yes.*"

"You'll call me when you have the money?"

"Y...yes."

"Do you remember the words you put all over my ride?"

"*Mmm hmmm,*" she panted, "I...I...I'm sorry."

"Did you mean them?"

"Noooooooo. Nooooo."

"Who's is this?" I asked in a cocky manner as I held onto her waist and took another sip of wine with my free hand.

"Yours, Reggie. All yours," she breathlessly replied as the slapping sound of flesh-on-flesh increased. The candlelight flickered, casting our shadows on her apartment walls. Part three was a success. Shit, Trina was lucky I didn't hit her up for the car rental bill as well.

30 Neal Wallace

Shenita had to rely on the alarm this morning to wake her up. When she nudged me after getting dressed for work, I was still sleeping like a log.

"Huh?" I asked as I turned over in the bed to look up at her. She was wearing her bright blue Questcom shirt with a pair of jeans this morning. I noticed she was wearing blush too. She must have gotten up on time for a change.

"You still pissed?"

"Nah. I still don't want my pops coming over here though."

"You need the car today?"

"Nah. You go ahead. I just want to sleep."

"What time did you come back last night?"

"Ten or eleven. You were already asleep."

"Yeah, some of us have to work in the morning. Your eyes look red…You been drinkin'?"

"Umm. Yeah. Just a little." Not now. It was too early for this.

"Where'd you go?"

"Nowhere really. I just hung out with…Me-Me…and Reggie last night and had a couple of margaritas." Oh shit, oh shit, oh shit. I sort of lied. I turned back over in the bed and hoped that Shenita would leave with no further questions. I looked at the clock under the lamp on our nightstand. She needed to be to work soon.

"…Want to have lunch with me tomorrow at the mall?"

I couldn't hide my surprise. I rolled over again to face her and smiled.

"Sure, baby," I said.

"Alright," she said with an emotionless look on her face and then she grabbed her purse and walked off.

I heard the sound of our car driving off and went back to sleep. Me-Me's incredible singing was the soundtrack to my dreams as I dozed off again. Last night had turned around from being completely shitty into something really special and I owed it to Me-Me. She was indeed a good friend to me when I was in need of one. I could see now why Reggie was so eager to protect her from harm…because now I was too.

I woke up before noon and decided to take a bath in the whirl-pool instead of my usual shower. My head was not at one hundred percent yet, thanks to the margaritas. Besides, I deserved some relaxation every now and then.

After my long bath, I had some spring in my step. I threw on my robe after toweling off and went downstairs to put on my Zapp CD. I cooked a late breakfast and tried to reach Reggie at work. I wound up getting his secretary, Ruby, and decided not to leave a message. I would just call him back later.

I had the phone in my hand and decided to make another call. I ran up the stairs to look for the item in my pocket from last night.

"Hello?"

"Hey, it's me…Neal."

"I know! I didn't forget you from last night already. I still owe you for having me make a fool out of myself."

"You didn't make a fool out of yourself. How many times do I have to tell you?"

"Yeah, yeah. Whatever, boy. What you doing over there? Sounds like you're havin' a party."

"No party. Just listening to some music and unwinding. Thanks for talking with me last night."

"Hey, that's what friends are for. I see you made it home in one piece."

"Of course. I went straight home after we left from down-town."

"I don't know much about real estate, but you could do something with those places. Thanks for letting me see them, *Mr. Restaurant Owner.*"

"You are quite welcome, *Ms. Houston.*" I was getting silly with her again and sprawled out across my bed. I was looking up at the ceiling and feeling like I was in college…and single all over again.

"Neal?"

"Huh?"

"I don't mean to rush off the phone, but I gotta run. I'm off and need to shower and get some shopping in."

"Oh…I see. Well, alright then."

"…Unless you feel like tagging along before you go in to work this evening."

My foolish self was feeling pretty good just then. I opened my mouth, but actually took a second to think and come back down to Earth before answering, "Nah. I'll pass."

"Alright, friend. You take care…alright?"

"Yep."

I took a deep breath and hung up the phone. Our honeymoon photo was stuck in the frame of the mirror where it had always been. Me-Me had purely innocent thoughts, but I was feeling something else at the time. I was deluding myself into taking Me-Me's kindness for attraction of any kind. I hadn't had my ego stroked in quite some time and desperation was setting in on my old ass. Man, I really needed our trip to New Orleans.

I started searching for clothes to put on and realized that my loud music downstairs was suddenly annoying. That was when the phone rang again. I stared at the phone on the bed as it rang.

"Yeah?"

"Damn. You act like you were expectin' me to call."

"Shenita?"

"Nah, fool. Haha! It's me…Kelly!" Shenita and her sister always sounded alike. Only Shenita's time in Houston had made a difference in their voices. You still had to listen very hard though.

"Hey, sister-in-law! What's up, girl?"

108

"I'm waiting on y'all, big boy! *It's my birthday! It's my birthday!*"

"What you gonna be? Twenty-one?"

"Hell nah! I wish. Twenty-six. You knew that."

"Yeah. Just messin' with ya. We're supposed to be getting on the road this Friday."

"Reggie still comin'?"

"*Yeeeesss, Kelly,*" I replied dryly. Women always had the hots for his devilish ass. "You lookin' for your sister?"

"Yeah. She at work?"

"You guessed it. You got the number, huh?"

"Yeah. I'll call her there. I can't wait for y'all to get here. We're going to have some fun! Talk to you later, bro. I love ya!"

"Love you, too Kelly."

"Yeah. Heh, we are going to have some fun," I thought aloud to myself. I took the piece of paper with Me-Me's number on it and flushed it down the toilet.

31 Reggie Collins

I hadn't heard from Lila since she left for Dallas, so I left a message on her voice mail on Thursday. We were leaving for New Orleans tomorrow and I just wanted to hear her voice. It was still early morning when I got a call of a different sort.

"I got your money," was all she said.

I decided to meet Trina at her job where the chances of her blowing up were a little less likely. I arrived at Northwest Mall just before lunch and parked on the opposite end from where Trina's job was. The walk through the mall would help me think...and plan.

I walked slowly as I struggled with what I was about to do. I took in the faces of every woman and child that I walked past. I don't know what I was searching for in their eyes; maybe forgiveness.

Before I knew it, I was standing across the walkway from Trina's store. I heard my dad's voice in my head again saying, "Life is hard, son. You have to be harder." I took his words with me as I stepped forward.

Trina was carrying boxes into the storeroom. She saw me as she walked into the back and gave me a wink. I smiled back. There were two employees on the floor at the time, but no customers. I walked around and looked at the shoe displays like I was interested. A pair of shoes that I would like to see Lila in actually caught my eye when I noticed Trina approaching me. She had a wrinkled envelope in her hand.

"Hey, baby," she said as she gave me a discreet peck on the cheek in front of her employees.

"So, you came through, huh?" I asked while motioning toward the envelope.

"Yep. It's what you wanted me to do, Reggie. I didn't sell my car though."

"Oh."

"I took a loan out and used the car as collateral. They got my title and I got fifteen hundred. That's all that's in the envelope," she said as she put it in my hand. "Here."

I opened the envelope and confirmed what she said.

She added, "I'll get you the rest, but it'll take a while."

"Th…that's okay. It's enough."

"So when do you want to move in together, baby?" Trina grasped my right hand and held it in hers.

I pulled my hand away and answered with a cold smile, "Never."

Trina's eyes widened and she tensed up.

"Game's over. Don't call me ever again."

"What??"

"You heard me. I didn't stutter. Who did you think you were fuckin' with? You thought I was going to let you get away with keying my shit?"

"No," she said with doubt still.

"Oh yes. I don't want to hear from you ever again. Don't think about doing anything crazy either. You see that white guy over there?" I said while pointing at a chubby middle-aged man in a suit that I had picked at random.

"Yeah, I see him. So what?"

"He's with Harris County and he's just IDed you. I reported you already and your ass is going straight to jail if you so much as breathe near me." All lies of course, but they had the desired effect.

"Y…you fucker. You piece of shit." Trina's traditional rage was starting to build.

"Aww, I thought I was 'little dick'. You really ought to make up your mind. Bye, Trina."

I backed up and walked off, coincidentally, right as the chubby gentleman moved from the wall he was leaning on. The split second improvisation had worked perfectly.

"I would have given you the money anyway, you son of a bitch!" Trina screamed at me as she finally lost her cool in the store. I heard a shoe display go crashing to the floor.

"I know," I whispered to myself under my breath. I was going to miss our encounters, so I was sure to get the most out of our last few. I had to end it on a final note to make sure I wouldn't be tempted to pop back in…literally. One bridge burned was another bridge closer to possibly committing to Lila if I so chose. I came close several times to ditching my plan, but stayed tough in the end.

I caught up with the chubby white guy just before the exit to the mall.

"Excuse me," I said as I tapped him on the shoulder. "This is for you."

"What's this for?" he asked as he eyed the hundred dollar bill.

"The great job you did. Merry Christmas!"

"What job? And I'm Jewish…and it's June??!!"

"Happy Hanukkah then," I said as I nodded and walked off with the fourteen hundred dollars left in my envelope.

32 Neal Wallace

Reggie surprised me when he passed by the house on his lunch. He normally stayed around the southwest side when he was working. Since we were leaving tomorrow, maybe he had taken off work early.

"What you doin' on this end, bro?" I asked as I gave Reggie some dap.

"I just left Trina at the mall, dawg. Figured I'd pop in and check you out too."

"C'mon in," I said as I motioned my boy into the house. "I don't understand why you'd keep messing with that crazy girl. Didn't she fuck up your paint job?"

"Yeah. She finally admitted it. It's all over now though," Reggie answered with an almost sad tone to his voice.

"What did you do?"

"I got her to pay me back the money it cost…or most of it." He handed me an envelope to look in.

"Damn. You are good. I don't know how you got money out of her and I'm afraid to ask."

"It's all over with her. She won't be calling me or anything anymore."

"And you're not going to be going over there tryin' to hit that?"

"…Nope."

I smiled and said, "Lila, Lila, Lila. I never thought I'd see the day."

"Hey! Lila's got nothing to do with this. I'm still the same ol' Reg. It's just that the whole Trina thing was bad for me."

"You can say that again. You still driving tomorrow?"

"Yep. I'll be your chauffeur for the day. If you two mess up my seats in back, you're payin' though."

"Nigga, please. Hey, before I forget…I need to ask a favor of you."

"What's up?"

"Umm, I told Shenita that I was out with you and Me-Me Sunday night."

"Neal! Tell me you were not out on a creep! Aww! This is wild!"

"No! It's not like that! I went by the restaurant and then Me-Me and me hung out at Casa Taco. That's it. I just told Shenita that you were there too. It's not really a lie because I was looking for you. I just didn't want her trippin', bro. Things were already bad off that day."

"Uh huh. No prob. I got your back, dawg. I know your woman ain't too fond of my lil' sis either. Speaking of that…you and Me-Me are getting kinda tight, huh?"

"Yeah. She's cool. Heh. I don't have to tell you that though. Bro, I got her to sing when we were at Casa Taco and she blew up the joint!"

"What?? Get the fuck outta here!"

"For real."

Reggie eyed my facial expression very closely before resuming the conversation.

He asked, "You got something to drink? It's an oven out there today."

"Yeah. It'll cost you some of that money in your envelope though."

"Shiiit. This is all going on my credit card bill. It cost me eighteen hundred to repaint my shit. Those Mexicans did a good job though."

I was peering in the fridge when I asked, "You want tea, water, or soda water?"

"I'll take a glass of water, dawg. Did you know Lila spent the night after the club?"

"Yeah. I heard."

"Damn. Me-Me musta told you. Anyway, I've been wanting to talk with someone about that."

I handed Reggie his glass and motioned for him to have a seat at the kitchen table.

"So, it is serious."

Reggie took a drink of water and sighed before answering, "Yup."

"You guys had chemistry that night at the club, bro. So, who made the move to take it in a different direction?"

"She did…and I went willingly. She's in Dallas now with her parents. She said she'd be back in about two weeks. We're going to have a talk then."

"Do you love her?"

"…Bro, I've done so much shit in life that I don't know if I can answer that."

"You just did. You sure you're going to be alright with this trip? With Kelly and all, I mean."

"Bro, I am a single black man now and might be one forever if I choose to. Believe me, I will be more than alright. Last time I checked, there were no papers on my ass."

"There are papers, Reg. They're just not completed yet, that's all."

33 Neal Wallace

"Hurry up, Neal! Reggie's gonna be here any minute!" Shenita said impatiently as she watched me.

"I'll try to hurry, but this won't be quick," I answered as I strained.

"Do you want me to get on top to help you out?"

"Unhh. No. I think I can get it. We might break something doing it that way. No offense, but I don't think it was built to take your weight. Just stay right where you are."

"O, okay, but you look like you're in pain."

"I'll be alright, baby. Th…this is just an awkward position, that's all."

"Don't stop, don't stop, don't stop. You are soooo close."

"There!"

"Yes, yes, yes! Get it baby!" Shenita squealed.

"Awww!" I shouted as I succeeded in my goal. "You happy now?"

"Oh yes! I love you, baby!" she said as she gave me a long, passionate kiss.

"Well, it looks like our little vacation has already gotten off to a good start," I said as I answered Shenita. "Here…these are for you."

"I knew you could do it, my big teddy bear."

Shenita reached out and snatched her yellow-lensed Gucci sunglasses out of my hand. She checked them to see if there were any scratches then ran upstairs to clean them. We had all our bags packed for the weekend trip, but Shenita was missing her sunglasses. She was wearing her lime green tube top and white denim shorts with her matching white canvass tennis shoes. If Shenita hadn't found her sunglasses, she was going to be very unhappy on the trip. She found them, but they had fallen off the top of the entertainment center downstairs and were scrunched between it and the wall. It took a lot of straining on my part and I almost pulled my arm out of its socket, but I managed to reach them with Shenita being my eyes since I couldn't see what I was reaching for.

I stretched my arm out and walked over to the downstairs bathroom to wash my hands. It was dustier back there than I thought. As I dried my hands, I heard Reggie arriving. I took another look at my fresh haircut in the mirror before turning off the light and walking out. I had gone to my barber first thing this morning and had everything lined up. We had decided on leaving around noon today, as Reggie wanted to sleep in and didn't want to fight Friday morning rush hour trying to get over here from his southwest-side apartment.

"Ready for New Orleeeens, dawg?" Reggie asked as I let him in. He was wearing black shorts and a tan ribbed crew neck shirt. I saw my reflection in his gold Ray Bans and the white of his teeth as he smiled. He looked like the Reggie of old; ready to prowl.

"Yeah. We got everything packed. Let me check the house one last time."

"You do that, bro. I'll start loading things."

"Hey, Reg!" I heard Shenita say as she came down the stairs. She was wearing her newly found glasses and was wearing a white short sleeve shirt now over her tube top.

"Look at you, dressed all cute to go back to da hood and all!" Reggie answered back while snapping his fingers in an exaggerated manner.

"Heeeeey! Don't I look good though? Uptown! Uptown! UPT! UPT!"

I shook my head and started my final walkthrough of the house.

Reggie had already grabbed the last bag and was loading it in the back of the Pathfinder as I locked the side door. Shenita was closing the garage door after moving our car inside. We all met up in the driveway.

"Get in people," Reggie uttered as he hopped into the driver's seat and turned the key.

I reached for the front door on the passenger side when Reggie stopped me.

"Nope. In back. Both of y'all. You two thought I was kidding before?"

I looked at the Mrs. and shrugged my shoulders before motioning for her to get in.

34 Reggie Collins

We worked our way down to I-10 then headed east on our way to New Orleans. I had my CD case on the front seat and was taking requests from Neal and Shenita up until we passed the Chevron plant east of town. The two of them got very quiet around that time and their heads started falling in unison. I put the cruise control on and turned up the volume on my radar detector so I could hear it over the music. I brought my cell phone along on this trip and had it inside the armrest console. I fought off the urge to call and leave a message for Lila. I decided to check in at work instead.

I was concentrating on the Jack In The Box restaurant to my right and my growling stomach when Ruby answered.

.She rattled off, "Stratford Circle this is Ruby how may I help you?"

"You could get me an Ultimate Cheeseburger for one."

."Reggie? That's you?"

"Umm. Yeah. Just messing with you. How's the fort?"

"Different day, same shit. You know how it goes."

"Tell me about it."

"Everything's okay, Reggie. Sam had a woman curse him out in Spanish while Loretta translated. You shoulda seen it. Nothing else as exciting. You left for your trip yet?"

"I'm on the road now, baby. I'll leave my phone on in case you need anything."

"Don't worry. I won't be callin' yo ass. Just have fun, boy."

"Heh. Thanks, Ruby. Any messages for me?"

"No. No messages. Now go away."

"Bye!"

One time through my R. Kelly album and half an hour later, we were passing through the "no man's land" between Houston and Beaumont. I checked my speed and dropped it down to seventy. No need having one of the local-yokel speed trap sheriffs that lurked around this area pulling me over. I watched a group of bikers roll by without a care in the world. It was just the road and them; the rumble of their pipes and the shine of their chrome. If only life were just that simple for me.

I looked into my rearview mirror in reaction to yawning from the back seat. Neal had slumped over across the seat and was motionless. Shenita was sitting to his left and was sitting upright with her head leaning back. Her eyes were flickering as she looked up, stretched and took in her surroundings. She saw me looking in the mirror and smiled back.

"*Yawn*. Where are we?" Shenita asked as she rubbed her eyes.

"Almost to Beaumont. You weren't asleep that long."

"Oh yeah. You okay up there?"

"I'm fine. I got music and I'm okay. You guys comfortable back there?"

"Sort of. Neal's all sprawled out and taking up a lot of the space back here now."

"Heh. Do you want me to pull over? Need to stretch?"

"Nah. We still got a long ways to go. You mind if I move your CDs and sit up front for a while?"

"...Be my guest." I handed Shenita my CD case, which she stowed on the floor behind the front passenger seat.

Shenita then began to step over into the front from the backseat. She placed her hand on my shoulder to brace herself as she crossed over. My attention was split between the road and trying to assist her. The same sweet smell of pears from before rose up off her left hand as it squeezed my shoulder.

"Nice shoulders," she said as she brought one of her legs over. Her white shirt was slipping off her left arm so she took her free hand and pulled it back up.

"Thanks, Nita," I replied with a quick look. Traffic was starting to slow up ahead as we got closer to the Beaumont city limits.

The quick look I gave Shenita was enough to distract me as a station wagon in front of me slammed on its brakes suddenly. There was a large piece of discarded tire tread from an eighteen-wheeler smack dab in the middle of the left lane. I still had my cruise control on and had to make a sudden swerve into the right lane to avoid smacking into the back of the station wagon.

I let out a quick "Oh shit!" as I cut the wheel to the right. Shenita was only able to let out a gasp before falling partially across my lap. I tapped my brakes and disengaged the cruise as we continued down the interstate. We had survived that scare and I took the time to slow to sixty miles per hour and remove my heart from my throat. My right arm was trapped underneath Shenita, as she was face to face with me. Her right elbow rested uncomfortably between my legs and her left hand was still on my shoulder.

"Whew! That was close," I let out as I pulled my right arm free from underneath Shenita's torso.

"Sorry, Reg," she apologized as she pulled herself up, bringing her eyes directly in front of mine. A nervous laugh came out of her petite mouth as her gloss-covered lips formed a smile.

"That's okay. It's my fault anyway. Should have been watching the road more closely. We're alive, so it's no biggie. You check on Neal back there?"

She looked back and laughed before answering, "He's still knocked out."

"He always was a hard sleeper. The big lug could sleep through a hurricane as long as it didn't blow the roof off. Heh. I remember some of the craziness I was up to when we stayed in Cuney. Nita, your husband slept through some wild shit back then."

"Heh. Yeah. I remember this time when I spent the night there. You were dating this dark-skinned sister…looked kinda like a model."

"Capri? Yeah! I remember her. She is actually a professional model now. Daaamn, that was years ago. How'd you remember that, Nita?"

"…I feel embarrassed admitting it…but this one night, you two were a little loud in the living room. Neal and me were asleep in his room."

"No! Not when we were…"

Shenita laughed as she covered her mouth and turned away. "Yeah! You two woke me up from a dead sleep. Sleepyhead in back there didn't miss a beat though. Zzzzzzzz."

"Y'all talkin' about my sleep habits up there?" Neal was still sprawled out, but his eyes were just starting to open. Shenita flinched at the sound of Neal's voice bellowing from in back. Her face went flush with embarrassment.

"Hell yeah, we're talkin' about your sleep habits! You finished hibernating, bro?"

"I guess. I miss anything?"

"Yeah, bro," Reggie answered, "You missed the station wagon I almost smacked into back there. You know better than to leave me driving unsupervised."

"Well, you obviously had my wife up there looking out and we're still rollin', so cut a brother some slack."

From looking at where we were, it seemed I wasn't asleep that long. Shenita was sitting up front now and I was lying across the backseat. Heh. I had probably run her off in my sleep by accident. She and Reggie were in the middle of a friendly conversation about my sleeping right when I came out of my dream. I only caught the end of what Shenita was saying, but if I didn't know better, I'd swear I had embarrassed her. That was a rare feat indeed.

My brief dream had me at the grand opening of my own restaurant. Press and photographers from all over were there as I stood in front with Shenita at my side answering questions and being witty. The flashes were blinding, but I could make out a face in the crowd. She was being subtle and trying to blend in, but I saw her. Me-Me was there for the premiere. Our eyes met and I mouthed a silent "hi" to her. She mouthed something back, but I couldn't make out the words. I gave her a facial expression that told her to repeat herself. I tried tuning out the questions and comments from all of Houston, but still couldn't figure out what she had said. Suddenly everything had gone silent as if a mute button had been hit. I was startled and when I turned my attention back to Me-Me, I had lost her in the crowd. I felt a rush of panic overtake me when someone spoke out. "You didn't invite your pops, boy?" came from behind me. I felt anger well up inside me and turned to face my pops when I woke up. I don't know why I still let my pops bother me the way he did, but it was something I was going to put to an end one day.

I was awake during the rest of our trip, as I didn't need any more wild dreams. The three of us talked about the old days and joked around about what we were going to do once we got to New Orleans. We crossed the border into Louisiana and stopped at a Texaco convenience store in this little town called Jennings almost an hour later. We still had some gas left, but Reggie wanted to fill up and get the black lovebugs off his windshield that were splattered all over. They were swarming at this time of year and they could ruin a paint job if left on too long. I knew Reggie wasn't going to let those bugs get away with something he didn't let Trina get away with.

"I gotta use the restroom," Shenita said as she put her shoes back on and exited.

She turned back around and looked at herself in the passenger door mirror before entering the convenience store.

I got out and stretched while Reggie pumped gas.

"You're making good time," I said to Reggie. The trip from H-town to New Orleans usually took from five to six hours depending on how you drove. Reggie, as was probably the case with most people in insurance, was especially paranoid of getting a ticket, but was still zipping along.

"I guess my time behind the wheel of that Mustang rubbed off on me. Maybe I should thank Trina, huh?"

"I'm surprised you still have a sense of humor over that, bro. I'm still shocked over how that whole thing ended. I'd be watching my back."

"Oh, I am. I think I put the fear of God in her though." Reggie was giving the gas pump handle a couple of quick squeezes as he finished filling up.

"I won't even ask about that. You're going through the car wash?"

"Yeah. I better. I paid too much money to let these bugs screw up this paint job."

Shenita was walking out of the store with a bottled water. She was talking on her cell phone. It was probably Kelly she was yakking it up with. I walked over to join her while Reggie drove through the car wash in back.

The Mrs. handed her water to me when I walked up and motioned for me to open it for her. I twisted the cap while she continued laughing on the phone. It was definitely her sister on the other end. Those two were as close as two peas in a pod. I was surprised Shenita hadn't tried yet to get Kelly to move into the house with us in Houston. We waited under the gas pump awning, out of the sun, until Reggie's freshly washed Pathfinder came around.

I offered to drive the final leg of the trip in order to keep myself awake. Reggie was okay with that so he jumped in the back and got comfortable. I adjusted Reggie's seat and mirrors to accommodate me and we were off down I-10 again.

Shenita put in the radio presets for the stations in Lafayette, Baton Rouge and New Orleans while I drove. She had made this trip more times than Reggie and I combined and knew the good stations along the route by heart- Q95.5 in Lafayette, Max 94.1 in Baton Rouge, Q93 and 98.5 WYLD in New Orleans.

"Looks like we're going to get there in time for the Finals. Feel like placing a bet on game six, Neal?" Reggie knew I was a diehard Western Conference fan because of the Rockets, while he was always pulling for the East.

"Shit. He better keep the little money he has," Shenita answered for me with disgust. Her arms were folded and she had slipped back into her PMS mode. I cut a pissed-off look in her direction, but I wasn't sure if she saw it.

"Gee. Thanks for your support, honey," I said dryly to Shenita. "I can always count on you."

"Well, if you—"

"Alright, you two! Let's move on to another subject! We're sup-posed to be having some fun! Okay??" Reggie interrupted Shenita from one of her profanity-laced tirades and kept things from erupt-ing. "We're going to be staying at your grandmother's, Nita?"

"We're supposed to be, but Kelly's talking about a surprise now so I don't know."

"Yeah. Kelly's full of surprises, Reg," I chimed in. "This is sure to be a memorable birthday for her…and probably for all of us as well. Heh."

We continued on our trip without much noise until we were crossing the Atchafalaya swamp between Lafayette and Baton Rouge. This area was one big wetlands with only the elevated in-terstate that ran through it. I couldn't swim and the thought of somehow falling into the waters filled with who-knows-what made me uneasy. I ignored the posted speed limit and sped up to clear this thirty-mile stretch of highway.

"I hate this spot," Shenita mumbled. "I used to dread this part of the trip when I used to come visit you back in the day."

"Yeah, baby. Me too," I replied. Traffic was thin and I decided to stay in the left lane.

"Neal?"

"Huh?"

"I asked Kelly to come stay with us in Houston." Shit. I jinxed myself by thinking about it earlier. I loved Kelly to death, but didn't want to live with her on anything resembling a permanent basis.

"Oh. You mean like *to visit*?"

"No. I mean *to stay*."

"What about your grandmother?"

"My auntie can take care of her."

"What'd Kelly say?"

"…She said she didn't know. She likes home."

"Excuse my being blunt, but did you ever think about asking me before inviting Kelly to move in with us? Am I that non-im-portant to you? You think that maybe you could include me in some of your decisions that affect both of us?"

"Oh. You mean like you've been doing with your restaurant *bullshit?*"

"Bullshit, huh? I'm busting my butt tryin' to give a better life to your crabby, unhappy sourpuss ass and you wanna call it 'bullshit'? Damn, woman! All I want to do is make you fuckin' happy!"

"Fuck you." Shenita looked like she wanted to throw something. Luckily, Reggie's CD case was in the back with him. He was still fast asleep.

"Fuck you too! I am so sick of your shit."

That was the last comment before we heard the siren behind us and saw the flashing lights. If I had been paying attention instead of arguing, I would have noticed the lights on Reggie's radar detector flashing slowly at first and getting increasingly brighter...and brighter. As I pulled over onto the shoulder, Reggie began waking from his nap.

"You stupid motherfucker," came from Shenita's twisted mouth as she rolled her eyes.

36 Reggie Collins

Okay. I take a quick nap and then I wake up to: two spouses sparring, one trooper writing (a ticket) and a paaaartridge in a pear tree. Cute, huh?

"I saw Dateline, y'know!" Shenita screamed at the stoic blonde officer in the blue Smokey Bear hat and uniform. "Saw that Texas license plate and couldn't resist, huh?"

Shenita was about get us thrown under the jail. I heard Neal mumble for her to shut up. The trooper continued writing and didn't say a thing. Shenita didn't stop though.

"That's why I'm so glad I don't live in this state no more. You need to be fixing these roads instead of trying to harass Black folk!"

"Shenita. Shush," I said. I couldn't take it any longer. I don't think the trooper noticed me in back until I spoke. He peered in and lowered his sunglasses while eyeing me up and down before ordering all of us slooowly out of my ride and into the hot sun.

We stood behind in the back of the Pathfinder, feeling guilty in the eyes of the cars that slowed and looked as they drove by. The trooper slowly, methodically searched our bags and shit while we stood around and grumbled.

"Umm. I know I'm coming into this a little late, but were you watching the radar detector, dawg?"

"No!" Shenita answered for her frustrated husband. "He was too busy trying to act like he got a spine all of a sudden." She then walked over to the cement guardrail to cool off and peered over at the murky greenish-brown water below.

"Dawg, what happened while I was napping?"

"Nothing. I just got tired of her shit. Sorry about this, man. I should have been paying attention."

"It's all good, bro," I said as we slapped hands. "I just hope ol' Cletus over there doesn't plant some Mary-Gee-Juana in your bags."

"Aww, dawg. You're kidding, right?"

"Haah! Gotcha! Just how fast were you going when he pulled us over?"

"I honestly don't know."

"Why don't you go try to talk to your wife over there. I'm not about to continue this trip with you two at each other's throats."

"Unh uh. You go over there first. 'Cause if she says something stupid, I swear I'm going to throw her off the bridge."

I looked at Neal, then looked over at the trooper to see if he had heard Neal's comments. He didn't hear it, as he was too busy trying to find something. I took a deep breath before approaching the war zone known as Shenita.

"Hey, Nita. You alright?" I approached her with my hands out at my sides. She looked like she was going to snarl, but then retracted her claws.

"Yeah. I'm fine. Thanks for asking."

"Hey! It's not me. Your hubby over there is the one worried about you. Girl, y'all two gotta get a handle on this. I'm not as young as I used to be and my nerves can't take this."

"Heh. Boy, you need to stop. It's just different now. All different."

"Is it different or are you different?"

"It. Me. Hell, I dunno, Reg. I just feel so frustrated and…and angry."

"You need a Prozac?"

"How about a hug instead, boy?"

I didn't get a chance to respond before Shenita had wrapped her arms around me and was giving me a bear hug. I stood by awkwardly and gently patted her back. Neal was now talking with the trooper and signing his speeding ticket. We would be on our way again, but I was driving this time.

I drove the rest of the way into New Orleans with Neal as my passenger up front. Shenita had regained her composure and the two of them were even exchanging a few words here and there. This trip really gave me something to think about if I ever decided to take the...*gulp*...plunge.

Our little pit stop on the Atchafalaya added about an hour to our trip. When we arrived in the New Orleans area, I started asking for directions from the Wallaces. I was heading toward downtown and started smiling when I saw the Superdome ahead on my left. Funny...I always liked it better than our old Astrodome, but once we got our new football stadium, that would be another issue entirely. Neal and Shenita told me simultaneously to exit onto Claiborne Avenue. When we came down off the interstate, we were on Shenita's turf, Uptown, New Orleans or the UPT, as she liked to call it. I didn't know what Ward we were in, but I'm sure it was one that we were in now. Just as we had our Third and Fifth Wards, so did New Orleans have its own. Shenita told me to slow down as I was going to be making a left turn soon.

I made a left turn onto First Street and waited in the median area for the other traffic on Claiborne to pass before continuing. Shenita's grandmother's house was on Second Street but these were a bunch of one-way streets and I would have to go down First Street and come back. I noticed that the streets were worse out here than in Houston and had to slow down to navigate over the bumps and potholes.

We went down two blocks before turning right to head over to Second Street. Neal pointed out the house on the left that was half a block up. Shenita's grandmother's house was an old white shotgun-style home with green trim that was a split residence. It had been kept up in comparison to the similar houses on either side of it. There were two separate dwellings under one roof and our destination was the residence on the left. There was no driveway so we had to park out on the street in front. The chainlink fence surrounding the house took me back to my old house in Victoria and to the good times I had before that dreaded day in April many,

many moons ago. I wondered briefly about where my mother could be before putting the Pathfinder in park and moving on to other more pleasant thoughts. Thoughts like Kelly. Oh Lord, yes!

The black iron burglar bars on the front door opened up and Kelly spilled out onto the porch in all her earthly goodness and bounded down the steps barefoot. Kelly was wearing a white knit tank top with a thin black wrap skirt that revealed the silhouette of her legs underneath. I was glad that we had at least another hour of sunlight so I could enjoy the view. Kelly was a couple of years younger than Shenita, but you'd swear the two were twins if you didn't know better. Both sisters were golden brown, around five foot five, one twenty or one thirty pounds and gorgeous. In fact, looking at Kelly really made me realize what a good-looking woman my boy, Neal, had in Shenita. Now, if only she and Neal could reclaim what they had in the beginning. The main difference between the two sisters was the hair. Shenita's hair was still black and in a medium length bob. She liked to wear it flipped to one side. Kelly, on the other hand, had a short, short haircut that fit her head shape and wore it a shade of orange-blonde that kicked ass with her skin tone.

Shenita and Kelly started screaming and laughing as they frantically hugged each other on the sidewalk. Women had a habit of doing that shit. Kelly then screamed at her brother-in-law to give her a hug, which he did while being careful not to crush her.

"Reggie, you're not happy to see me?"

"Heh. Of course I'm happy, Kelly. It's been a long time, girl." I stuck out my hand to shake hers. I was smelly and sweaty from hanging out in the sun during our traffic stop earlier.

"It's my birthday and I'm not going to accept anything less than a hug! C'mere, boy!"

Kelly pulled me toward her with a laugh of delight and held me tightly. I noticed that the two sisters had a lot of similar mannerisms except that Shenita was more on the fiery side, while Kelly was more of an upbeat soul. I felt awkward with Shenita's hug earlier, but her little sister's was a different matter. I let myself enjoy the embrace and bent over slightly to return the hug. My face rested momentarily by Kelly's neck and I took in the fragrances off her skin.

To my surprise, the girl wore Gucci Rush just like my baby, Lila. I smiled and inhaled deeper. It was the same intoxicating smell, but different…probably due to a different reaction with her skin. The familiar mixed with something different turned me on and made me anticipate what was going to possibly go down in New Orleans all the more.

37 Neal Wallace

"Kelly…you can let Reggie breathe, y'know," I said as I went around to the back to get our luggage out.

"It's my birthday and I can do what I want, Neal. Can't I Reggie?" Kelly wrapped her arms around Reggie more tightly in response. My boy was enjoying himself.

"Yep. I'm not complaining. Mind your own business, Neal," Reggie said with a laugh.

"Leave those bags in there, brother-in-law," Kelly said as she broke her grip on Reggie to motion at me. "You're not staying here tonight."

"Huh?"

"Yeah, my little sister decided to surprise us," Shenita interjected as she walked through the gate toward the house. "Tell 'em."

Kelly cut a mischievous look at her sister before replying, "We're staying in the Hyatt by the Superdome this weekend!"

"You got us a room?" I let our travel bag that I had just grasped drop back down. Reggie had an uneasy look on his face for once.

"Nope. A suite! Two bedrooms, living room, dining area, kitchenette…and a bar!"

"Oh shit," Reggie mumbled to himself. "It's on!"

"You can afford that?" I asked with a bit of rudeness. Shenita started laughing as she went inside the house to see her grandmother.

"Hell nah! Our Uncle Mack is a concierge over there. He hooked up his darling niece, *yours truly*, for her birthday."

"Shit. He's got any connections in Houston?" Reggie spit out without thinking. He was half-kidding, but half-serious too when

133

he asked. Kelly slapped his shoulder with her hand and gave him a "shush".

Kelly led us through the front gate and up onto the porch. I saw the neighbor peek out of their door on the right and stare me down. I politely smiled at the little girl, but she continued to stare blankly. I was feeling childish just then, so I gave her one of my monster faces. She responded by screaming and retreating inside.

"If that little girl's momma comes out shootin', you're on your own, bro," Reggie whispered as he trailed behind me.

"Don't worry. I'll just lock these burglar bars and leave you on the porch."

Reggie tapped me on the shoulder to slow me before I went inside.

"Do you need help with the speeding ticket?" he asked.

"I dunno. I don't even know how much it's going to cost. Probably a hundred or two."

"I got it, bro."

"Aww! Thanks, man."

"It's the least I could do. Besides, you wouldn't have gotten a ticket if you had been driving your slow-ass car instead. See, it's all my fault!"

"*You so funny*. Want me to start talking about Lila all night?"

"This is me shutting up *now*."

Me and my boy took a step into the tight confines of the house that were made tighter with years of accumulated stuff. The cream-colored walls were filled with a mixture of memorabilia: an old picture of JFK, a black Jesus painting, and family photos. Some of the photos had frames; others did not and were held up with either pushpins or old clear tape. On the walls, were also numerous browned newspaper clippings of weddings, obituaries, and honor roll lists that had probably been placed there by their grandmother. Even though the house wasn't that wide, it went back a lot further than you would suspect from looking at it outside. Most of the rooms were all in a row and you could walk through almost every one on your way to the back door.

Shenita and Kelly were involved in a hushed conversation at the rear of the living room next to an antique dining table. My wife was probably giving Kelly the details about our argument and my speeding ticket. Reggie had moved over to the air conditioner unit in the window and was letting the cool air blow into his shirt. I was looking forward to a nice shower and clean clothes myself. I sat down on the edge of the multi-colored upholstered couch to take the load off. The plastic covering crackled beneath my weight.

"Kelly, is your grandmother here?" I asked, interrupting her chat session with my wife.

"Yeah, Neal. She's in the bathroom now. She'll be out in a few. My auntie will be here soon. Then we can have some birthday cake."

"Who's going to be watching your grandmother this weekend?"

"My auntie. We're going to lock up the house and she's going to stay with her. Auntie Rita lives on the next block and has been watching her a lot more recently." That explained how Kelly would be able to move to Texas if she took my wife up on "our" offer. Kelly had been working at the makeup counter at the Saks in Canal Place and hadn't really found her niche since graduating from SUNO. It would be easy for her to pack up and join her angry sister in H-town.

I heard the squeaking of the floorboards and the noise of door hinges as Mama Baptiste hobbled out into the living room. I stood up in response to her entrance. Mama Baptiste was as sweet as can be in her old purple sundress. Her long hair was graying at the roots and was rolled up in hairpins. She squinted from behind her thick eyeglasses and gave everybody in the house a once-over before smiling. She didn't speak much these days, but her face showed her happiness in seeing us. Shenita gave her grandmother a long, loving hug along with a kiss on the cheek, then helped her over to a chair at the table.

Mama Baptiste had raised Shenita and Kelly since high school. Shenita had told me the story one night after we were married.

Their dad was a captain in the Air Force and died in a plane crash in Italy. Their mom, who chose to stay home in New Orleans with them, went into a deep depression after their father's death and overdosed on sleeping pills one night while they slept. While thinking about Shenita's mom, my eyes located her obituary nestled amongst the wall décor.

I wondered just how much of Shenita's anger was actually from our situation and how much was rooted in her past. Maybe I didn't really know the woman I called my wife. Maybe our marriage was an escape for her.

All of us gathered around the table and I gave Mama Baptiste a hug and kiss as well before introducing Reggie to her. Reggie didn't know her, but was feeling at home as most our people felt around each other and gave her a hug and kiss also. Shenita went into the kitchen in back to help Kelly with her birthday cake. The sun was going down, so I turned on the lamps in the living room for us.

Reggie and I talked to Mama Baptiste and kept her entertained while she nodded in amusement. Later on, Shenita came out of the kitchen fanning herself while she removed her earrings.

"Whew! It's still hot in there as always." My wife was looking at her watch. "Auntie Rita better hurry up. I can't wait to get to the Hyatt and take a nice long bubble bath. I am funky."

Shenita walked over toward the front door, but stopped at the air conditioner to cool off. I got up from the table and came up behind her.

"I'm sorry, baby," I said as I brought my hands to rest on her shoulders. I think she started to flinch, but relaxed instead, as my hands felt good there. I could feel the stickiness of sweat on them.

"It's okay, Neal. It's going to be alright."

I turned Shenita's head slightly and brought our lips together in a soft, lingering kiss.

The banging on the front door cut our intimacy short. It was Auntie Rita.

"Hey, y'all! How my nieces doin'?" she proclaimed as she came through the door I had just opened. "Hey, Neal! Hey, baby!"

"Hey, Auntie Rita!" Shenita hugged her aunt who was clad in a black and white Reebok jogging suit and holding her purse under her arm.

Just then and as if on cue, Kelly came out with her birthday cake. It was a freshly baked yellow cake with chocolate frosting and candles on it. Shenita and her aunt went back into the kitchen to help Kelly bring out the punch, napkins, plates, and cups.

When everything was in place, we all gathered around the table to sing *Happy Birthday* to Kelly. Kelly, being her usual carefree self, started taking bows once our awful attempt at singing began. Mama Baptiste quietly sang along with the rest of us, but I think I was the only one who noticed. When it came time for Kelly to make a wish, she looked at Reggie and smiled slyly before closing her eyes and blowing the candles out. It didn't take too much imagination to guess what Kelly wished for her birthday and my boy, Reg, was more than ready to oblige.

We stayed around for another hour before leaving for the hotel. We hadn't eaten any dinner, but ate some leftover gumbo and baked spaghetti that was in the fridge. After we ate, Kelly had made herself comfortable on the arm of the couch next to Reg and Shenita had to pull her away to get her bags and stuff. My eyelids were feeling like lead weights around that time and the look on Shenita's face told me she was running out of steam as well.

A couple of members of the neighborhood welcoming committee were standing outside under the streetlight and looking in our direction when we walked out onto the front porch.

"They're checking out the out-of-state plate on Reggie's shit," Kelly said matter-of-factly. "That's the car theft corner there. You never park your shit down there or it's...*phfft*...gone."

"I'll break someone's neck if they mess with my ride again," Reggie snarled as he cast his gaze back at the young brothers on the corner. He was still testy from it being keyed.

"Let's bounce, *killer*," I said.

"Yeah," Kelly said, "I doubt they'll hold the room much longer. I thought we'd be there by now. Luckily, it's not during the Essence Festival."

"Now you know Uncle Mack couldn't hook us up with a suite around that time of year anyway," Shenita laughed. "He ain't got that kind of stroke!"

38 Reggie Collins

Neal climbed up into the front to ride shotgun with me as we waved bye to Shenita and Kelly's aunt and grandmother. Shenita and Kelly still had stuff to talk about, but Neal just arched his head back against the headrest and zoned out. I didn't feel like bothering him, so Kelly talked me through the twists and turns of New Orleans and over to the Hyatt by the Superdome.

We were travelling down Girod Street and all I saw was the big Macy's sign up ahead that kept getting bigger. I didn't see the entrance to the hotel until Kelly had me make a final right turn. That brought us down a dark street that was actually the driveway entrance to the hotel. The partially bricked driveway separated the hotel from the parking garage and the New Orleans Centre that were next to it, but was covered overhead by a canopy of cement, brick and steel that served to connect the two structures. This gave me the impression of entering a long, dark tunnel until I came to the hotel entrance on my right. The area was lit up and the bellboys were scurrying to and fro to accommodate the other guests who were arriving in their cars and limos.

"I'm beat and don't know where I'm going. I'm valet parking this badboy." With that said, I moved into the valet lane next to one of the mini water fountains. Kelly handed her garment bag over to one of the attendants and rushed through the glass door to check on our reservations.

The sound of doors opening and closing and the echo of the entranceway woke Neal from his snooze session. He wiped the drool from the corner of his mouth and joined Shenita next to the bag cart while I handed over my car keys. I was about to get out when I remembered to get my cell phone from out of the armrest. The valet drove off with my Pathfinder before I had a chance to give him a tip, so I joined the Wallaces.

The three of us walked into the lobby and looked around for Kelly. She was at the check-in counter to our left, so we walked across the maroon carpets and marble floors under the light of the chandeliers with our carted bags trailing behind us, courtesy of the bellboy.

"Please tell me they kept the room," I begged Kelly as we approached behind her.

Kelly turned around with the two magnetic key cards in between her ringed fingers.

"Is this what you want?" she replied teasingly. "Twenty-fifth floor, how ya luv that?"

Our party boarded the glass-walled elevator that we had been guided to and headed up to our suite. On the way up, I looked down at the large atrium and convention area below while Neal paced around trying to stop the tingling in his leg that had fallen asleep. Shenita rested against the wall and Kelly hummed to herself, reminding me briefly of my lil' sis, Me-Me.

"First time to New Orleans?" the middle-aged bellman asked me.

"Nah. Don't come here that often though. You got a nice place here."

"Best in New Orleans if you ask me. Yassir."

"You know Mack Wilson?" Kelly asked our bellman.

"Yeah. That's your people?"

Kelly smiled and nodded. "Yep. That's my uncle."

"Mack? Why didn't you say so??!! Well, we gonna hafta take care of y'all. Ma name's Willie. You need anything, just ask fo me."

Willie led us down to the end of the hallway where our suite was located. Kelly did the honors by popping the card into the electronic lock and opening the door.

"Shit. This is better than my apartment," I proclaimed as I walked in behind Kelly.

Willie put our bags down next to the dining area table and then gave us a quick tour of our suite. The suite came with two full bedrooms; one with a king-size bed and the other with two double beds; a small dining area with kitchenette and bar and a living room. The master bedroom had the combination whirlpool tub/shower in its bathroom, while the smaller bedroom on the other side of the living room had just a shower. I slipped Willie a twenty-dollar bill for his trouble and gave him some dap.

"Whoo hoo! This da bomb!" Kelly yelled as she ran through the suite taking everything in.

"Sister, I know it's your birthday and all, but do you mind if your big sister calls it a night tonight?" Shenita had taken a seat on the sofa. Neal was moving the bags around and looked at Kelly with puppy dog eyes while nodding in agreement with Shenita.

"Nah. Y'all go on and get some sleep. We got this room until Sunday, so we'll make up for things tomorrow."

"You damn right!" Shenita responded, "But we need to clear up the room situation now."

Kelly looked at the three of us then shrugged her shoulders. "Y'all two are married, so take the big bed."

"But it's your birthday, Kelly. Me and Neal can take the room with the two doubles." Neal flinched on that remark, but said nothing.

"No! It is my birthday, but I couldn't do that to y'all. Neal…put y'all's stuff in the room with the king-size." Neal didn't hesitate to snatch their bags up and head off into the bedroom.

"I'll make it easier on y'all as well. I'll take the sofa out here. It looks like it has a fold-out bed in it anyway."

Shenita looked at Kelly and me in response to my suggestion and then left us alone to join her husband in the bedroom. I could hear Neal unzipping their bags in there before the door closed.

I had walked over to the royal blue sofa and was peeking under the cushions at the bed. Kelly had kicked her shoes off and I saw her bare feet walk up from behind me.

"Hey," she said softly. I turned around to respond and wound up getting her lips on mine. Her mouth tasted of butterscotch and her tongue of cinnamon. Kelly brought her arms up and put them around my neck. I let my hands slide slowly, gradually down to her ass as we kissed for several minutes. Damn, Kelly was a good kisser.

"So…," she said as she broke off the kiss and looked up into my lust-filled eyes, "you still wanna sleep out here tonight?"

"No. Never did. Just didn't want to push anything. There are two beds in there, but I didn't want to be presumptuous. You're the birthday girl so it's all up to you."

"Heh. If it's all up to me, we're going in that room and not coming out until checkout time, sexy."

"You want to go out for a little while? I'm as beat as Neal and Shenita in there, but I don't come here often and wouldn't mind seeing the sights. Maybe the French Quarter?"

"Okay. We can go out for just a little while. Thanks, Reggie. I need to clean up a little first."

"Ha! I think I need that more than you do. I must reek."

"Nah. You smell fine, baby. But since you are a guest, you can use the shower first."

"Ladies first," I said. "Besides, I need to unpack some stuff."

"Allllright. I'll try not to hog *our* bathroom then."

Kelly carried her garment and overnight bags into the bedroom. I heard the shower running later. I followed into the bedroom shortly with my bags and placed them on the bed adjacent to the one with Kelly's stuff on it. I slipped my sweaty shirt off over my head and did a quick pose-down in the mirror to make sure I still looked good. My abs could have used a little work, but otherwise everything was in place on me. I looked toward the bathroom door and could hear Kelly singing to herself in the shower. I started walking toward the bathroom, but stopped when thoughts of my last shower…with Lila crept into my head. A woman had finally succeeded in messing with my mind.

I let out a short scream of frustration and walked out of the bedroom. I retrieved my cell phone from my pocket and checked it for messages. As I sat on the sofa, I scrolled through the menu until I came to the message section. I was surprised to find a message left on the phone since I hadn't heard it ring all day. It turned out the message was left around the time the phone was in my armrest while the policeman was searching my ride. Most importantly, the message was from Lila. I looked at the time. Damn. It had been hours since she called.

"Reggie?" The voice was groggy, but wonderful to hear. My pulse shot up instantly.

"How'd you know it was me?"

"Heh. Caller ID, silly. I got your messages and called you back, Champ. It's nice to know I'm missed."

"How are your parents?"

"They're about the same. My mom's doing better with her treatments, but my daddy's pretty weak still."

"You know when you'll be back?"

"Next weekend maybe. Maybe that Monday after. I may hire a nurse for them so I won't worry as much."

"I wish I could be there for you."

"I know, Champ. This is something I have to do myself...Maybe in the future."

"Okay."

"So...how's New Orleans?"

"It's fine. We got out here a little late."

"Car trouble?"

"No. Just driver trouble. Heh."

"Should I ask?"

"Nah."

"How's the birthday party going? It sounds quiet over there. *Yawn*."

"...Well, everybody's asleep now. We had cake and stuff earlier."

"Where are you at?"

"...At Shenita's grandmother's."

"Oh. Where are you sleeping at over there?"

"…On the sofa. Actually I'm on it now." *Well.* I was sitting on the sofa just then.

"Hey, I hate to be rude, but I have to get up before daylight to bring my folks to the hospital for their treatments. You okay with that?"

"Of course. Get some sleep. Pleasant dreams."

"Oh, they will be now…I love you, Champ. Bye."

"Bye."

I sat there reflecting on my thoughts until I realized a pair of eyes was looking at me. I was so deep in thought that I hadn't noticed Kelly. She was finished with her shower and stood in the bedroom doorway on the side of the TV console that was directly in front of me. She smiled innocently while wearing nothing but a towel and a smile.

"Sorry about hogging the bathroom."

"S'okay."

"I thought you might come join me."

"…I was. I got a call though." Sorta. I wiggled the phone in my hand for emphasis.

Kelly walked over to the sofa with beads of water rolling down her legs with each step she took. She plopped down next to me and placed her hand on my knee.

"So, what have you been up to in Houston? Seeing anyone?"

"…Nothing serious. How about you?"

"Heh. Nothing serious." Kelly tightened her towel around herself and moved on the sofa so she could put her feet across my lap. I took that as a hint and began massaging them, starting with her arches.

"*Mmmmmmm.* That feels good. You've got the touch just like I thought you would."

"Just consider it a birthday present."

"How's work? Shenita tells me you got a raise or something."

"I got off my probationary period as supervisor. The job's going great. It could always pay more though."

ERIC E. PETE

"Yeah. I heard that. Y'all got a lot of jobs in Houston. Y'know...my sister asked me to move down there."

"Oh?"

"I'm not sure about it though. Jobs don't pay here, but it's my home. Maybe I'll go down there to visit. *Ooo, that feels good.* Reggie?"

"W...what?"

"You're about to fall asleep on me, boy. I saw your head dippin' just now. Why don't we just go out tomorrow? You okay with that?"

"Yeah. I'm sorry I'm being poor company."

"No. You're excellent company compared to some of the knuckleheads out here. I've liked that about you since I first met you at the wedding."

"Thank you, Kelly." Kelly had arched one of her legs causing the cotton towel to slide down her thigh. Our eyes met and a player like me knew what came next...usually.

"Kelly, would you mind if I took a shower...and then just went to bed?"

"Heh. No! Of course not. Like I said...we don't check out until Sunday."

"Thank you," I said as I stopped massaging her feet. I then moved her legs to get up to shower. I did give her a nice long kiss though before leaving her alone on the sofa. I saw her turning the TV on with the remote as I disappeared into the bedroom to shower and sleep.

Something was wrong with me. I had a work of art on the sofa in the next room, in just a towel and I was heading in the opposite direction. Nine times out of ten, I would have been running up in it. Something had happened to me to drop that figure from ten out of ten. That "something" had just four letters and started with an "L". I'll let you guess which word, as I'm sure you and your friends could spend hours arguing over whether it's "Lila", "Love", or something else entirely. Heh. Goodnight, y'all.

145

39 Neal Wallace

I felt like I had slept a week and probably could have if Shenita hadn't disturbed my sleep early Saturday morning. Not that I'm complaining, mind you. The Mrs. was feeling frisky, probably due to the change of scenery, and decided to play nice with me. I felt my boxers being slipped off and Shenita climbing on top all in one quick move. I already had my normal morning "wood", but with my awareness of what was going on came the rock-hardness.

"C'mon, baby," she said as she started down the road toward her climax. I blinked a couple times as I was roused into gear by the motion of her body against mine. I was still somewhat groggy and half-asleep while moving, but knew what I was doing. My wife's nude body was doing its dance on me and slid up and down as I was worked over for every inch of me. I reached behind Shenita and gave her ass a quick spank that startled her, but also kicked her into overdrive. I then sat up to face her and took one of her breasts in my hand to suck gently on her bulging nipple. She responded by speeding up her riding motion. I held her tighter against me as our sweat covered bodies both rushed toward eruption.

"Oh, my gawd! Oh, my gawd! Oh, my gawd! *Yessssssss*," Shenita screamed as she crumbled lifelessly down onto me. I felt the same, but couldn't speak. The moistness from our encounter was running down the sides of my thighs and onto the crisp white sheets. I was glad the other bedroom was on the other side of the suite from us. If Reggie was on the couch, he may have heard us though. I think I would have probably been more embarrassed if I had seen no action on this mini-vacation.

"Oh, that was *good*," I finally managed to get out my mouth once I caught my breath.

"Hell yeah," she responded before popping up and heading to the bathroom.

I sat up a few minutes later and stretched out before standing. Shenita had the tub filling with water and was at the faucet taking her pill in the meantime. I walked as lightly as my big ass could over to the bedroom door and cracked it just a little. I stuck my head out far enough to see the sofa and loveseat. Reggie wasn't there. That didn't surprise me as Kelly had made it obvious that she was interested and it was her birthday after all. I chuckled then ducked my head back in.

"He's in there with Kelly, huh?" Shenita asked as I closed the bedroom door back.

"Looks like it."

"Heh. I guess her wish came true after all. Joining me in the whirlpool?" she said with a wink.

"Does a fish swim?"

It was only nine o'clock when we came out of our room. Shenita was wearing a pair of her tight-fitting blue denim shorts with a blue denim sleeveless blouse that tied in front. I chose to wear my blue and white "no-name" jogging suit. In the daylight, I really got to take in my first real look at the suite. Reggie and Kelly were still in their room so Shenita went back into our bedroom to get her boom box. I walked over to the window by the loveseat and looked out at the view. I could see the rest of the hotel as well as the top of the Superdome and the puke green sports arena next to it. The skies were clear and I could tell that it was hot and muggy outside already. A knock on our door interrupted my taking in the view out the window.

"Toldja I was gonna take care of y'all!" It was our bellman from last night, Willie, and he came bearing gifts. Lots of them. Willie had a food cart stocked with breakfast food—bacon, eggs, grits, toast, grapefruit, milk, juice, cereal and more.

"Willie, you da man! Come on in!"

"Good morning! I talked with Mack this morning and he told me this was for his niece's birthday. I told him I would pass by early to take care o' y'all." Willie hurriedly pushed the golden covered cart into the suite and away from prying eyes in the hallway. Shenita had placed her boom box on the dining area table and was plugging it in when she saw the breakfast bonanza.

"Mmmm! This is right on time," she said as she ran over to the cart and sniffed. The sight of the food was making my stomach growl now.

"Kelly and Reg better get up soon or this is gonna be all gone," I said as I rubbed my hands together in anticipation.

"Oh, that's not all," Willie said with a sneaky smile. The door to the suite was closed, but he still looked around suspiciously before squatting down. He reached under the cloth that covered the lower section of the cart and immediately we heard the sound of glass clanking.

"No…No. Nooo. Yes. Yes!" Shenita said, as her eyes got wider. At first one bottle came out, then another, then another, and another. Oh shit. It was all there; Gin, whiskey, bourbon, rum, tequila, and vodka, even Reggie's Absolut. Willie, the bellman extraordinaire, even brought the mixers.

"Y'all need to keep this strictly on the DL. Alright?"

"Whatever you say, Willie," I said as I handed him a twenty for his extra service. Willie gave us a wink and tipped his hat to us before backing out of the door.

"Somebody will be up later to pick up the cart," was the last thing he said on his way out.

Me and Shenita looked at each other like two little kids on Christmas. Our smiles ran wide like two Cheshire Cats.

"Ooooo! Wait till my sister sees this! Kelly!!"

40 Reggie Collins

I was too tired to even dream when I went to bed Friday night. After showering, I thought I might find Kelly in the bedroom, but she was still on the sofa watching TV. That was good for me because that may have been one of those rare nights, other than that one time at summer camp years ago, that I would have been incapable of servicing a woman. I hoped that I didn't snore too much. I did hear Kelly come to bed later on and asking me if I was awake, but I thought it was a dream. I opened my eyes once in the night and could make out Kelly's outline under the covers of the other bed.

I started stirring Saturday morning in response to voices and music from the other room. Soon, Kelly's voice was with them. I heard *Joy and Pain* playing and knew that Kelly's birthday had resumed...New Orleans-style. The clock read "nine thirty-five" and I knew any further sleep was out of the question. I wriggled out of the sheets that I had rolled around me like a burrito and got in the shower.

"Reggie's up, y'all!" Kelly said with her usual enthusiasm. She wore a lavender sundress and tan sandals and had a platinum armband that wrapped around her right arm like a snake. Her earrings, that complimented her armband perfectly, danced about in sync with each movement of her lovely bobbing head as she danced about.

I was caught up checking out Kelly and hadn't noticed all the breakfast food spread out across the dining table. Neal was sitting down to a plate of bacon and eggs and gave me a nod and smile before turning his attention back to his plate. Shenita was as caught up in the music as her sister, but was at the bar mixing drinks. I didn't know where all that...damn...alcohol came from, but decided not to ask.

"Absolut?" Shenita asked between notes of the *Maze* song.

"You got the drink right, but it's a little too early for me still. Let me have some of this breakfast first."

"Suit yourself," she replied as she resumed freshening her gin and juice.

"Good mooorning," Kelly said as she gave me a wink. She then picked up her drink from the bar and took a sip, all the while keeping her eyes on me. Our eye contact spoke volumes. She had forgiven me for last night, but I wasn't getting off as easy tonight.

I helped myself to a couple of croissants and grits before sitting across from Neal.

"Who brought all...*this* up here?" I asked Neal as I gulped my orange juice.

"That dude, Willie, bro. Couldn't believe it myself. This is some good shit. So, how'd you *sleep*?"

"We'll talk later, dawg."

"Later" came that afternoon at the Hyttops Sports Bar in the third floor atrium. Shenita and Kelly had walked through the connecting doors to the New Orleans Centre on the second floor to check out Macy's and Lord & Taylor. All of us had a serious drink-on already, so Neal and me copped a seat and had some appetizers and pizza rather than accompany the women.

"I see you and Kelly shared the room last night, Reg."

"What'd she tell y'all?"

Neal laughed and replied, "Nothin'! Was she supposed to?"

"Nah."

"Did you do something wrong?"

"No. Don't laugh, but nothing happened."

"What?? Not that anything's wrong with that, but I'm just a little shocked since it's you two. Heh. Heh. *Diet-Player. Just one calorie, not quite player enough.*"

"I was tired, dawg. Cut me some slack. I wanted to see how it was to live the *married life* for one night! Haha!"

"Fuck you. I'll have you know that me and the Mrs. got it on this morning, so you know where to put that 'married life' comment."

"Yeah. Whatever. You're *regular* all of a sudden, so you wanna get cocky now."

"You better get used to it. Once Lila gets back from Dallas, your life's gonna change too."

"...I spoke with her last night, bro."

"Huh? When?"

"While Kelly showered."

"You just too smooth for me, bro. Do me a favor though?"

"Yeah. What?"

"Don't be flippin' Kelly's mind. Okay? I mean...you two are adults, but don't have her thinking there's more than there is. She *is* my sister-in-law."

"Cool. Besides...I fear Shenita more than you." I started laughing as I sipped through my drink straw and almost choked.

"Oh yeah?" Neal said as he reared up like he was going to punch me. Even he had to laugh.

We finished our pizza and drinks and decided to trail the women. We headed toward the middle of the shopping center and walked past a store that was filled with tourist gear. I still needed to get Kelly a birthday present, but that wasn't the place for her. Maybe I would snag something there later for Me-Me.

I spotted the Afro-American Book Stop on the first floor by the Lord & Taylor entrance and gravitated straight to it. Women usually liked books, so this was perfect. It was comforting to confirm that it was locally owned too. New Orleans was one of the few predominantly Black cities in America, but it was obvious that with increased numbers there wasn't always the increased economic opportunity to go along with it for its residents.

I started out browsing through the inspirational selections, while Neal was reading the backs of romance novels. He was probably trying to find the right one for the Mrs. I snagged an inspirational book for Kelly and thumbed through the romances for one with a happy ending. That was for Lila. Neal had already finished his purchase as I approached the register. He waited for me in the store entranceway.

"Bought something too, bro," I said to him as I walked out. Neal's book was small and he quickly stowed his book and bag halfway into his jogging suit pants pocket.

"Ready to go find them?"

"Not yet. I bought a book for Kelly as a birthday present and want to bring it up to the room first. I got one for Lila too…for when she gets back from Dallas. I see you bought a little sumthin' sumthin' in there too. A surprise?"

Neal hesitantly replied, "Yeah…Let's go."

Shenita and Kelly joined us back at the room with their bags from their downstairs-shopping trip.

"Macy's had sales we couldn't pass up. Shenita didn't want to shop, Neal. It's all my fault," Kelly said as she dumped her shopping bags onto the table that was previously covered with breakfast food. Willie must have sent somebody up to clean up. The cart and the breakfast remains were gone, but they didn't touch the liquor.

"Me and Reg walked around the shopping center too...after we ate."

"Did you see the bookstore?" Shenita asked as she walked past me with her shopping bags. She was heading straight for the room to put her stuff up.

"Yeah. We went in there and checked it out."

"What? We must've just missed y'all," Kelly said with a giggle. "Shenita thought about buying you a book, but she said you don't read much."

"Yeah...that's me. What's up for tonight?"

As she pulled her shopping plunder from the bags and inspected them, Kelly thought to herself. "Hmm. What about dinner at Top of the Dome and a little gambling at Harrah's?"

Reggie said, "It's your birthday, girl. Whatever you say goes. I'm not much of a gambler though."

"So we hang out at the slots and get some complimentary drinks. Can't beat that, right?"

"Okay. It would be nice to see the casino," I responded.

Shenita came back from our room a few minutes later with something behind her back and presented it to Kelly. It was a digital phone from Questcom in Houston. Shenita got it with her employee discount to replace Kelly's that was stolen at a party last year. We had meant to give it to her earlier, but had gotten sidetracked. Kelly was thanking us when Reggie ran into the other bedroom and came out with the book he had bought her. Kelly thanked her sister and me for the birthday present with a hug and thanked Reggie with a hug…and kisses.

We kicked back and unwound some more in the room over the next few hours. Shenita drank some more and then fell asleep in our bedroom. I sat down on the sofa scanned the local cable channels. Reggie and Kelly carried on cracking jokes with one another while playing music on the boom box and getting a few card games in. I started to join them at the table, but decided to give Kelly her quality time with my boy.

The clock struck eight when the four of us walked into the Top of the Dome restaurant for dinner. Some of us were more rested than others, but we all looked good considering the amount of "blood in our alcohol systems". The restaurant revolved, so I was going to avoid concentrating on the windows, just in case. Shenita and Kelly wore matching knit halter-dresses like a pair of gloves. Kelly's was a fiery red meant to draw attention to her, while my wife's was her favorite "out" color, black. I knew that women normally didn't like wearing the same thing, even if a different color, but they were sisters. My boy, Reggie, busted up in a sky-blue open silk shirt with white undershirt underneath and steel-gray pinstriped slacks. A pair of black Grimaldis on his feet finished everything off. I was a little further down the fashion scale; White T-shirt under a gray cotton V-neck sweater and black slacks was my calling card for the night.

The maitre d' had one window spot left, but with my luck, I got the seat with my back to it. It didn't stop me from looking out at the Superdome roofline from over my shoulder. I didn't have the money to spend, but splurged on lobster anyway. Shenita had the shrimp, and both Kelly and Reggie had the filet mignon based on our waiter's recommendation. Reggie ordered the first bottle of Cabernet Sauvignon and I picked up the tab for the next. I had called our waiter aside earlier and mentioned Kelly's birthday, so she got surprised with a gift straight from the Chocoholic Bar…a chocolate cake/chocolate ice cream concoction with a candle in it. While there, my thoughts went back to owning my own restaurant, but I didn't tell Shenita as she would have either blown me off or gotten pissed off again. I looked around and committed the sights, smells, and sounds to memory. I would share them with Me-Me upon my return home.

We left for the casino after closing out the restaurant. None of us were in the right state to be driving, so we caught a ride on the complimentary bus meant to look like a trolley. Kelly and Shenita played around with the multi-colored fish sculptures that were mounted in the sidewalk in front of Harrah's. Reggie wanted to take some pictures, but had forgotten his camera back in his Pathfinder.

I started at the quarter slots on the first level along with everyone else, but wound up in the Mardi Gras themed section at the blackjack table where I foolishly let a couple of hundred dollars get away from me. I wasn't much of a gambler to begin with, so I kept trying to win back what I lost and got deeper and deeper. Shenita was going to go ballistic. Even in her drunken state, she had stuck to the slots with Kelly. I was pissed off and disappointed in myself. Reggie found me as he made his sightseeing rounds in the place.

"You lost, huh?" he asked with a look that told me he already knew the answer.

"Damn. It shows?"

"Yup. You were a happy mutherfucker coming in here. Not now. I looked the same way on this trip I took to Vegas one time. How bad?"

"Two hundred."

"Haha! That's it??"

"Yes. I'm broke, bro. It doesn't take much these days. Finished laughing?"

"I'm sorry. I just thought you lost more. My stupid ass had lost a grand when I looked *just* like you. That was just a laugh of relief."

"I'm still screwed, bro."

"Here." Reggie cautiously removed his wallet from his back pocket and counted off three Benjamins before slipping them into my hand. "Don't expect *shit* from me for Christmas, nigga. I kept some of the money I got from Trina in cash just in case I needed it on the trip."

Words could not express my appreciation for my boy at that time. We always had each other's back, no matter what. As different as we were in so many ways, it was still as if we were blood brothers.

Kelly was truly the birthday girl, as we found out when we caught up with them. She had won five hundred dollars on the slots. She and Shenita were trading high-fives while almost spilling their complimentary drinks on their dresses. It was almost midnight and time to return to the room after we took a walk down Bourbon Street.

The gambling fever had taken hold of the women, as they wanted to play spades with us upon returning to the room. The first chance I got, I made myself comfortable and yanked my V-neck off and threw it in our room. Reggie turned on the boom box again and we listened to Q93 the rest of the night. He also took his turn at bartender and took our requests before fixing himself his usual Absolut. An old song that only someone from New Orleans would know came on the radio and the fellas were treated to Shenita and Kelly trying to do something called the "doggy hop" in their tight-fitting dresses. Both of them wound up on the floor as we laughed. To make things even, we alternated teams while playing spades. Shenita wasn't the best card player much to her mouth's dismay.

The spades game ended and Kelly brought up a game of quarters. It was my turn to lose then and I wound up taking a break on the sofa after four losses.

"Man, I need to get my camera before this night is over," Reggie said with a slap of his forehead. "These are going to be some funny-ass pictures!"

"It's in your ride, huh?"

"Yeah. I've got the valet ticket so I guess they can tell me where it's parked."

"Watch out for ghosts down there. *Whooooooo!*"

"Shit. It's the living my drunk ass needs to watch out for."

We quieted down while Reggie called downstairs and tried to sound completely sober. Reggie motioned for someone to write down the garage location of his Pathfinder. Shenita found a piece of paper and scribbled the info, while Reggie spoke aloud. He had his remote to open it, so he didn't need the keys at the front desk. Shenita handed him the paper after he hung up. We turned the radio back up and resumed the party while Reggie left for the parking garage. It was time for either Shenita or Kelly to lose at quarters.

42 Reggie Collins

The directions I was given led me straight to my Pathfinder in the Hyatt's parking garage. I wasn't sure I was at the right Pathfinder until I pushed the remote and the doors unlocked. My drunken state and the garage lighting had led to my uncertainty. I thought I had placed my camera in the hatch area and started my search there. All I found was the empty case for it. I started cursing to myself for letting someone park it instead of me. I slammed the hatch down and started to storm off when I remembered something. Our stuff was thrown all about during the traffic stop when the trooper was searching everything. Maybe my camera was thrown into the backseat.

I opened the car door and started digging around on the floor of the backseat area. All I found was my CD case, an old Houston Chronicle, and an old phone number I must have gotten from some woman that I could no longer remember. My rage started coming back only to fade away when I took one final look under one of the floor mats after noticing a hump. The camera was thin and had been partially covered by the floor mat.

"Yeah," I said to myself. I began backing up to exit my ride when a pair of small hands covered my eyes.

Bam! I was startled and smacked the top of my head on the ceiling. The hands were still covering my eyes, but the laugh was familiar. I had been hearing it all night…or at least I thought, with my usual confidence.

"Okay, girl. You scared the shit out of me. Happy?"

"Maybe…Hee. Hee. Keep your eyes closed," she whispered in a low, sexy manner.

"Heh. Okay."

I was up for going along with the birthday girl's game, so I didn't resist. She turned me around in the door of my ride and removed the camera from my hand. I kept my word and kept my eyes closed. Using one's imagination can be fun at times. I felt a pair of hands undo my belt and pull my undershirt from out of my pants. I felt their soft touch as they ran playfully up under it, caressing my stomach and chest. Damn. My stupid ass had messed up the night before and had to be all tired and shit. Oh well, no time like the present.

Light, gentle kisses followed the hands across my chest, with her stopping to run her tongue over my nipples, making them sensitive and hard. I had to do something with my hands and ran them down her back, feeling the fabric of her halter-dress. When I got to the small of her back, she took my hands and ran them under her dress to her panties. At that time, our lips met. We had exchanged a few kisses since my arrival in New Orleans, but they were different, more intense this time. Also, the taste of butterscotch on her lips was missing this time. The ol' rod came flying to attention almost on cue. Her body was pressing up against mine and was calling for a serious working-over right there in the parking garage.

She took her hands and guided mine in removing her panties. I let out a laugh of enjoyment in between our intense kisses, which was responded to with a moan or two on her part. She reached down for her panties, then placed them over my head covering my eyes completely. Boy, this was turning into some wild shit. As we continued kissing, I smelled the alcohol on her breath and something else from the panties...something sweet and somehow familiar. I brought my hands between her legs and began stimulating her further with my fingertips. It was already wet and inviting.

"Umm. I think we need to go back to the suite," I said as we continued to kiss and caress. "They...*mmm*...might have a camera in the garage. And I've got your draws on my head. Heh." I was still buzzing, but my common sense was starting to return.

"So," she replied breathlessly, "let 'em watch." That's when it first struck me like a wet fish across the face. Something was different with her voice…wrong. I continued kissing, but really homed in on the sweet smell. Pears. Oh my God…it was pears. I quickly brought my hands up toward her hair only to have her pull them back down to her waist. I was praying that I would feel her short cut and confirm that this thought was insane, but now I was feeling just the opposite. I yanked one hand free to pull the panties off my head. My eyes came…into…focus.

"Nita? Wha…what?" She simply smiled and pulled me toward her to continue kissing. Memories of her body from the night she woke me up on their couch at home came flashing back into my head, but I shook them off.

"Don't stop, Reg," she said as we locked into a passionate, intense kiss again. I gave in ever so briefly, but then shoved her away.

"What are you doing?? This shit ain't right! I know we've all had a little too much to drink, but let's get real. Okay?" We stood there at five paces; Shenita with her black dress raised slightly up on her fine shape and me with my belt undone and shirt raised up. It was a pitiful sight indeed.

"I'm not drunk, Reg. I know exactly what I'm doing." She started walking toward me and I backed away and against my ride in response. "Reg…remember when we were talking about you and that girl back in Houston, the model? The one you were with that night I was at the apartment with Neal."

"Yeah. Capri. What's that got to do with…with…any of *this*?"

"I saw you two that night…and watched. *Heh*. I almost admitted it on the ride out here, but Neal woke up." Shenita had closed the gap between us again and was reaching out with her lips to kiss me again.

"Make love to me, Reggie," she said softly as her tongue ran playfully across my bottom lip. "Do me like you did her that night. I want to feel your dick inside me."

Part of me wanted to puke, but some part of me that hid in the dark recesses of my soul stirred as well. Lust was clouding my judgment although I could have blamed it on the alcohol. Maybe deep down, the thrill of the forbidden had always lurked there with Shenita. She definitely would have been someone I would have done in a heartbeat back in the day...if she weren't my boy's girl. I had a million questions to ask her, but this was time for either retreat...or action. My belt was already undone, so Shenita helped me along some more by unzipping my pants. I pushed her hand away, so she couldn't complete the job and gave her a scowl. She stood there staring at me for what seemed an eternity, but was actually just a few seconds. I couldn't read what was going on in her head until she pushed me aside...and climbed into the backseat of my ride.

"Nita...what in the fuck are you doing?"

"What does it look like? I know a guy like you doesn't need an explanation," she said with added emphasis as she sprawled across my backseat with her legs spread open revealing the forbidden treasure that was now being offered to me. "Come...here."

I always knew Shenita had balls, but they had to be the size of watermelons. Right at that moment in time, she was the most confident woman ever...and it turned me on even more causing my hard-on to swell beyond belief.

I still resisted though.

"No," I said with a resolve that I didn't know I had in situations like this.

Shenita chuckled, but stayed put. "Well, at least give me my draws then."

I hadn't realized it, but her panties were still clenched in my hand. Shenita still didn't move, but motioned for me to hand the draws over. I took a deep breath to steady my nerves, when I realized that I was trembling. I leaned over into the ride to hand her panties back...and wound up on top of her and liking it. She celebrated her fresh kill with delight and wrapped her legs around me. I began a closer inspection of her tonsils with my tongue as she paused to slip her dress over her mane of black hair, revealing those breasts I had taken a guilty glance at before. I was rushing headlong into insanity and was pulling my pants down when I tried to reason my way out of this again.

"But...Kelly," I said in desperation.

"Shhh. I saw you first, remember? I'm oldest, so I should get first dibs anyway."

My feet were dangling out of the Pathfinder door as I plunged inside Shenita and felt that tiny part of me that I considered "good and pure of heart" die.

"Where are you going? You lost! It's your turn to drink!" I shouted triumphantly at my wife. I had finally won at quarters over her and wanted to see her pay the price.

"I don't feel so well. Maybe something's not agreeing with me. I'm going walk around in the atrium...get some air." At first, I thought Shenita was just trying to get out of drinking, but took her at her word. I had lost more times, but Shenita did weigh less...and had been drinking all day. Kelly still seemed okay in comparison.

"Need me to go with you, baby?"

"No. I'll be fine. I just need to walk around. Keep my little sister company until Reg gets back."

"*Sigh*...okay. Be careful, alright?"

I let Shenita off the hook for not killing her shot and Kelly and me continued the game without her. Half an hour passed without Shenita or Reggie showing up until Reggie returned.

Slam! Reggie came in the door looking as if covered in dried sweat. It was probably the alcohol sweating out of his system.

"Hey, dawg. You okay?"

"Yeah. Why?"

"You look kinda creepy, bro. Did you find your camera?"

"Oh. Yeah. Got it right here. I...couldn't find my ride in the garage. I walked around on two different levels in the heat. *Phew!*"

"Probably bad directions, Reg...or maybe Shenita wrote them down wrong. Did you see her downstairs on your way up?"

"Nah. Nah. What's she doing downstairs?"

"Claimed she needed some air."

"Oh."

"Ready to take some pictures?"

"Yeah. I can do that. I really need to shower though."

We decided to take a few pictures and then wait for Shenita to come back. That way, Reggie could take his shower. Reggie insisted on taking pictures and didn't want to be included until he cleaned up, but I twisted his arm and got him and Kelly to take one together. Reggie seemed a little uneasy hugging Kelly in the picture. It was probably because he wanted to make sure the photo never crossed Lila's path by accident one day.

We excused Reg from the room and took a break from playing quarters to wait for Shenita to return. I was beginning to worry and had decided to go looking for my wife.

I opened the suite door to see Shenita messing with her hair in the hallway.

"Baby," I shouted out of relief, "I was going looking for you! How you feelin'?"

"Better. I just feel sooo worn out," she said while holding her side, "I think I've had enough to drink for the night."

Shenita did look worn out. Her dress was looking wrinkled and slightly twisted as well.

"Where'd you go, baby?" I asked out of concern.

"I went down to the atrium and walked around for a while. I then had to go to the bathroom suddenly and couldn't make it back up here. I wound up running around like a chicken with its head cut off down there while looking for a bathroom. I'm ready for bed after all that mess."

"C'mon sis," Kelly chimed in, "The night is still young! We've got pictures to take. You're not getting old on me, huh?"

"Kelly, y'know I love you…but that clock says 'three-thirty' and I am '*too through*'. I can barely walk and I am carrying my ass to bed. We can take some pictures tomorrow…*oops*…later on to-day when we check out. Good night, y'all."

That left Kelly and me alone at the table with Q93 playing in the background.

"Well, checkout is at noon. You feel like calling it a night, Kelly?"

164

"Not really, but go join your wife. Reg will be out the shower soon and I'm sure he'll keep me…um…company the rest of the night."

"You sure?"

"Yeah, brother-in-law. I enjoyed the time all of y'all have spent with me. I do need to start de-toxin' for work Monday. Haha!"

Kelly stood up from the table and gave me a big hug.

"Neal…you and my sister alright? I've been wondering since she asked me to move out there with y'all."

"To tell you the truth, we have some serious differences and difficulties especially as of late. Kelly, it's like we can't stay away from each other's throats. I think things would be much better if our financial situation was better, but we disagree on how to better that too. Look, I'm tipsy and talking too much now. I'll just say that I do love your sister and that I hope this trip marks a turning point in our lives for the positive."

"I'll pray for y'all, Neal. Things will get better. She loves you too and wouldn't do anything to hurt you intentionally."

"I know Kelly. Now, I am going to bed with my lovely wife. Goodnight, girl."

"Goodnight, brother-in-law."

I walked into the bedroom and closed the door behind me. Shenita was just in the bed, but was sound asleep. The bathroom door was open and the shower steam from it had filtered into the bedroom. She had a smile on her face that was almost angelic. I curiously wondered what she was thinking about as she dreamed.

Shenita left her dress on the floor, which really told me that she was tired. She normally was a lot more careful with her expensive clothes and would have placed that dress on a chair or something. I picked it up off the grayish carpet and laid it across a chair. I left my wife briefly to go shower before returning to join her in bed. She was nude beneath the covers and I considered waking her up to see if she wanted to make love, but passed. She was sleeping so peacefully that I decided to simply cuddle up behind her. We had succeeded in having a good time since arriving in New Orleans without arguing and I was happy with that.

44 Reggie Collins

"Kelly, are we still taking those pictures?" I asked as I walked out of the bathroom with my towel around my waist. I had just finished scouring every physical trace of Shenita off my body when I heard Kelly enter the bedroom and close the door.

"No. Party's over. Shenita came back…and went straight to bed."

"Oh? Was she okay?"

"I guess. She claimed she had too much to drink and was exhausted. I just told Neal to go to bed too. That leaves just you…and me." Kelly walked over to "her" bed and sat on it. I watched her shape move under the red dress that resembled its black twin I had just been touching.

"Nothing wrong with that," I said.

"Reggie?"

"Do you find me attractive?"

"Haha! Of course! What would make you ask something like that?"

"I dunno. Maybe I meant to ask if you find me desirable. I mean, last night you were tired and all, but when we took that picture just a little while ago, you seemed uncomfortable then too…like you didn't want to be next to me."

"That had nothing to do with you. I was all sweaty and nasty and just felt awkward, that's all. Nothing else to it." I had sat down on "my" bed opposite Kelly and took her hands in mine as I leaned forward.

Kelly smiled from her seat across from me on her bed, having been reassured in her womanhood. I took my right hand and started rubbing at the base of her neck. Kelly welcomed my touch and kissed my arm as she twisted her head to the left. My thoughts and emotions were still in turmoil from what had just gone down with her sister, but I still continued…maybe in a vain attempt to erase the past hour. Before I knew it, I was tasting the familiar butterscotch on her lips as I bent over her while she continued to sit on her bed. Kelly really needed this right now and as horrible as it was, I was still thinking of her sister's body, her sister's touch, and the smell of pears while with her. I tried to ignore it and walked over to the bedroom door and locked it.

I turned the lights off and removed my towel as I walked back toward Kelly. Kelly stood up and pulled the covers back on her bed. She then pulled her dress off over her head, revealing the silhouette of her lovely body, before getting into the bed and under the covers. I slowly slipped under the covers with her in the double bed and went to work on fulfilling Kelly's birthday wish. When I had joked to Lila before that it was hard to pigeonhole myself when I was all things to all women, I never knew how prophetic that smart aleck crack would come to be. Someone could have written a book based on this crazy shit I found myself in the middle of, but nobody would believe it. Yep. Straight up fiction.

Kelly and me eventually fell asleep, but while my body rested my troubled mind would not. I went back to the parking garage where I was in the middle of hate-fucking Shenita. We were going at it hot and heavy in a delirious state and she let out laughs of delight with each thrust I made deeper inside of her. I had dropped all reservations or fear of someone seeing us now and had fallen prey to the flesh…until I saw the headlights moving down the aisle.

"Shit," I said, as I froze in mid-stroke.

"What? Don't stop," Shenita said from under me and she dug her fingernails into my ass cheeks to prod me on.

"Oh shit. It's hotel security!" I could now make out the white Ford Explorer whose headlight beams were now right next to us. It moved slowly through the parking lot and was getting closer.

"Where are they?" she asked.

"About four cars down." I was still inside her, but managed to close the door that was still partially open. The interior light in the Pathfinder went off.

"Do they see us?"

"No. I don't think so," I answered while looking down into her eyes in the dark. Logic was starting to enter back into my head as I cooled off and the sweat dripped off my chest and onto her stomach. "We...we've gotta stop this. I mean...what about Neal?...Kelly?...I can't do this."

The security truck was passing directly in front of us now and I pressed myself closer onto Shenita to stay out of sight. By doing that, I unintentionally went up in her further causing her to respond with pelvic thrusts of her own urging me to involuntarily continue.

"They'll never know," she said with that fiery, determined look in her eyes. "And you're already *doing it*. Now...fuck the shit out of me."

I obliged and the security truck rolled on by.

I jerked suddenly as I woke up from my flashback. It was five in the morning and I was rattled.

"What were you dreaming about?" I heard from the warm body next to me.

I groggily and without thinking answered, "Nita."

"*Huh?*" Kelly said as she pressed up against me. Shit.

"...Shenita. I just had a crazy dream, that's all. Too much alcohol."

"Yeah...that's strange. I was just dreaming about my sister and Neal too. I guess we've both got them on our mind, huh?"

"Yeah. Too much, I guess," I said as I rolled over to face Kelly.

"I probably shouldn't say this...but she used to have a thing for you back in the day when she first met you and Neal. Heh. She told me about it back then once, but probably forgot she told me."

"No!"

"Yeah, but Neal stole her heart and she forgot about her little crush. And if you tell anyone I told you this, I'll deny it!"

"Please. I've already forgotten that you've said it. Besides…that's way in the past."

"I'll say one thing though, Reg…My sister, Shenita, just doesn't know what she missed out on. Oh well, her loss. Heh."

"Yeah. Her loss," I said as I immersed myself in Kelly once again to her delight.

Daylight came too soon for us…or should I say, for me and Kelly. Checkout wasn't 'til noon, but I could hear Neal first, then Shenita moving around the suite with bags and stuff. I was not in a hurry to face Neal or see Shenita for that matter, as I still didn't know how I would react, so I lay there motionless with Kelly in my arms. Kelly didn't mind, as we didn't fall back asleep the last time until around seven-ish. The ploy worked until ten when Neal knocked on the door. I faked being stirred out of my sleep and Kelly woke up for real.

"Good morning."

"Heeey, Reggie," Kelly said as smooth as butter. Satisfaction showed all over her glowing face.

We got up and showered in time to take some pictures together before checkout. Neal didn't break my neck, so I figured I was safe for the moment. I still avoided eye contact with him out of guilt. Shenita carried on as if the previous night hadn't even occurred. If it weren't for the look I saw in her eyes when nobody else was looking, I would have sworn that she had complete amnesia.

The bellman came up to the suite to help us with our bags and I took a final goodbye look out the suite window down at the glass roof of the New Orleans Centre and the Superdome grounds below. I was going to miss New Orleans, but not the chaotic state my being had been thrown into as a result of this trip.

At the front desk, Kelly and Shenita finished checking out, while I gave the valet my ticket. Neal had gone to find a restroom earlier and was returning out in front when my Pathfinder came rolling up. Nothing seemed out of the ordinary...I thought.

"Ready to roll, Reg?"

"I guess, Neal. It'll feel good to get back to H-town. I hope Lila comes back soon...God, I miss her."

"Had enough of Shenita and Kelly, huh?" Neal said with a laugh. I had given the valet my ticket and a tip and had my keys in my hand.

"*What did you say?*" I asked with uncertainty as I slipped my keys back onto my key ring.

"Had enough of putting up with the sisters' carrying on and stuff?"

"Umm...yeah. Yeah!"

"The two of them together can really wear anyone out, Reg. You don't have to say it. Heh." My boy was completely clueless and I was a piece of shit.

The concierge had walked up to help load up my ride, so I walked toward the back hatch...and stopped dead in my tracks. I hadn't noticed it before because the black color blended in with my paint job, but there they were waving at me. Shenita's panties were dangling from the bottom of the rear passenger door where they must have fallen last night. They must have been forgotten in our haste and the door must have closed on them otherwise they would be on the parking garage floor.

Neal was walking up behind me and my heart skipped a beat.

"Um...Neal. Could you go tell Kelly and Shenita that we're almost ready to go?" I was stopped between Neal and the Pathfinder so as to block his view and waited for him to turn around and head back into the hotel before scurrying quickly to the car door. I popped both the hatch and the passenger door open with my remote and quickly snatched the panties up and scrunched them into my pocket. Neal and the gang came out and we departed for Kelly's grandmother's house once everything was loaded in.

Kelly rode in the front with me. She wore a plain white T-shirt, jeans, and sandals and you could tell she was sad to see our visit come to an end. I held her hand and could tell that we were under Shenita's gaze from behind her sunglasses in the back. Shenita wore a yellow tank tunic with white capri pants and white sandals. She also wore a straw hat that she had sloped over her sunglasses.

"What's that *smell*?" Kelly asked as she sniffed the air and twisted her face in disapproval.

"Oh yeah. The air is stale in here from the long trip still," I casually replied before lowering all the windows with a flip of the door switch to air my ride out. I then cranked the A/C up to the max and turned up the jazz on 98.5 WYLD to cut down on any further conversation this Sunday morning. I would stop at the Auto Zone later to pick up one of those "tree air fresheners" as well.

We said our final goodbyes at Kelly's grandmother's house and I shared a long goodbye kiss with Kelly before exchanging numbers with her. Shenita and Kelly talked some more while Neal and me waited in the ride with it running. I watched them intensely from behind my Ray Bans and tried to read their lips as they slapped hands and laughed. I was pretty sure Kelly was filling Shenita in on our night, but wasn't too concerned about that. I was looking for any reaction or changed facial expression on Kelly's part that would have come with a sudden Shenita confession. It didn't happen and I breathed a sigh of relief as Shenita gave Kelly one last sisterly hug and started walking to the ride.

"Want me to drive, Reg? You look like you had a rougher night than me, my brother."

"Nah, dawg. I'll be fine. Just ride shotgun with me up front, in case I suddenly get sleepy." I wanted to keep some distance between Shenita and me. I couldn't bear to look at Neal, but I *really* couldn't bear to have Shenita next to me on the trip back to H-town.

Most of the trip was in silence with the radio providing the soundtrack of the trip. I smiled and was as cordial as could be, but Neal and Shenita did most of the talking. I used the excuse that I was tired to explain my uncharacteristically "Al Gore–like" manner, but one of the Wallaces knew the truth.

I watched my speed and…radar detector, especially while crossing over the Atchafalaya and even got an embarrassed laugh out of Neal during that stretch. Shenita smacked her lips at Neal, signifying a shift to her crabby mode. She didn't know that I was paying for Neal's speeding ticket. I wanted so bad to tell her to shut the fuck up, but for obvious reasons, chose to keep my mouth shut. Maybe if I had kept my mouth shut along with my zipper in the hotel parking garage, I wouldn't have been having this dilemma. I told myself that I was tricked…and I was, but I didn't have to close the deal.

We stopped in the little town of Iowa, just outside of Lake Charles, to fill up on gas and to make a restroom stop before heading across the border back into Texas. Shenita got out and adjusted her hat before entering the convenience store. I chose to stay outside by the pump with Neal who was springing on the fill-up, but stole a sneak at Shenita's backside that was nesting inside her capri pants. It was going to feel good to get back to H-town and put some distance between me and her…some distance and other warm bodies.

Neal and me had some small talk while he pumped the gas about what was going to be the first thing we'd do once we got home. I went to put my hands in my pockets out of habit and realized what was still in one of them. I yanked my hand back out and played it off by rubbing my head. I needed to make a pit stop in the ol' john anyway. I ran into Shenita as she came out of the ladies' room. I subtly reached down into my pocket.

"I think you're missing this," I said as I removed her panties from my pocket. I held them low at my side for obvious reasons. This was our first real conversation, albeit a short one, since…y' know. "Maybe you need to go back in the restroom and put them up somewhere."

"Thank you, Reg. I was wondering where they went. That was sweet of you to keep them for me." She opened her hand and I let them fall into it.

"Nothing sweet about it. I don't care if you burn them, throw them away, or even put them up in your hat." I moved to pass her, but she stepped in front of me, bringing our bodies into contact with each other.

"Reg...are you mad at me?" she asked with a devilish smile meant to fuck with me.

"*You*? I'm mad at myself. I don't feel anything for you," I replied with a straight face. I then gently moved her aside and walked into the men's restroom...and locked the door behind me.

45 Neal Wallace

Monday…the first day of most people's workweeks. My schedule was different than most, but I did have to go in that evening. Shenita had taken an extra day of vacation, so we didn't have to set the alarm clock for her that morning. We had arrived back in Houston Sunday evening and grabbed some fast food at Jack In The Box before unpacking and passing out. I left the Mrs. in the bed just before noon and went to get the mail and check the lawn out. I would need to cut and edge it this week before the neighborhood association started complaining. The two days of mail that had accumulated didn't amount to much: A few bills and a reminder for Shenita's next dental appointment. It was going to be another hot day; the same as it had been in New Orleans. My blue T-shirt was already developing a wet spot in the chest area from sweat.

I walked back to the house and left the mail on the kitchen counter while I fixed myself a big glass of water. All that drinking in New Orleans and lack of sleep had me feeling groggy and dehydrated during just my short walk to the mailbox. I probably needed to start hitting the gym consistently again as well. I took a quick pinch of my waist and came up easily with more than an inch.

"Got the mail?" Shenita came walking lazily down the stairs while holding the railing. I was surprised to see her up and about. She was wearing just her yellow shirt from the trip back that she had fallen asleep in.

"Yeah, baby. On the counter. Time for your dental checkup."

"Damn. I better not have another cavity," she said as she thumbed through the mail, "Oh. Another bill too. Your loan payment for that chef school is due, huh?"

"That's *culinary institute*, Shenita."

"Yeah. Whatever. Just another bill we don't need." Yep. Home again.

Shenita was on the phone with Kelly running up our long distance bill when I left for work that evening. I didn't bother asking her if she needed the car this time. Don't get me wrong, I looooved our time away, but it felt good to get back into my routine and my element, the kitchen.

Mirage was slow on my first day back, which was good for me. We had to place orders for restaurant inventory and the early shift had left that job to me. I was known as Mr. Accuracy when it came to that sort of stuff, so it came as no surprise and would give me something to do.

I was going through our stock of tomatoes with the clipboard in hand, when I heard the songbird of Mirage. I had brought a bag into work with me and ran into the back office to get it. I returned to the kitchen with the bag in time to see Me-Me and Tookie entering from off the floor. Tookie had walked in to place an order and Me-Me was keeping her company.

"Welcome back, Big Neal!" Tookie said as she interrupted her girl-talk to acknowledge me. She had noticed me before her singing coworker. Me-Me responded a second later by running up and giving me a hug.

"Yeah! Welcome back, buddy! We missed you in the kitchen!"

"You mean you missed the fast service you get with me back here!"

"Haha! That is true! I'm not gonna lie, but we missed you as well! You had fun in the Big Easy?"

"I did. I did. Heh. I was so tired though when we got back last night."

"Well, that's the sign of a good vacation!"

"Hmmph. You can say that again," Tookie added in before she left us to head back out on the floor.

"So…" I said nervously to break the silence that marked Tookie's absence.

"So," Me-Me said, mimicking me as she smiled.

"Um. I got this for you." I reached behind me and removed an item from the bag.

"Aww! A book? For me??" Her eyes lit up from behind those glasses of hers and her mouth came to life with expression.

"Yep."

"This is sooo sweet! Thank you, Neal! This is so thoughtful!"

"It's nothing. I was looking at books in this African American bookstore out there and thought you might like a little gift. D...do you like romances?"

"Yeah. I could use more of that in my life, but this book will have to do for now. Haha! Thank you...again." Me-Me was tall, but still had to lift herself up when she gave me a kiss on the cheek. I felt a blush coming right as Me-Me began pulling away and as Tookie came walking back in.

"Oooo! I caught ya!"

"Oh, be quiet, Tookie. I was just thanking Neal. Look! He got me a book out there!" Damn. I should have waited to give the book to her. It was just a little gift and a token of friendship.

"Umm, Neal? Where's mine? Why's little Miss Melissa here so special?"

"She's not...I mean...I, well...I just didn't get a chance to get...umm—"

"Because I'm his buddy! Aren't I, buddy? Huh?" Me-Me's silly ass had saved me from making a further fool out of myself. Tookie decided to spare me and simply made a fake pouty-face at me and stuck her tongue out at Me-Me before leaving another order and exiting.

"Thanks for the save," I said to Me-Me as my blushing ended.

"Please. I didn't do a thing. Tookie didn't mean anything by it anyway. So, did Reggie behave?"

"*Does he ever?* No...actually he did behave himself. I can't even much front on him. Reg was a class act on the trip. I owe him big time." I was thinking of my speeding ticket and the money I lost at the casino on the trip. He also agreed to come on the trip, thus getting Kelly off me and Shenita's back.

"So…when are we gonna hang again? A friend of ours from back in the day is having a party this weekend down in Sugarland. I don't know yet if Reggie's coming, but you want to tag along with us?"

"I'll have to take a raincheck. Thanks though. I'm working this weekend anyway and besides…we just came back and I want to spend some time with the Mrs."

"Nothing wrong with that. I guess you gotta work to keep those home fires burnin'. When I find Mr. Right, I'll be doing the same."

"Sugarland, huh? Maybe you'll find a rich Mr. Right at the party."

"One can hope, Neal! One can hope!"

46 Reggie Collins

"Hey…it's me. I'm back in Houston. We had a safe trip and all. I miss you…Bye."

Short and simple. I had already been home for a full day, but waited until Tuesday to call Lila from work. I had gone to New Orleans hoping to have a wild time with no complications before Lila returned and had come back with a suitcase full of drama. I still wrestled with the idea of telling my boy, Neal. I had seen similar situations though, but with the male/female roles reversed. In those, the couple always stayed together and the woman that brought everything out into the open wound up looking like the slutty troublemaker. My rep and "tendencies" didn't help me either. Shenita, after all, was Neal's wife and would probably say that I came on to her and caught her in a vulnerable state or something. The thing was bad all around and probably best for me and my possible future with Lila that I kept it to myself and just sucked it up.

I had started Monday off fresh and was the first person to arrive at work. As chaotic as my personal life could be, there was no reason to let it intrude into my career.

I was still one of Stratford Circle's shining stars and couldn't be slippin' on the job. I even wore the blue Zegna suit that Lila had surprised me with as a Christmas present.

Nothing had jumped up to bite me on the ass while I was away, so I closed my office door and had spent that morning catching up on the usual reviews. Normally, I would have called Neal and hollered at him, but I knew Shenita was off. A knock on my door disturbed my deliberation.

"Reggie! It's good to see ya!" It was the Houston-area manager and my boss, Bob Briceland. Bob was a west Texas native who managed to rise up through the ranks without leaving his home state. That feat was becoming rarer and rarer these days. He was a good-hearted soul who was usually "hands off" when it came to letting his supervisors do their jobs.

"Bob! What brings you down to Sharpstown?" I stood up and shook his hand over my desk. I motioned for him to have a seat. Bob's office was located in the Jersey Village area of Houston, northwest of here.

"I'm just making my rounds and visiting the troops down on the front line. Y'all are doing an outstanding job and I wanted to salute each of y'all personally!" Bob always used military jargon from his days as a wannabe in the National Guard. He was goofy, but harmless.

"Heh. Well, thanks. Everybody's motivated at our office and performance has skyrocketed since you made that brilliant decision to promote this young African American to full-time supervisor recently," I said facetiously.

"Haha! Never afraid of being overly modest, huh? Well, if you keep your nose clean, there are bigger things ahead for you, son."

"And I look forward to them."

"Umm. Yep. We never want to do anything that might jeopardize that." Bob didn't mean "we"; He meant "me". Bob was nervous whenever he was uncomfortable with the subject and this wasn't just a visit to the "troops". I should have known as Bob was always at the Lochinvar Country Club on Mondays for tee time. Had Trina tried to sabotage my job while I was gone?

"What's on your mind, Bob?" I hid my discomfort behind a face of nonchalance.

"The plaintiff attorney…Lila Reed. I don't even know if this is true…and it's none of my business, but rumor has it that you've been seen in her company."

You're right. It is none of your business is what I wanted to shout at Bob. Someone from that day at Copeland's when I was with Lila had blabbed and the rumor mill was now running full steam ahead. That was the one thing I loathed about Stratford Circle.

"Yes. She is a friend of mine. Is there a problem?" was my PC answer.

"I know this is ridiculous…but there are also wild rumors that you might be…um…sharing confidential information with her. I can attest that I have seen nothing of the sort and don't believe it…But that doesn't mean that others in the company feel the same as I."

"That's preposterous! You know me better than that, Bob!"

"I do. I shouldn't even be discussing rumors with you, but I felt you should know. Like I said…we don't want to do anything that might jeopardize bigger things for us in the future."

"I understand. Thanks, Bob." He was telling me to ditch Lila. I really wanted to reach out and pimp-slap his dopey ass, but he was just passing the info on. I started trying to guess who started this shit, but stopped before I wound up making myself sick.

After Bob left our office, I took the rest of Monday off and went home. But enough of those thoughts, this was a different day and it was lunchtime now. I needed to get out and I needed someone I could talk to. My phone started ringing before I could forward it. It could have been Lila returning my call, so I answered it.

"Stratford Circle, this is Reggie."

There was silence on the other end, but I could hear people in the distance…like at a mall.

"Hello?" I called out into the silence.

"Hey," the voice on the other end said in a low tone. It was Trina.

"What do you want?"

"I miss you, baby…and just wanted to talk."

"No can do. I thought I spelled it out loud and clear for you. YOU CALL ME OR COME AROUND ME AND YOU GO TO JAIL. Got it? Leave me the fuck alone!"

"Please. Don't do this to me. I'm sorry. Okay?"

"No. Not 'okay'. Don't call me again."

"Reggie! I—" *Click.*

I didn't have the time or patience for her crazy ass. I forwarded my phone and told Ruby not to expect me back for a couple of hours.

"*Who is it?*"

"It's me…Reg. You busy?"

"*Hell no, boy. I'll buzz you in. Watch the gate though. It sticks sometimes.*"

Me-Me lived in an apartment on the southwest side, same as me, but hers was a little lower on the plush scale. Her one-bedroom apartment on Fondren ran her about three-seventy a month. The complex looked nice and it did have a security gate that worked most of the time, but Me-Me's neighbors could get a little rowdy. 9-1-1 was on Me-Me's speed dial as a result and the most used number too.

Me-Me opened her front door for me and then ran back to her TV. She was wearing red jogging suit pants, white anklet socks and a black Reebok sports bra with the red emblem. *Days of Our Lives* was on, which was her favorite soap. She motioned for me to close the door behind me and have a seat on the leather couch next to her.

"Did Bo ever find Hope?" I asked as I took a seat. Me-Me was hunched over and staring at the old nineteen-inch screen.

"That's old. He's been found her. They just got married again."

"Oh?"

"And she just had her baby."

"Bo didn't waste no time, huh?"

"This one's not his."

"What? Well, who's the father?"

"Either John or Stefano."

"What?? So Hope became a ho??!!"

"No. She was someone else when she slept with them."

"I'm confused. Fuck it."

"Don't worry, Reggie. It's going off now."

My lil' sis was free to give me her undivided attention now. I tried not to look like I had a world of troubles, but she saw right through it.

"Want something to eat…or drink?" she asked.

"Whatcha got?"

"Nothing."

"Figures. And you're always talking about me having nothing at my place."

"Yeah. I can do that. Hee. What's wrong? I talked with Neal yesterday. He said you were on your best behavior while in New Orleans."

"*Oh really?*" I couldn't talk with Neal about the New Orleans situation, but then I couldn't really talk to Me-Me about it either.

"Don't even act like that. It's okay to be a good guy sometimes, y'know."

"Heh. If you say so. I don't feel so good right now."

"What's wrong? Lila?"

"No, not directly. It's…" I paused as I noticed the new book on the arm of the couch next to Me-Me. It was unmistakable, as the one Neal had bought in New Orleans at the bookstore. I decided not to say anything.

"*It's…?*" Me-Me repeated back to me.

"It's just that…things are going weird at work all of a sudden. That, and so many other things that have something to do with Lila in one way or another. I just came back from a short vacation, but feel like I need another one right away or else I'll crack."

"What does Lila have to say about all of this?"

"Oh yeah. We haven't really talked since Sunday before last at my apartment. Lila's in Dallas."

"Heh. I'm surprised she let you out of her sights. Sooo, that's why you're over here now. Otherwise I wouldn't see you, but every once in a blue moon."

"C'mon, girl. You know it's not like that…Things 'may' be getting serious between Lila and me in the near future. I don't know yet if and where it's going to go. Everything's over with Trina though."

"Congratulations! That was long overdue there! Lila had something to do with that I'll bet."

"Not directly. Trina was bad for my health…and sanity anyway. Y'know, I miss hanging and talking with you lil' sis."

"I miss you too, Reg. When's the future Mrs. Collins coming home?"

"Next week sometime, I think."

"Want to hang this weekend? Like old times?"

"Sure. I'd like that. What's up?"

"Remember Easy Al?"

"Yeah? He's got that big ass crib in Sugarland now." Albert or "Easy Al" as most of us knew him, grew up with us in South Park back in the day. He sold out in high school and attended Jack Yates over in Third Ward by TSU and U of H, instead of Jesse H. Jones like the rest of us. The boy later went on to play b-ball in the NBA before being cut and going on to play in Europe. I used to hate his ass because when he was a young buck, he would steal your momma's dentures if her mouth wasn't closed. He outgrew that foolishness, but I still had a bad vibe left over from that.

"Well, I saw him this weekend at Mirage. He had stopped by with his entourage for dinner. He's having a party at his crib and we're invited. It's this Saturday."

"Hmmm."

"I'm going. Please say you'll come with me. Please!"

"Why not? It'll be fun."

"Are you going to call your dad?"

"To invite him over?"

"Yeah."

"…I don't know. I know what you told him, but I've still got some serious issues with him."

"He's not getting any younger." The meaning of those words came through loud and clear and cut through the redness of my rage that normally came with a conversation about my pops.

It was Thursday around lunchtime and I was sitting at Manchu Wok in the Northline Mall with Shenita. She was on her break from work at Questcom and had agreed to have lunch with me. Shenita had been a lot mellower since our visit to New Orleans. It looked like the trip did her some good and the change in her mood was good for me as well.

"…I guess I could try to be civil. When were you thinking about having him over? I'm still not calling him and asking…but if you invite him, I won't make a stink."

"Or punch the wall again?" she sarcastically replied while eating her beef and broccoli.

"I'll *try* not to punch the wall again."

"Okay. I'll call your dad. How's this weekend?"

"Bad. Working, of course. I need to tell you about that. I found out yesterday that the chef who works days is quitting. He found a better gig."

"And?"

"I'm going to start alternating the lunch and dinner shifts next week until things clear up. The good thing is that I'll have weekends off…at least for a little while. Maybe we could do next week-end."

"I've been thinking…we never did a housewarming party. Maybe just a few people? Like Ramona and her husband and a couple of other neighbors. It could be potluck. You could invite Reggie. We haven't heard from him since we got back."

"And Lila. She'll probably be back by then."

"…And Lila," she huffed as she hesitated, then gave in.

"Yeah. Just enough people that I can talk to when I need to get away from my pops. He's bound to say something to piss me off."

"Was life that awful with him?"

"…He loved me. Life was still awful. My moms had the worst of it. I'll leave it at that."

"Okay."

"He's wondering when we're going to have kids."

"Oh?"

"Yep," I said as I took another sip of cola through the straw. I don't know what made me pull that sledgehammer out and slam it onto our table. Maybe I thought she was a little too mellow and wanted to stir her up a little. All I got was silence as she continued chewing her food.

"Time for me to go back to work," was all she said.

I walked Shenita back to her job inside the mall without mentioning children again. She gave me a quick kiss on the cheek before going back on the clock and disappearing behind the digital phone display counter to help an elderly lady who didn't know how to operate her phone.

As I left the mall, I realized that I had the rest of the afternoon to myself and didn't feel like going home to be a couch potato. I started to call Reggie to invite him to our get-together, but he had dropped off the radar since our return. I decided to pay him a personal visit instead and give him a hard time.

I took I-45 into town and caught the 59 for my trip to the southwest side where Reggie's big green and white office was located. I didn't know if he was even in when I stopped, but it didn't matter. If he wasn't there, I would just take a walk through Sharpstown Mall that was nearby. I hadn't been in there in about three years and it would be nice to see one of the old hangouts from the school days.

When I told the receptionist who I was, she called to the back. Reggie was in and she told me to have a seat in the lobby. Reg had told me that they were sticklers for security ever since somebody walked in with a knife and tried to stab an employee. I remembered seeing something on Channel 11 about it. It was an ungrateful job my boy was in. Everybody was always upset or unhappy. It was not the place where somebody would call you just to say "hi". It was always negative and took a certain kind of individual to handle that kind of pressure. I guess Reggie was that kind of person.

"Say, bro," he said as he came out the door from in back. His white dress shirt had the sleeves rolled up. It was a sign that my boy was actually earning his paycheck today.

"What's up, dawg?" I said with a smile. "Working hard?"

"Hell yeah. They're bustin' this Black man's ass today. A bunch of last minute reports. How you been?"

"Good. We thought we'd lost you, bro. We ain't heard shit outta you since we came back."

"Nah. I'm still here. Just been busy. Let me holler at you," he said while motioning with his eyes toward the exit. I led the way out into the parking lot.

"What's wrong?"

"Shit. They're trippin' about me and Lila. Somebody's starting rumors…saying that I've been sharing confidential shit with her. Straight bullshit. Feel like I need a cigarette…and I don't even smoke. Heh."

"What?! Sounds like somebody in the company is trying to screw you, bro."

"I'm not letting it get to me. I won't let anybody stop me. Believe that."

"Lila back yet?"

"No. Haven't heard from her. Her parents have her busy, so I ain't mad at her. Gonna hang out with Me-Me this weekend."

"Oh yeah. The party."

"Yep. You two sure talk a lot."

"Yeah. It's work. We're always running into each other and she's easy to talk to."

"I know. She's special, Neal. The right person's out there for her somewhere. Just wait 'n see."

"Umm...what are you doing next weekend?"

"Nothing really. Hopefully Lila will be back by then."

"Well, me and Shenita are inviting the two of you over. We are going to try to 'entertain' at the house. Y'know...a couple of neighbors...and my pops."

"...Okay. I'm sure she'd be okay with that. I didn't even know your father was alive. Damn."

"Long story. It's sure to be interesting. Trust me."

"We should be there then. If something comes up and Lila can't make it, I'll let you know. I should be there anyway."

"Good. Maybe the four of us will start doing the married couples thing more often."

"*Yeah*, right. Umm...How are things with you and the Mrs.?"

"Y'know...that's a good question, bro. Shenita's been so...so mellow since we got back. That is good...very good. Maybe someone put a voodoo spell on her while we were down in 'Weeziana'. Haha. Did you see anything strange going on with her out there?"

"...Nah. Nothing I can think of...Look, I hate to run you off, but I've gotta get back in there. Reports, y'know."

"Alright, dawg. Holler at me later." Reggie was definitely not himself since returning from the trip. Heh. Both he and Shenita had that in common. Maybe somebody had put a voodoo spell on the both of them.

"That's a church."

"No it's not."

"Look at it. That's a church."

"No."

"Look at how big it is. That's a church. It's gotta be."

"That's his house. Look at the cars over there," I said while pointing at a black Range Rover, a white Lexus IS300, and two Corvettes that lined the street on Sugar Creek Boulevard in front of the large red-bricked Colonial style house on our right.

"Daaaaaamn, Reg. It still looks like a church."

My Pathfinder had entered the Sugarland area southwest of H-town, specifically, the Sugar Creek neighborhood. The reflecting pool and columns had greeted us as we drove through the entrance and past the country club. We followed the directions down the winding street past homes ranging from only a couple hundred thousand to over a million dollars and over the waterways that were scattered throughout the golf course community. There was a lot of money down in this area and Al was far from being the only athlete in this hood. Hell, he was probably on the lower end of the income scale around here. You did get more for your money out here though.

Me-Me and me headed to Al's crib for the party after starting our Saturday first with an early evening at Drexler's Barbecue on Dowling. I had picked up Me-Me at her apartment and she was hungry so it was off to Drexler's, one of our old hangouts.

"My hands still smell like barbecue sauce?" Me-Me asked as she shoved her hands quickly in front of my face. I was looking for somewhere to park close to the large home and her sudden jerky movement had startled me. She was unusually self-conscious and it made me think that she wanted to impress ol' Easy Al.

"Yeah. I can still smell them. That's good though. Makes brothers want to lick your fingers. *Slurp*."

"Boy, you just too nasty," Me-Me said as she shoved my hand with her hand.

"But the women love it," I shot back with my normal cockiness.

I hadn't really unwound without any plots, plans, relationships, or issues hanging over my head in a while and it felt good to be around somebody that would let a dog be a dog. Me and my lil' sis had that kind of bond and respect that allowed us to kick it in our element without fear of being criticized and that was liberating. Even with all that said, I still missed Lila and was seriously leaning toward making that change when she returned. I had put that Shenita shit behind me and was moving on. Case closed. Tonight, I would try to unwind and regulate...Okay! Okay! Maybe somebody in the party was going to get "dicked down", but that was going to be off-the-cuff.

Me-Me was wearing a gold sleeveless polyester/spandex fringe dress with matching sandals that looked like something fine ass Beyonce' had worn in a Destiny's Child video. The little fringes danced around her thighs with every bouncy step of her body as we walked toward Al's playa palace. Her specs were on lockdown inside her handbag for the night. I was going to have to watch her closely as she was trying to look all cute and flying blind as a bat in the process.

"You got sauce on your dress," I said right as Me-Me's finger was about to push the doorbell.

"No!" she screamed as she turned around and started looking all over.

"Haha! Just fuckin' with you."

Me-Me scowled at me for my prank and then rang the doorbell. I had never been here and frankly didn't know what to expect; A house full of honeys in bikinis would have been right on time, but this wasn't one of those times. One of our host's flunkies opened the door. He was a lanky, yellow brother wearing Sean John gear who had a half-empty bottle of Cristal in his hand. Don't get me wrong, there were some women in there when me and Me-Me walked onto the scene, but the place was filled mostly with brothers hanging out or playing NBA Live on the PlayStation 2 hooked up to the large flat screen TV that took up a whole wall. Some of the faces looked familiar. Either I had seen them growing up around the hood or on TV warming the bench in a basketball game. All the brothers' eyes were on Me-Me as their "fresh meat" alarms went off. My girl was looking stunning with her braids up and glasses off. On her right shoulder were the initials "JB"...Joseph or Jo-Jo Bonds, her brother and my best friend.

"Look who rode up in here," Al said as he walked into the white-walled, mirrored foyer to greet us. His tall ass was dressed all in white and iced up in platinum with a bracelet, three rings and a chain with the traditional diamond-encrusted cross as a status symbol. I could tell that the two catty-looking sisters, one in a black bra with short denim shorts and the other all in leather, that trailed behind him were recently under his arms, but kept my mouth shut, as I wasn't sure.

"Easy Al!" I said with fake enthusiasm. He still wasn't one of my favorite people.

"Reggie Collins! Haha! People, I remember when this nigga here used to be afraid of pussy. But look at him now...the ladies' man...got the Perry Ellis on! Boy, I'm proud of ya," Al said in his loud booming voice as he tried to cap on the brother before his paid-for audience.

"Heh. Yep...that was me. Right until I fucked your girlfriend...*oops*...*my* girlfriend after that! I didn't realize how friendly pussy was until then. I guess I should say 'thanks', bro."

A chorus of *ooos* rang out from Al's boys. I halfway expected Al to take a swing at me or kick me out.

"Long time no see, Reg," Al proclaimed with a laugh as he gave me a brotha-hug instead. It was cool between us.

"Yep, dawg."

"How ya livin'?"

"Awight. Awight. Not a big balla like you though."

"*Ahem*," Me-Me said as she cleared her throat, "Are y'all two finished throwing the testosterone around?"

"Umm. Sorry, Me-Me. I apologize for the rude language, but I ain't seen this muthafucka…oops…in years," said Al as he bristled at the thought of offending Me-Me. He even reverted to his college English he used to use for his interviews.

"Al, this place is off the chain," Me-Me said in awe as she turned around in a full circle to see all she could. Al's crib was tight, I had to agree. The large white leather sectional down the stairs in the living room had to be worth at least as much as Me-Me's Corolla.

"Here, let me take you on a tour, Me-Me. Uh…Y'all want somethin' to drank or eat first?"

"I'm fine," Me-Me said, "I'll have something later." She was eager to see something she hadn't tasted in life.

"We ate a little while ago, but I'll take a drink," I replied. I didn't want to go on the tour anyway and I'm sure Me-Me didn't want me being overprotective and smothering her.

I walked over into the kitchen, once the sister in leather pointed me in the right direction. I was going to have to get her number later, but was ready to get my drink on first. The kitchen was stocked with alcohol more than anything. Cases of Cristal, Moet, Alizé, Heineken, and Tequiza were in full supply in the extra large stainless steel fridge that was built into the kitchen wall as well as on the kitchen counter. This nigga must have bought the stuff by the crate.

I interrupted this dreadlocked brother in camouflage from getting busy with this Asian hottie next to the fridge and apologized. They were both fucked up already and rolled their eyes before moving on to somewhere more private in this big ass crib.

"Here…let me get that for you," the sister in leather said as she walked into the kitchen. I had her pegged as one of Al's groupies earlier, but wasn't too sure. She reminded me of Aaliyah, but older and with more body.

"I got it. Thanks though. I would appreciate it if you would get me a glass."

"Here," she said as she honored my request. "What's your name?"

"Reggie. Sorry. Your boy didn't introduce us earlier."

"Angelique. Pleased to meet you. You play ball too?"

Angelique and me started shootin' the shit in the kitchen over drinks. Even though she was a gold-digger, she was a good conversationalist, so I didn't mind. I only had hard dick and soft music for her anyway...and the music wasn't playing tonight.

Al came into the kitchen about an hour later with his arm around Me-Me. I gave Me-Me "the look" to make sure everything was okay as she approached. She gave me the "all-clear" sign and then smiled as she eyed Angelique then looked back at me. I ignored her smile intentionally and gulped down the last of my drink. The four of us talked briefly as Al filled a bucket of ice from the freezer for his champagne. Al mentioned the hot tub out back that might be jumping later on, which seemed to get Angelique going. I was starting to feel real good myself and was thinking about having her take me on a personal tour out back sooner than later.

Al and Me-Me left us in the kitchen again and we broke open another bottle before walking around the rest of the ground floor. I slowed to check out the video game the brothers were still playing with Angelique on my arm. Their game was almost over and part of me wanted to play a quick quarter with the Rockets to see what Steve Francis could do on there, but Angelique wasn't too interested and moved me along.

We took a brief tour of the other rooms and eventually made our way to the back deck by the hot tub and swimming pool. The full moon was shining down on us through the clouds. There was sure to be some craziness tonight. Somebody inside had discovered Al's stereo system and it came blasting to life. UGK's *One Day* came on as we stood by Al's hot tub, taking me back about six years and several 40 ounces ago. I involuntarily began nodding my head to the rhythm. I was feeling good, but Angelique was feeling even better as she took a seat. She had taken her shoes off and was letting her legs dangle in the bubbling waters of the hot tub. It was still humid outside and I took my jacket off to get more comfortable. I squatted down and called Angelique over to me. She hiked her leather skirt up and walked across the hot tub to give my drunken ass a kiss. We were getting to know each other a little better when *Wobble, Wobble* by the 504 Boyz came on, sending Angelique into full freak-mode. She went into one hell of an exotic dancer routine in the water, while I watched on and hoped nobody would walk out and interrupt my private dance.

I had been drinking way too much and asked Angelique to excuse me once the song ended. I discretely entered back into Al's house to take a quick leak. The party was jumpin' inside now and I almost wanted to stay. I found my way to a bathroom under the stairwell and tried to open the door.

The occupants inside shouted, "Go away!" leaving me to try to quickly find another one.

I decided to try the upstairs area and jogged up the polished mahogany stairs. Just my luck, I found an open bathroom at the second door on the right and relieved myself with a sigh of relief.

I was zipping my pants up when I heard a thud and noises through the wall. I didn't think much of it and finished washing my hands. If I took too long, Angelique might have become bored and moved on to someone less suave and debonair. I was about to run back downstairs when I heard the same noises, but a little more distinct this time, from down the hallway. It was a woman's voice and it didn't sound happy. The music downstairs would have drowned it out to everyone down there. The hairs raised up on the back of my neck and I paused to listen more closely.

I figured out which room the sound was coming from and began running, slowly at first, toward the large closed door before me...and kicked it in.

50 Reggie Collins

I thought I had broken my ankle when it hit the latch on the door. The door was solid, but it gave right where it was supposed to. If I wouldn't have been drinking, I probably would have tried simply turning the knob. Oh well. I wouldn't feel the pain 'til morning.

The door flying open had the dramatic effect needed as it caused Al to pause. His pants were down to his knees and he had Me-Me pinned down on the four-post bed by her wrists. Me-Me's leg was up to kick him away when I charged in, but she wasn't going to get it done. Al was almost seven feet tall and solid. Heh. As if I was going to have an easier time.

"Man, I'm gonna excuse that door. Why don't you go back down there 'n handle your business with Angelique? We just got in a little argument, s'all. Everything's cool."

Me-Me didn't even need to give me the "*not* all-clear" sign as he released his grip on her wrists. I had seen enough. This was going to be painful.

Me-Me responded before I could move on him. Her nails raked across Al's face as he looked at me. Al let out a scream as he grabbed his face in pain. Al raised his fist up to rain down on Me-Me in response, but it wasn't happening. This was my lil' sis' night. I had to jump up to connect on Al's jaw, but it did the trick and threw him off balance. I didn't stop to give him a chance and started droppin' them bones in a flurry. I thought it was over when Al's backfist tagged me, making me see stars. Al's nose was bloody and his face was bleeding from Me-Me's scratch, but he was still up and snorting like a mad bull. His pants were still down and Me-Me let out a scream as she planted her heel square in his cashews. A deep moan was all that came from Al's throat and he fell to the floor holding himself. His pants had tripped him up. Me-Me was still wound up and landed square on Al's back and continued tearing into him. Her braids were flying all over. Al rolled Me-Me over in one move and was on top of her until I kicked him upside his head with my best punt. I was straight-up O-Dog from *Menace II Society* just then and Al was just another victim of my wraith…a tall one, but a victim nonetheless.

The kick knocked ol' Easy Al cross-eyed before he went smooth out. The problem was that Me-Me was trapped underneath him.

"Ugh! Get this big MF off me!" Me-Me screamed as she tried to muscle his frame up.

I caught my breath then pulled Al off her. He was starting to come around already and was beginning to blink his eyes. The beige carpet was stained red with his blood.

"You okay, girl?"

"I am now. Let's just get outta here, Reg."

"I don't think your boy is inviting us back," I said just before I stomped on his head one last time. Told you I couldn't stand his ass.

I led Me-Me down the stairs and we quickly headed out the front door. Some of the partygoers looked at us strange, but our fake smiles disarmed them. Somebody in there had to be strapped and we didn't need that kind of mess. I had left my jacket out back with Angelique, but smartly decided to ditch it. The two of us laughed all the way to 59.

"Me-Me," I said as my mood turned serious again, "are you sure you're okay?"

"Yeah, boy. I'm fine," she said casually. Me-Me grew up one tough customer and it was showing, but I was still concerned.

"Do you want to press charges?"

"Nah. He got worse than he gave…Thanks. I owe you…again."

"I told you I'll always be there for you."

"I believe you, Reggie," Me-Me said as she gave me a gentle peck on the lips. It wasn't anything hot or passionate, just sweet and light. We never kissed on the lips, but she took comfort in it so I didn't make a big deal out of it. I think she was hoping for something different from Al than what she got and was hiding her pain.

"Do you want me to take you home?"

"No. No home. Not yet. Let's just hang like we used to do. I want to get fucked up."

"Well...umm. I'm kinda already waaay ahead of you in that department. Matter of fact, you might have to drive before the night's up. The adrenaline's wearing off and I'm still buzzed."

We found ourselves at a tiny hole-in-the-wall on the north side of town called McEnemy's. It was just off the 610 Loop and I'm still not sure how we wound up there, but the music was good and they even had a little dance floor. Me-Me got a chance to let her hair down as I attempted to dance with her on a few numbers. I was too tipsy, so I told her to dance with someone else while I watched from the bar, but she passed. We sat at the bar the rest of the night and just talked over drinks like we used to.

"You having a good time?"

"Reggie, I'm having one of the best times of my life!"

"For real? Even with what went down earlier?"

"Yes. If you hadn't kicked in the door to save the day when you did, it might be a different story. Thank you...again. It's so comforting having you around. No matter what happens, I hope you're always in my life."

"Please. I already told you I'm not going anywhere." My world had begun spinning and I knew I was at my limit for the night. Besides, the place was about to close anyway.

"No. That's not true. Once you settle down with Lila and tie the knot, it's 'bye-bye Me-Me'."

"Heh. Honestly though?"

"What?"

"I don't think I deserve Lila. I've done...bad things," I said as something triggered memories of Shenita in the garage as well as my friendship with Neal. "I think that maybe…I'm just no good for her or anyone for that matter." A wave of intense sorrow was overcoming me as I was finally breaking under the pressure of the last couple weeks. Maybe it was just too many drinks talking, but my soul was feeling tortured.

"That's not true, Reggie Collins!" Me-Me hollered at me like my own personal cheerleader, "You are kind. You are caring. You are loyal…"

"Heh. *Loyal.* Yeah…right. I thought that once. You just don't know, girl. Maybe I don't know myself."

"Stop beating up on yourself. You've got something you want to talk about?"

"…No. Not this time. It's just something I'll have to learn to live with. Umm…are you in any shape to drive?"

51 Reggie Collins

"Look…you can take my ride and just bring it back in the morning," I said to Me-Me when she woke me upon arriving at my apartment.

"Nah. I'll help you up the stairs. Besides…I don't want to be alone in my apartment right now."

"I understand. You can take the bed, Me-Me. I'll take the couch."

"Nonsense. You take your bed. I'll just hang around to make sure you're okay then head out."

Me-Me helped me up my stairs and into the apartment. The alarm started counting off and I gave her the code while I continued on into my bedroom. I made it out of most of my clothes before Me-Me helped me out of the rest. She then put me to bed in my blue silk boxers. I last heard Me-Me walking around in the living room before I fell fast asleep.

It seemed like I was asleep for an eternity and that time stood still. The spinning of the room had stopped without my puking or anything and I was now resting comfortably. I heard footsteps, but couldn't open my eyes. I thought that Me-Me had already left, but apparently she was still with me. It was still dark and all was silent as I heard the ruffling sound of clothes. I tried to talk, but only let out a groan that was responded to with a giggle. I lay there flat on my back with the breeze from the ceiling fan blowing across me. I then felt the bed shift as a body got into the bed next to me. Me-Me had discarded her dress and had snuggled next to me nude. I managed to get an arm around her as we lay there and pulled her closer to me. It appeared Me-Me had a need for comforting this night as much as I relished having a warm body next to me. It was odd, very odd indeed…especially for the two of us to be laying together like this, but this was not a usual night. I was exhausted and had no intentions of this taking a sexual turn…but things don't always go as planned in my life.

It started maybe just a few hours before sunrise. I was sleeping hard and dreaming about Lila as usual. Me-Me's hand brushed, accidentally I suspect, against my usual hard-on causing me to begin stirring from my dream state. On reflex or partially out of habit, I pressed up against Me-Me in response. Me-Me's hand returned, nervously at first, but stayed around this time and began working me up through my boxers. It was slow, almost unintentionally at first as her hand caressed me, then the motions became intentional and her grip tighter, more intense. I was smiling in my sleep and my hands began roaming as well, first across her shoulders then down to her breasts, which caused Me-Me to stir as well.

Before I knew it, my lips had found their way onto her body to where they received a welcome gasp from Me-Me. I was in that half awake/half asleep state where there could still be a turning back…but it had to be soon. Things were escalating quickly and my eyes flared open to face Me-Me. It was as if I was looking at her through new eyes.

"Do you want to do this?" I asked Me-Me in all honesty as I ran my hands through her braids and kissed on her neck.

"What do you think?" she replied as she moaned again. "I haven't had any in a while."

We had decided at that moment that we both needed this right at this time. Hopefully, things wouldn't be permanently ruined between me and my lil' sis, who wasn't looking very little at the moment nor very "sisterly".

We recklessly proceeded as I took to mapping every square inch of Me-Me's long frame with my mouth and tongue before giving in to her pleading and slowly, gradually entering her tight confines.

I felt the arrival of Sunday morning as the sunlight entered through the bedroom window. I was still on top of Me-Me where I had collapsed inside of her in an explosion of delight hours before, but neither of us was moving still. I honestly don't know if we could've moved, even if we wanted to. Neither one of us had anywhere to go nor anything planned for the day, so there was no rush. Besides, waking would have brought on an awkward conversation that I didn't think either one of us was prepared to deal with just yet. I had spent most of my life protecting her to see it all go out the window by doing something in one night that could wind up hurting her. Heh. I was good for that. As I lay silent, I started realizing that Me-Me's feelings for me may have been far from what I thought for quite some time, but that I had put blinders on when it came to her out of respect.

I eventually rolled off Me-Me and was on my back with my mouth open and catching flies, when noises in the apartment caused me to awake. It had to have been around noon now and Me-Me had probably gotten up to fix something to eat. That would have been the case, except that I could feel one of her braids as it still rested across my face.

My head was killing me as I went through multiple images in a split second. Me-Me had pushed my front door closed, but had she locked it? She didn't know that it would pop open if not locked. Somebody could have simply walked right in...and had. My baseball bat wasn't nearby either. The sound of somebody standing in the bedroom doorway caused me to open one eye cautiously at first...then the other. The image was blurry at first as I brought my vision into focus.

It wasn't a burglar or axe murderer. It was worse...incredibly worse.

"I guess we don't need that talk after all, Champ," she said accusingly. Her smile was there, but it carried a different meaning than normal.

I sprang up from the bed and in sheer terror at how things looked to Lila. I tried to come up with something to say, an excuse or rational explanation, but could only stare in shock and look busted. I was greeting Lila with a naked body that smelled of Me-Me, as she lay in my bed asleep with a smile on her face. It was exactly two weeks ago that Lila and Me-Me's roles were reversed in this very apartment. At that time, I was on cloud nine. Now I was stuck in one of the inner circles of Hell.

"I…I…How did you get in?"

"Your door was open. I thought you had seen me coming and left it open to surprise me. Well…you *surprised* me."

"Um…when did you get back?" I asked while quickly picking my boxers up off the floor and putting them on.

"Last night. I wanted to run over then, but figured I'd wait and surprise you. You are lower than I ever could have imagined," she said as she looked down at Me-Me from behind her tortoise shell sunglasses.

"No. No. Let me explain," came weakly from my mouth, sounding like a tired, old excuse, "Me-Me was almost raped last night and…I was just comforting her—"

"By *fucking* her??? You are a sick motherfucker! What was I even thinking? J…just how long have you two been *close* like this?"

I was preparing to answer when Me-Me woke up. Her eyes had to adjust too, as she wasn't wearing her specs, but she knew it was Lila. Me-Me gasped then reached for the sheets to cover herself. Me-Me looked at me with shock and sorrow in her eyes. I turned away to concentrate on Lila.

"Th…this just happened by accident, Lila. Let me put some clothes on and talk with you."

"Forget about it. Just forget about it. I can't believe I let myself fall for a son of a bitch like you." Lila's eyes were blinking behind her sunglasses as she took them off and turned to walk out.

"Lila! Wait!" I screamed as I ran behind her. A small gift-wrapped box fell from her hand onto the floor and bounced in front of me. I hopped over it as I closed on her and grabbed her shoulder.

"Don't fucking touch me!" she snarled as she slapped me across the face, almost knocking a tooth out. The blow startled me for a second, giving Lila time to leave out the front door.

While barefoot and still in my draws, I ran down the hot stairs after her. To hell with the neighbors or my feet, which burned with every step on the noontime pavement.

"Lila! Stop! Waaaaaaaait!"

My screaming at the top of my lungs finally got through to Lila as she paused in the doorway of her car.

"What? You have something you think you can say?" she asked. In the bright sun, she was absolutely radiant. If only I could just rewind everything back to two weeks ago.

"Please. Don't go. I've been waiting this entire time for you to come back…Please. Let me try to explain…again."

"Reggie, Reggie, Reggie…I can't do this. I had prepared myself for everything else—Your past, all the women, the hoochies, but you topped yourself with this Me-Me thing. I can't deal with you, Mr. Collins. I'll only end up hurting myself more than I just did. Goodbye, Champ. It's been real."

"No!" I shouted as I grabbed her shoulder. She swatted it away as she turned the key and pushed the "start" button, which sent her convertible roaring to life. Lila began putting it in gear as I continued yelling to her.

"Wait! I have something to tell you!" I screamed desperately as Lila began backing up. She wasn't having it and I didn't blame her. I stood in front of her car in my draws in an attempt to stop her. No go.

Lila floored it, taking me off my feet and sending me landing on her hot car hood. On the short parking lot, She got the S2000 up to third gear with me as a screaming involuntary passenger before slamming on her brakes to discard me. I rolled off the hood and landed flat on my back. Lila stopped to make sure I hadn't broken anything and then whipped her little car around me and sped away.

"I love you," I whispered with tears in my eyes as I rolled onto my stomach just in time to see Lila disappear out the apartment gate. I lay on the hot, dirty pavement motionless for several minutes until a pickup truck came along and started honking at me.

I took my hands off my face and brushed myself off. I was too shattered to be embarrassed as I walked past my curious neighbors, some of which who offered to call the police for me. I would live…but I was dead. The funny thing, if there was one in this, was that Lila only knew the tip of the sordid iceberg.

I slowly limped up the stairs back to my apartment. I had totally forgotten about Me-Me. She was sitting in the living room and had put her dress back on. She had been crying.

"I am sooo sorry," she sobbed, "You think she will listen if I talk to her?"

"…No. Are you going to be alright?"

"Heh. Yeah. I'm fine. I'm sorry for screwing everything up. I was just feeling so lonely last night and you had always been there for me. I…I just needed someone to make me feel good about myself."

"Me-Me, you don't need anyone to make you feel good about yourself. You are a beautiful, strong black woman who can take care of herself…Heh. Maybe I should ease up on trying to shelter and protect you as much as I do…I've always considered you as just my lil' sis, but you're not. You are a woman. I've come to realize that. And I'm still sorry for letting what happened happen last night."

"Don't apologize, Reg. Okay? It was wonderful. There's nothing to apologize for. If I'm not mistaken, there were *two* consenting adults in there. I knew what I was doing. You know what?"

"What?"

"I don't hold you responsible for what happened to Jo-Jo. Never did. You need to forgive yourself, Reggie. There was nothing you could have done, except wind up in the ground with him. Y'know…I didn't just stop growing the day he was shot. I think your image of me became frozen that day."

"Not anymore, Me-Me. Not anymore," I said as I gave her a hug. It was a goodbye of sorts…but a hello to a new friendship between two adults.

"Can you give me a ride home now?" she asked as she put her specs back on.

"Yeah. Let me put some clothes on first." I started limping toward the bedroom.

"Uh…Reg?"

"Yeah, Me-Me?"

"What happened to you out there? You've got bruises on your back."

"…Nothing."

On my way to the bedroom, I picked up the gift-wrapped box Lila had dropped.

I sat on the bed and opened it slowly. It was a sno-globe with a miniature view of downtown Dallas in it. There was a note attached and I began crying as I read it.

It read:

Dear Champ,

Just bought this little trinket to let you know that you were on my mind the entire time I was here in Dallas. While I was gone, I may not have been in touch with you as much as I would have liked, but you were always in my thoughts and in my heart. Perhaps we'll grow old and gray together and will have this reminder of the wild, crazy times that we put behind us.

Love Always,

Lila

53 Neal Wallace

I hadn't seen Me-Me since last Monday. We were on different schedules for most of last week and she had called in sick the last two nights. She was probably hung over from that weekend party she had attended down in Sugarland with Reggie. She returned to work Wednesday evening and I made it a point to holler at her.

"Normally, I just listen for your humming to find you," I said as I walked out onto the restaurant floor from the kitchen. I was going on break.

"Heh. Normally I feel like humming."

"So, how was the party? See anybody famous?"

"No. Just a bunch of assholes," she said with a look that was a mixture of disgust and sadness.

"Are you alright?"

"Never felt better," she muttered aloud sarcastically.

"Oh. Well, I'm going on break. Talk to you later?"

"Yeah."

I turned and began walking to our break area.

"Neal," she called out at the last minute.

"Yeah?"

"You got time to talk?"

"For you? Of course."

"I'll be on break in five."

"Alright."

Me-Me joined me at the table while I drank a Sprite with a lemon in it.

"What's up? You look like you're the one who wants to take a road trip to Galveston this time. Something happen at the party?"

"Heh. You could say that. That motherfucker, Al, tried to get physical with me. I shoulda known better."

"He tried to rape you?" I whispered in disbelief. I was feeling the rage welling up inside of me instinctively.

"*Tried* is the key word. He was taken care of."

"Reggie?"

"Yep. He saved the day. Let's just say we're off Al's party list from now on."

"Whew. I was about to ask for this Al's address. Reggie's the man though. You sure you're okay? Have you called the police?"

"No, I'll be fine. That turned out to be one of the milder parts of the night."

"Speaking of parties…We're having a get-together at the house this weekend. It won't be as glitzy as Al's, but I can promise that it won't have that kind of drama either. I know you and my wife aren't best friends, but I'm sure she won't mind if you come. What do ya say? Reggie and Lila are coming too."

"Heh," Me-Me laughed, "Um. That's what I left out. If Lila and Reggie are there, I don't think Lila would want to see me."

"Why? Did something happen between you and Lila? She's back?"

"Oooh, she's back alright. Nothing happened between me and her, but…rather between me and…Reggie," she finished with an embarrassed whisper.

"What??!!" I asked in sheer disbelief. "Are you saying what I think you're saying?"

"Shhhh! Not so loud…Yeah. Lila walked in on…on…on us…in the bed," she said as her eyes started watering at the memory.

"That bum," I mumbled as I fumed.

"It wasn't his fault, Neal. I wanted to sleep with him. Hell…it's something I've always wanted to do, I guess. Now I've ruined his life and his future with Lila."

"That's bullshit, Me-Me!" I snarled, "He's my friend and you've been around him even longer, but you don't know this guy. I've personally seen some of the shit he's made women do. He…he's got a way of getting in women's heads. Damn. I've gotta have a talk with my boy, next time I see him. He was wrong for doing this to you." The feelings I was experiencing were unsettling and I tried to ignore them.

"Neal! He didn't do anything to me! I told you that already. Damn. I wish I wouldn't have told you now. Why are you so hot-headed all of a sudden? You were calmer when I mentioned Al."

"…That's not true. Sorry about blowing up like that, Me-Me. I'm…I'm just rattled by all of this. That's all. I should be listening instead of judging. So…so what happened with Lila?"

"Nothing. She left, Reggie ran after her, I put on my clothes, and then he came back. That's all. I mean…there was more to how it happened, but I don't feel comfortable going there. Maybe they can patch things up. I even offered to talk to her for him. He really loves her."

Damn. Just like I had said. Reggie must've messed with Me-Me's head and probably whispered some sweet nothings in her ear and shit. I guess he couldn't leave any stone unturned in his conquests. I kept my mouth shut, but I was still going to let him have it.

I had tried to reach Lila all week, but she was screening her calls. I went so far as to try to charm my way past the female security guard at Lila's place, but had no luck. She had probably told the guard about me. I tried to focus on my career that was suddenly in jeopardy from somebody within the company, but found myself placing several unreturned calls to Casey Warner and Associates for her.

When I woke to pouring rain and thunderstorms on Thursday, I knew what I had to do if I was ever to have a decent night's sleep again. I called in sick to Stratford Circle for a start, then walked to my bathroom where I stared at myself in the mirror for several minutes. I put the shower running, then slowly walked to my closet to find something to wear.

I arrived at LBJ General Hospital, which used to be known around here as Sam Houston Hospital, by taxicab and paid the driver extra to wait for me. The rain was only getting worse and I had to open my umbrella to keep somewhat dry. I approached the information desk for the room number, then took the elevator up. I confirmed her condition as stable at the nurses station and was informed that no visitors were allowed still. She was going to live and that was most important to me. There were people milling about on the floor who looked like they could have been relatives, but I didn't ask. I got directions to the hospital florist, then moved on. The cabby wasn't going to stay much longer. As I walked, I said a silent prayer.

"Will that be all?" the florist asked as he completed the room delivery form for the get-well bouquet.

"Yes."

"And the patient's name?"

"Holliday."

"…And do they have a first name?"

"I'm sorry. It's Trina. Trina Holliday."

"And do you want to include a note or something?"

"No. Just include this envelope. She'll know who it's from," I said as I handed over the sealed envelope containing nine hundred dollars cash. The rest was spent already, but this was better than nothing.

I had heard about Trina last night. Apparently she had tried to commit suicide by driving head-on into another car. I don't even know if that had anything to do with me, but it was another life scarred by my touch nonetheless.

"Where to next?" the West African cabby asked as I ran in from the rain.

"Downtown. Wells Fargo Building."

The yellow cab splashed through the puddles as we approached Lila's office building. If the rain continued at this pace, there was going to be some local flooding. I paid the cabby extra again to wait for me and ran past the large red, white, and blue outdoor sculpture and into the building.

I had been to Lila's office before, so I knew it had an outer lobby and an inner one for security purposes. The receptionist greeted me as if she knew me when I walked up.

"I'm sorry, Mr. Collins," she said after calling to the back, "Ms. Reed is currently out of the office and I don't know what time she will return." Her answer was too pat. I doubted that she had even called Lila's office in back.

"It's okay. We talked earlier and she's expecting me. I called her on my way up," I said with a wink. Her hesitation confirmed that Lila was here. She reached to make a real call to Lila in back as I smiled on.

She had just started talking to someone on the other end of the line when the outer lobby door opened up. Two attorneys were leaving out for an early lunch. I made a mad dash for the door before it closed and was into the inner office right as the receptionist screamed out. The two attorneys turned to stop me, but I shoved them aside. I desperately tried to find Lila's office from memory before security caught up with me. When I saw the gray uniforms at the other end of the hallway coming toward me, I knew my time was up.

I ran past Lila's office and then right into it by luck. She was sitting in a leather chair behind her large mahogany desk and was looking like she expected me. I didn't say she looked happy…just like she was expecting me.

"Lila! I have to talk to you. Please."

"I don't want to hear it."

"Please. If we ever had anything…"

"Okay. I'll give you five minutes. My mind is made up though. After that you are leaving," she said while motioning to the two burly security guards who overheard her time limit. They nodded and moved back into the hallway.

I could tell it was hurting her to look at me. I had never seen her look this pained before.

"You look like shit, Reggie. Of course, I feel like shit on the inside so I guess we're even."

"Haven't been sleeping well. Things have been crazy. At work too. Someone started a rumor that I've been passing confidential information to you."

"Ha! That's a laugh. I'll bet it was that 'hot tamale'. She looks like a schemer."

"I'm not here to talk about Loretta…or anyone else. I love you, Lila…with all my heart."

"What about Me-Me?"

"What about her? That was an accident. We're not like that. That's all it was. You have to believe me."

"An *accident*. Hmmm," she repeated as she swivelled in her chair, "An accident that it happened…or an accident that you two were caught?"

"Please. That was the only time…ever. Me-Me's even willing to talk to you. You want me to call her?"

"No. Reggie…it's over. When I realized that I couldn't do the bed-buddy thing with you anymore, I came clean. I gave you over two weeks to get your stuff in order or to decide on what you wanted to do. I just realized that I can't handle life with you when I saw what I saw."

"Lila…that's behind me. All that stuff. The women are all gone…for you."

"That's the problem Reg. They have to be gone for you. Otherwise, they would have found themselves creeping into our life if we would have decided to have one…together."

"I had a present at my apartment for you. Umm. I didn't get a chance to give it to you though," I said as I pulled out the romance novel I had purchased for her in New Orleans. She took it in her hand, which was a good sign.

"Thank you. It's still over."

"Lila, I—"

"Reggie, I may be moving."

"What?"

"Back to Dallas. My mother is dying, Reg. I think there's a greater need for me up there than there is here. Heh. The funny thing is…I couldn't get you out of my head…even with all that going on."

"Yeah. I read your note that came with the sno-globe. Lila, give me another chance and I will show you that we can have that life…that we can grow old and gray together."

"It's stupid of me to admit this, but some part of me will probably always love you. You're no good for me though. Goodbye, Champ. Please leave."

"Lila…I can't…I can't do that," I said as my heart was realizing what was happening. "Please."

"Sorry about knocking you down on the parking lot, but I wanted you to hurt the way I was at the time. Are you okay?"

"Yeah," I said as I wept in the chair across the desk from her. "I'm...I'm okay."

"Good. Now please leave," she said as she motioned for security to return. She then turned her back to me and put her hands over her face to hide her tears.

"Lila. Lila. Don't do this. Please," I begged as security grabbed me by both arms. "Lila, I love you!" She didn't respond and security proceeded to drag me out. I tried to resist, but was emotionally and physically drained and didn't have much success.

I was escorted down to the street by the goons and thrown out onto the sidewalk in the middle of the rain. The downpour soaked me to the bone and washed my tears away as they dropped from my eyes. My umbrella was left in the cab...and even it had left me. If I weren't so miserable, I would have laughed.

I tried to be hard and suck it up, but it didn't work this time. A woman had actually succeeded in making me cry. My dad's words about having to be harder than life came to mind. Heh. The funny thing about being hard is that sometimes you are so hard that you become brittle...and then shatter. My hopes for the love of my life had been shattered.

Saturday had arrived and I was in the kitchen frying up catfish for the party. I had mowed the lawn at the crack of dawn while Shenita cleaned the house. Her friend, Ramona and Ramona's husband, Rico, were bringing baked macaroni tonight. Besides Ramona and Rico, we really didn't associate with many of our neighbors since moving here, but Shenita had met a pair of newlyweds recently and had invited them as well. They were going to be interesting to meet. On the other hand, there was my pops, whose encounter with I was not looking forward to in the least.

I was enjoying the weekend nonetheless, as it was the first of many that I would be off. Starting Monday, I was going to be working the day shift at Mirage thus giving me free weekends most of the time. Shenita would have been thrilled except that we now had to figure out the car situation for our jobs, since I was going to be due at work around ten or eleven every weekday. I was sure we would have it out tomorrow night over the car, but I wasn't going to let it intrude on our Saturday.

"You call my pops?" I asked Shenita as she looked over my shoulder at the frying fish.

"Yeah. While you were cutting the grass. You doing anything else besides the fish?"

"Yeah. This sauce I made up. What'd my pops say?"

"That he's comin'."

"Are you gonna pick him up?"

"Nah. He said he's drivin'. I gave him directions though."

"What?? Nah! Nah! Tell me he's not drivin'."

"Why?"

"Because he's a menace on wheels, Shenita!" I said as I battered another piece of fish.

"I don't know how he still has his license. You know what this means?"

"No, but I'm sure you're going to tell me," she replied while rolling her eyes.

"It's going to be dark. Someone's gonna have to drive him home."

"…Or he can spend the night," Shenita added to my dismay.

Rico and Ramona were the first to arrive as they lived in our cul-de-sac. Rico worked for West-Tel, the main rival of Shenita's company. As West-Tel paid more than Questcom, I'm sure Ramona had him putting out feelers for a job opening for Shenita over there. We had them put the baked macaroni on the dining room table. Shenita kept them entertained while I finished up the fish.

It was dusk when the familiar faded-red Crown Victoria that was my pops' came rolling slowly into our cul-de-sac. That car was his gift for best sales back at the dealership years ago and was still his prized possession, even with all the scrapes, dings, and dents it had now. In my opinion, it was probably prized even more than his family.

My pops parked next to the curb in front of our house rather than pulling into the driveway and was wearing his favorite blue polyester shirt and black slacks from years gone by. His walk was a little slower than I remember and it made me wonder about his health.

"Hey, boy," my pops said as he walked up the driveway.

"Hey," I replied as I met him in the driveway and we stood face to face. I still had no handshake or hug for him, but he was welcome in my home. It was going to take most of the night for me to feel any warmth for him.

"Boy, you gain some more weight?"

"Heh. Probably. I do love food."

"Just like your mother. God rest her soul. I do miss her. Sometimes, I think all the good in you came from her. I've always been the bitter sort."

"Nice of you to admit it, pops. Want to see the house?"

I introduced my pops to Rico and Ramona, and then Shenita took over and gave him the house tour. She got along better with him and I still had to wrap up things in the kitchen.

As much as Shenita hated it, I put on my Zapp CD to loosen things up while she was upstairs with my pops. Heh. Nothing like *More Bounce* to bring out the "colored" in us "colored folk". Ramona and Rico were already starting down memory lane with their old dances on that number when the newlyweds arrived.

I answered the door and met Andre and Vivian for the first time. Both of them were short and petite, like they were made for each other. Andre was a brother, but looked like he had some Filipino mixed in. Vivian was a brown-haired sister with braces who still had that starry-eyed newlywed look on her face. I silently wished them luck on keeping the fires alive. With them, they brought a green bean casserole and a carrot cake for dessert.

We arranged everything on the table and blessed the meal before everyone started serving themselves. Shenita was playing the faithful daughter-in-law and fixed my pops' plate. If only the three of us could coexist like this on a daily basis.

"Where's Reggie?" Shenita quietly asked as we ate from our plates on the sofa.

"I don't know," I gruffly replied. I still hadn't had my talk with him about Me-Me.

"What's wrong with *you?*"

"Nothing."

"Is Lila coming with him?"

"Why don't you ask him?" I answered with a question of my own right as the doorbell rang probably announcing his arrival.

"Well hello."

"Sup, Nita," I replied. I was really having second thoughts about showing up now.

"We thought you weren't going to make it."

"Almost didn't. Believe me...I didn't make it on your account."

"Aww, Reg. Why so hostile? Was it...that...bad?" she whispered in a tone that I had recently become very familiar with.

"Don't fuck with me. You have no clue what kind of mood I'm in."

"Excuuuse me. Where's Lila?"

"Are you going to let me in the door before your hubby becomes suspicious?"

"...You didn't come here to tell him, did you?" she asked with a sudden fear in her voice.

"Thought about it. You want me to?"

"Boy, no!"

"Oh, so now you suddenly care. You weren't too concerned in the garage."

"Shhh. Keep your voice down. Come in," she said as she hurried me into the house and let out a fake laugh for the rest of the house to hear.

I had seriously planned on not attending my boy's get-together, after my heart being ripped out and recycled. I changed my mind, as I didn't want to be rude and was afraid of what I would do if left alone for too long over the weekend. Once I had changed my mind, I had the dilemma of whether or not to come clean with Neal about the garage romp with his wife. I decided to leave well enough alone. I didn't want to hurt Neal and even with the bullshit, there was a chance for the Wallaces still. It was one of those times for me to suck it up and put stuff behind me.

"Shenita," I said as she was turning to walk off, "Here. These are for you and Neal."

She took the two tickets to Marc Anthony at the Pavilion and eyed them, then me.

"I hope the two of you have a good time. Please. Try."

Shenita squinted as if not knowing what to make of me then let out a, "Thank you".

She proceeded to give introductions from across the room and left me to circulate. I saw Neal and his father having a long over-due talk and gave him a nod. I would holler at him later, but was surprised by his less-than-enthusiastic look when he nodded back. Maybe he had something on his mind, maybe I was making too much of it.

I fixed myself a plate of food, then sat with their neighbors, Rico and Ramona. The two of them were cool, except that I was picking up vibes from Ramona. She was going to be the next to pull a "Shenita" with somebody out there. In my "old days", I probably would have been willing to be the one. I didn't really know Rico, so it would have been fair game. Poor guy. There was some-body out there that hadn't been through my shit and would be receptive to Ramona's call. I excused myself and moved on to meet the other couple. I could see Shenita showing the Pavilion tickets to Neal as she fluttered about in front of his father like a loving wife.

It was a totally positive vibe with the short newlyweds. You could see the love in their eyes as they sipped their wine. It turned out I knew some cousins of the dude, Andre. One of them worked at the Stratford Circle claims office in Conroe.

I went to the kitchen to pour myself a glass of Pepsi as Shenita began playing their Lucy Pearl CD on the stereo. The other couples got up and started dancing and Shenita made her father-in-law feel good by dancing with him. I was getting my laugh-on at Neal's old man catching Soul Train flashbacks when Neal walked up with the tickets in his hand.

"Thanks, bro," he said as we gave each other a brief, manly hug.

"No prob, dawg. How ya been?"

"Okay, okay. This is going to be a nice concert. Shenita loves Latin music."

"Yeah. I had them already, but my plans changed. Sorry I rushed you off the other day at my job, Neal."

"That's alright. You've gotta do what you gotta do. Reg, I need to talk with you about something. Want another drink first?"

"Nah. It's just Pepsi."

"Huh? *You?*"

"Yeah. Been drinking too much lately. Had to cut it out."

"Oh?" Neal asked with a curious look. He motioned for me to join him at the kitchen table. There was an uncomfortable manner about him.

"That drinking's got you in trouble recently, huh?" he asked while staring me straight in the eye. I mean…you were drunk that night, right?"

"…What are you getting at?" I asked with uncertainty.

"How could you, man??!!" Neal roared at me as he pounded his fist on the table. I was beginning to feel very warm and uncomfortable. Had Shenita flipped the script and filled him in to paint me as the villain? I looked toward the others in the house, but they were still dancing and ignorant of what was going down. I tried to get a quick read off Shenita, but she was busy dancing too.

"What are you talking about, bro?"

"Man, you know damn well what I'm talking about!"

"You were drinking and you slept with her! I thought better of you…no matter what anyone said. That was low! What kind of a man are you??"

"Um…look. Neal…I'm sorry. I'll admit it. I was drinking a lot that night, hell we all were drinking, but I didn't initiate it. I swear. I should have told you and I'm sorry."

I bowed my head down at the table in shame. I guess Shenita did flip the script on me, but Neal was taking this waaay better than I expected. Until...

"You didn't initiate it? Please! That's the same thing she said, but I know better. And what...do...you mean '*we* were all drinking'?"

"You know...at the Hyatt that night. I still should have told y...*Uh, Neal?* Just what are *you* talking about?" I asked as I had a feeling that we were in the same store, but in different departments. Neal's face was turning red and trembling all of a sudden. I made a quick confused look toward Shenita, then back at Neal as my eyes widened. Oh shit, oh shit.

"...Me-Me," he answered in a low tone. The quiet before the storm. Neal cut a look at Shenita, who happened to be turning around, that froze her dead in her tracks. I don't recall hearing any music from that point on. Shenita's smile disappeared and was replaced with a look of terror I had never seen before as she looked back and forth between Neal and I.

As the table between us was flung aside and Neal came at me, the last thing I was thinking about before seeing bluish flashes of lightning was, "How could Me-Me tell him about what happened between us?" Heh. Funny ain't it?

57 Neal Wallace

"Boy, I will kill you!!!!" I screamed at the top of my lungs. The kitchen table had already landed with a crash by the dishwasher. My forearm was stinging from swatting it like that, but nothing compared to the pain I was about to inflict. I hadn't felt anger like this since...well...since never, I guess.

I thought Reggie would put up more of a fight. Hell, I *wanted* him to put up more of a fight. He simply closed his eyes as my right crashed upside his head, then my left. The music was still playing, but some of the women were screaming now. Reggie fell onto the kitchen floor in a heap before his instincts to fight back kicked in. He rushed me and tried to take me off my feet, but I just tossed him up against the kitchen door.

Glass went flying as the door window shattered under the force of Reggie's weight.

I felt Rico's hand reaching to grab me, but I shoved him away and gave him a look that dared him to try something stupid like that again.

"Stop it!" Shenita shouted above all the noise as she ran around screaming in a panic. I paused to look at her once as I caught my breath. Her ass was next.

"...Sorry. Sorry," came out of Reggie's busted lip as he tried to steady himself.

"Sorry this, bitch!" I screamed as I punched him dead in the nose, sending his head flying back into the glass. Reggie fell down onto the floor amidst all the glass, giving me a chance to stomp on him.

"You havin' a good time now, you son of a bitch? Huh? Feeling real sorry now, huh?"

"S…stop, bro."

"I'm not your brother, you piece of shit! Get up!!"

"Neal, stop it!" Shenita screamed as she got in my face. Reggie's eye was swelling shut as he crawled on the floor behind her. He was still blubbering apologies while trying to breathe.

"You fuckin' ho. How could you?"

"Stop making a fool of yourself," she chose to say instead of answering me. Life had been bad between us, but I had no idea. I was feeling like such a fool right now. The thought of Shenita laughing at me behind my back while fucking my best friend sent me into a rage again.

"Bitch! Who in the fuck do you think you are? I loved you!" I belted out as I reared up before her. Shenita tried to outscream me and hold her ground, before I took a swing and punched a hole in the wall next to her head. She had closed her eyes as she thought the wall was her head…and it almost was. She opened her eyes and ran off in a panic.

Just then, Rico and Andre tried to get me under control under encouragement from their women.

"*Step the fuck back!*" I yelled as I stuck out my hand, halting the brothers in their tracks. The two of them looked at each other, not knowing what to do. Reggie was up on his knees now and crawling across the kitchen floor. Funny. My knuckles weren't even hurting yet. I bent over and raised Reggie to his feet by his neck and put him up against the wall.

"I should kill your punk ass," I whispered with clenched teeth as I began choking him.

"Stop," he wheezed, "I…told her it was wrong. I'm sorry. Y…you gotta believe me."

"Do you ever stop? Me-Me? *My wife*? You were my boy! I …trusted you, man," I said as my rage was shifting to pain. My eyes were tearing up.

"Stop, boy," I heard as a hand landed on my shoulder. I turned to face my pops.

"Get your hands off me, old man! You don't tell me what to do anymore!"

As I released Reggie's throat and let him drop to the floor again and as everyone in the house looked on, I went eye-to-eye with my pops. It was almost as I had imagined it would be, with neither one of us budging, except that I didn't see the rage equal to mine. In my pops' weathered eyes, I only saw remembrance...and familiarity. He was seeing something in me that he had lived with for all too long...and it saddened him.

"I'm sorry," was all that he uttered as he nodded in acknowledgment. "Let him go, boy."

I looked into my pops eyes further for any sign of that bitterness to combat at last, but couldn't find it. I sighed as I rubbed my head and stepped aside, letting Rico and Andre pull Reggie to safety and beyond my reach.

"Get him outta here. Hell...everybody get the fuck out! Now! Party over!" As if they didn't know. Ramona was the first one out the door and was talking up a storm on her way out. We would be the talk of the neighborhood for the next twelve years. Fuck it.

The newlyweds said some quiet, polite good-byes to Shenita as she stood by the front door, arms folded and looking rattled. Rico was outside attending to a disrupted Reggie.

"You can go too, pops," I said as I unconsciously extended my hand to him. "Thanks. For stopping me."

"I don't want no thanks, boy. I'm your father...and I was just stopping you from becoming something awful like me. I know you hate me, boy. I see it in your eyes, in your voice, I feel it deep in here," he said as he put his fingers on his chest.

"But you know what?" he continued, "You can never hate me as much as I hate myself. Tell you what...my ass can't drive at night. I'm gonna stay put if you don't mind...just to keep an eye on things."

"…Alright. But I'm not going to hit her, if that's what you're thinking. Feel free to spend the night."

Shenita was sitting down at the foot of the stairwell and wiping the tears from her eyes. Makeup was running down her face and she was looking toward the front door that was now closed.

"Upstairs," I said as I walked up to her.

She just turned and looked at me like I was stupid.

"Scared, baby? Heh. I thought you had brass balls. We need to talk…alone. Now."

58 Neal Wallace

Shenita cautiously watched me over her shoulder as she walked up the stairs. I wanted to yank her ass down them, but was through dishing out pain for the night. I could hear my pops trying to clean up the broken glass in the kitchen. I didn't care how the house looked and probably never would again. It could all go to hell. My whole world was shit. Betrayal by one's wife and best friend can really ruin someone's day.

"Close the door," I said with an eerie calmness after walking into the bedroom past her. I didn't hear the usual lip smacking that came along with her doing something she didn't want to do. I think she was spooked at the thought of being alone with me. I took some perverse pleasure in finally having this hellcat in check. It was a small consolation for the hurt I was enduring though.

"Why do we have to talk up here?" she asked as she stood by the armoire and out of my reach.

"Why, Shenita?"

"What do you mean?"

"Don't fuck with me! Was New Orleans the only time or have the two of you been playin' me for a fuckin' fool all these years?"

Shenita gave up her stalling tactics and quietly replied, "No. That was it."

"Awww, you sound sad, baby. Wanted more, huh? I guess I just wasn't what you were looking for, huh? *Huh?*…Man, man, man. I would have given my life for you, girl. I loved you, Shenita."

"…Sorry."

"Sorry my ass. I guess my stupid ass would have been in the dark forever. Is that what the two of you agreed to? When did this "happen" anyway? Where was I?"

"Don't Neal. Alright?"

"No. I want to know. Don't worry. You can't hurt me anymore, woman. I'm fuckin' Superman. See the 'S' on my chest? It's probably for 'sucker' though."

"Just forget about it. Shit's all fucked up now as it is. The house, the neighbors. Oh, they're gonna be talkin' about us. The laughing stock of the neighborhood. That's us."

"That's all you care about—the people, the neighbors. You don't even care about what's most important. What about us?"

"The garage."

"Huh?"

"The parking garage. You said you wanted to know, so there. Your 'boy' fucked my brains out in the parking garage. It was incredible. Happy? Is that what you wanted to hear?"

"I…I…"

"I screamed like I never did before…and loved every minute of it," she giggled to herself as she got her courage up enough to move away from the armoire.

"…When you left to get some air that night. Bitch." I had that crazy feeling coming back, but still wasn't going to strike a lady…or my wife.

"Whatever," she said with that familiar smack of her lips.

"Did you ever love me? Don't think I want to get back together or anything. I just want to know if you ever did, that's all."

"…No. I don't think I did. I was fond of you and you treated me so well, but…"

"Okay. I am a sucker. That's been established now. Heh. All these years. All this time I put in trying to make you happy and…all for nothing."

"I am sorry, Neal."

"Bullshit. I just beat my best friend to a pulp over a bitch that doesn't even love me. You just finished laughin' in my face about fuckin' him! Yeah, you're sorry alright. You just don't know how close you came tonight."

"Yeah. You actually grew a pair tonight. What? You were going to slap me around? Punch me too?"

"Is that what you wanted? Someone a little more abusive to you maybe? Maybe treat you like a dog? Would that have made you happy?"

"I said I don't love you. No need to drag this out. I'll call Ramona to see if I can spend the night with her and Rico."

"No. I'll leave. Besides…she might not want you around Rico," I said as I intentionally tried to hurt her.

"Where are you gonna go?"

I looked at Shenita with an amused look on my face and responded, "Like you really care. Don't worry. I'll board up the window on the kitchen door before I leave."

"You…you don't have to leave," she said as I got off the bed and began gathering clothes.

"Y'know what's so bad?" I asked as if not hearing my wife's last comment, "The newlyweds…Andre and Vivian. They shouldn't have seen this tonight and I'm to blame for most of that. This…this isn't what marriage is about. Marriage is about love, not some one-sided shit that this apparently was."

I slowed as I walked past Shenita with my gym bag. Part of me wanted to take the easy way out and try to work at returning to "normalcy", but the easy route was something I was not too accustomed to in life.

Shenita reached out with her hand to touch my shoulder, but dropped her hand to her side instead.

"Shenita, one last question. It doesn't really matter now, but I'd like to know. Who initiated it?"

She hesitated, took a breath, then shakily uttered, "Reggie. It was all his idea. He had it planned out before we even got to the hotel. I…I didn't want to at first, but he kept asking me…so I met him in the garage that night."

"Uh huh. My boy did all that?"

"Yep. Your 'boy'."

I started to say something, but decided not to. I came upon my pops in the kitchen. He had found our broom and had swept up all the glass. Bugs were flying in from outside, so I walked over to the switch and turned off the outside light. I then walked over to the front of the house and looked out the window. All was quiet on our street. Reggie's Pathfinder was gone and I could see the lights on at Ramona and Rico's. Shenita was probably on the phone with Ramona now, trying to put her spin on things and limit the gossip that was going to come about.

"Whatcha gon' do, boy?" my pops asked as he peeked out the window beside me.

"I gotta go. Just get away. I saw too much of you in me tonight…and didn't like it."

"I know. I know. I pray to God everyday that your dear mother up in Heaven will forgive me."

"She probably already has. She was always such a good soul."

"So, the missy upstairs was breakin' bread with your 'homeboy', huh?"

"Yeah, pops."

"I always thought she was so sweet. Y'know, I used to work with a Baptiste at the car dealership."

"*What*? For real?"

"Yep. Probably no relation though. Boy, I'm glad you didn't have no kids with that one."

"Heh. I'll probably never have any now."

"You never know. Funny things happen, boy."

"I'm leaving after I get some boards from the garage and seal that window up."

"Where you goin', boy?"

"Home. Back to Brookshire with you. Just for the night. It's too dark for you to be driving anyway. I'll drive. I'll check on getting a place tomorrow."

"I guess I could let you drive my car…as long as you be careful. That's my prize out there."

"I know, I know."

"Maybe tomorrow you can cook me some of that fancy shit you be cookin' for them white folks."

229

59 Reggie Collins

I drove home from Neal's house that night with one good eye. I had taken my shirt off to wipe the blood off as that guy, Andre, helped me to my ride. Not fighting back against Neal's big ass was probably one of the hardest things I had ever done. Not that I would have been able to beat him anyway, but just taking the ass kicking was not a pleasant experience. I deserved it. All of it.

I didn't take any calls Sunday. Just iced my face down and slept. I had showered before, but there were still little slivers of glass in my hair. I could see the glass sparkling when I turned my head under the bathroom light by the mirror. I placed one call to Lila's number at home to find it had been changed to a *non-published number*.

I was too swollen and achy to go to work when Monday arrived and didn't feel comfortable until Wednesday. My sick leave was dwindling to nothing over a period of less than two weeks.

My left eye was still swollen and looking like an armadillo when I arrived at work. I played it off by wearing shades and saying that a wasp had stung me. There were still whispers throughout as I walked toward my office. I saw Loretta talking by the copier with another rep and gave them a little wave. They continued their conversation, but I could feel Loretta's eyes watching my every move.

My usual comfort zone disappeared when I came upon Ruby's empty desk. It turned out she had been transferred to our Katy Freeway office while I was "indisposed". My one security blanket here had been removed and I was flying blind. I went on in my office rather than let everyone on the floor see that I was visibly shaken. I waited for my computer to boot up and then reviewed the intercompany E-mail to bring myself up to speed on everything.

"Reggie," Sam said interrupting my concentration, "you busy?"

"Nah, Sam. It's good to see you. C'mon in. Have a seat."

"So, you heard about Ruby?"

"Yeah. Just now. It's my fault though. I should have been checking in."

"What's wrong with your eye?"

"Oh. Wasp sting. The swelling's finally starting to go down."

"Reminds me of my eye when I got drunk one night and entered this toughman competition in Corpus Christi."

"Oh. Sorry I've been in and out so much. How have things been…besides with Ruby moving on?"

"Hectic. Um…Reggie. I know you've heard about the rumors around here. I just wanted to let you know that I don't believe that stuff about you leaking company information."

"Thanks, Sam. I just try not to let it get to me." Lord knows I had enough problems to choose from on any given day as my sore face was reminding me.

"I also want to let you know that I didn't have anything to do with those rumors about you and your lady friend."

"…Okay," I replied. I was bursting at the seams to ask him if he knew who it was then, but his face was showing that he was already way too uncomfortable, so I let it go.

Another week passed and I was still just numb with my surroundings at work. I had a new secretary, an abrasive old cuss of a woman named Dora who lacked people skills. I hadn't been in contact with Neal or Me-Me for obvious reasons and had given up on trying to get through to Lila. I was all alone…and feeling weak and needy. Easy pickings.

It was a late stormy Wednesday evening. I was thinking about what to replace a painting in my office with when my latest life-changing event strolled on in.

"Reggie."

"Huh?"

"You spend so much time in your office these days. What's wrong?" Loretta asked with a genuinely concerned look across her face.

"Easier to just concentrate on work and stay out of trouble."

"But that's not the real you."

"Heh. Excuse my bluntness, but what do you know about the *real me* anyway?"

"I know it's almost six o'clock and it's raining cats and dogs. And you're still in this dreary office. That's not you," she said as she made herself comfortable on my desk.

"Yeah. I'd rather be in bed right now. I am so tired…of everything. What about you? What are you still doing here, Ms. Juarez? Forgot your umbrella?"

"No. I just don't feel like leaving here…without you."

"Heh. Loretta. I'm not in the mood for this. Why don't you get out of here? Go on. Even if we went somewhere and hung out, I wouldn't be good company."

"Still with her, huh?"

"Who?"

"That attorney."

"No."

"Did your face have something to do with that?"

"What are you talking about, Loretta?"

"Please. I grew up in a hotheaded Latin family with three brothers. I know all about faces that looked like yours did. That was no wasp sting."

"Nah. It didn't have anything to do with her."

"Need somebody to talk to?"

"You don't give up."

"Nope. Not when it's something I want."

"I'm bad for everyone. Run. Run and don't look back," I said with a laugh as I leaned back in my chair.

"No, Reggie. I don't think you're bad at all. You just need someone who understands you and doesn't want you to be something you're not."

I hadn't noticed, but my finger was resting on the keyboard of my computer. The screen was filled with meaningless gibberish when I finally looked. Loretta's web was finally catching hold as my resistance was all but spent. I had started focusing on her more intensely with each word. Her eyes, her lips, her voice, the way her chest rose with each breath, were beginning to get me aroused.

"Get out of here, girl," I pleaded as I contemplated the alternative.

"Not without you."

"I'm not going anywhere, Loretta. I'll probably be here another hour. Bye!"

"Then I guess I'm staying too," she said just before she stood up and walked over to my office door and closed it.

"*Click*" went the lock on my office door right as lightning flashed outside and the office lights dimmed.

60 Reggie Collins

"Stop," I said as Loretta walked toward me. Our emergency power had kicked on as the bad weather had temporarily knocked the electricity out in our area. My computer terminal had blinked off and was just now rebooting.

"You don't mean it," she said as she began undoing one button at a time on her red blouse, which revealed a white-laced bra underneath. Her bronze breasts were heaving up out of them. I had fantasized about a moment like this with Loretta several times, but with all the changes in my life, this just didn't feel right. I was still her boss and couldn't put myself in this kind of position.

"I do mean it. Stop," I said as I clung to my last shreds of decency. There was a war going on inside me.

"You mean stop undressing? Why? You want to do it yourself?"

She still had one button left on her blouse and left it alone to undo her black full-leg pants that dropped to the floor of my office.

"Loretta. I won't do this. Get out of my office. Now."

"You don't me—"

"I love her. She's gone, but I love Lila still. And always will. She's the only woman I've ever loved. I've done a lot of rotten and wrong things in my life, especially lately, but as long as I have just a tiny hope for a future with her…I have to do things right with no more fuck-ups."

"*So, I'm a fuck-up*?? Is that what you consider me??" Loretta said with a trace of an accent in her pissed-off voice.

"No. You are a beautiful headstrong woman whose pants I've been dying to get in. Y'see…I'm the fuck-up…but nothing is going to happen between us. Not right now, not ever. Please…just go. I won't bring up any of this. Just leave."

Just then, the regular power was restored and the building lights came back up to full brightness. Loretta stood looking confused at me, as if this was the first time she had been in this position. To give myself further strength, I turned around, faced my monitor and went back to work. I heard Loretta mumbling curse words as she put her clothes back on and stormed out my office door.

I locked the office up that night around eight and drove slowly in the rain to my lonely apartment. That night, as I had a Stouffers TV dinner with a glass of wine and relaxed to my Boney James CD, I listened to my messages from the answering service. Me-Me had called for me. She was wondering how I was doing. From her voice, I couldn't tell if Neal had told her about Shenita and me. I still wasn't ready to talk. I deleted the message, finished my meal, and then prepared for bed. Tomorrow was another day at the office.

Thursday, I thought, would bring awkwardness in dealing with Loretta after our late night face-off. I said my hellos to Sam, Doris, and my new secretary, cranky Dora and went straight to my office that was becoming a second home lately. Loretta wasn't at her desk when I walked by, so that had spared me some uneasiness. As I dwelled on that fact, my mood changed. Had something happened to her last night? I had walked back out to ask Dora about her when Loretta came bopping down the aisle all smiles and sunbeams.

After what she wore last night, I wasn't expecting the business casual look of the traditional green and white golf shirt and khaki pants. This attire was probably best though. She gave a cheerful hello to me before sitting at her desk. I wondered if this perky demeanor hid any animosity and resentment from my rejection, but decided not to dwell on things I had no control over.

I hadn't been seated no more than five minutes when Loretta walked in. She was still all-smiles.

"How are you?"

"Fine. Just fine," she answered with that smile that I could tell was a fake one now.

"So, what's up?"

"A proposal. Can I close the door?"

"I would prefer that you not," I answered with one raised eyebrow.

"Very well. I want to run something by you to see what your thoughts are."

"Okay," I said, as it sounded work-related.

"Let's say you give me the highest raise possible on my next salary review, push for my promotion to supervisor within a year, and we forget about last night and start over again...tonight. At my place. Around nine?"

I sat there speechless. I was shocked at the ease with which she had just laid this shit out before me. Maybe I should have let her close the door.

"You're kidding. Tell me you're kidding."

"Look into my eyes, boss. Tell me I'm joking," she said coldly with arms folded.

"And the alternative?"

"Let's just say that it would be a lot *less* enjoyable."

"Are you crazy? Are you fuckin' crazy? You're a good rep and have a good future, but if you think I would let you blackmail me...then you need to think again."

"Is that your final answer?"

"*Is that my final answer*?? This isn't a fuckin' gameshow!" I snarled under my breath at her.

"Suit yourself," she said with that false perkiness before walking back out.

Fuck. She was the one who started the rumor about my passing stuff on to Lila. It had to be. I thought Loretta was just trying to be a player, but I was wrong about the game. Dead wrong.

61 Reggie Collins

The very next day, Loretta wasn't there and Bob Briceland showed up at my office. I quickly found out what the alternative was to Loretta's "proposal". She didn't waste any time. She had accused me of sexual harassment and was demanding a nice sum of money, of course, to go away. Of course, this stirred up the earlier shit about my leaking secrets to Lila.

This led to a wonderful six months of depositions, testimony, and all around misery at the office. Eventually, Loretta was given a third of what she wanted and disappeared into the sunset as America's newest almost-millionaire, after attorney fees of course. My loyal former secretary, Ruby, had called me during the mess and had offered to testify on my behalf that she had overheard Loretta planning the whole thing. Ruby would have been lying and I thanked her, but told her to stay out of the whole thing. There was no point in ruining her career as well.

Mine? My career with Stratford Circle was in the tank after that. I lost my supervisor job and was moved to the Conroe office where the cousin of Neal and Shenita's neighbor, Andre worked. Andre's cousin had heard about the incident at Neal's house thus giving me no escape. I did escape one day. I just disappeared into the sunset myself and never looked back. For some that would be hard, but for me it was easy.

Before I left the company, I had done some checking. In hindsight, I should have checked Loretta's background more thoroughly in the beginning. An off-the-record check would have revealed that her move to Houston from LA had involved some similar strangeness, but it was all too late now. It had been too late for me long ago.

Word got back to me on my visits to Houston that Neal and Shenita were separated...and that Me-Me had a baby. I guess Neal didn't waste any time getting that kid he always wanted. The important thing was for them to be happy.

62 Neal Wallace

It was a few years before I saw Reggie again. Shenita and I had tried counseling, but that was pointless. Our divorce had been final for a year now and I was finally at peace.

Our house was sold and due to the skyrocketing property values in our area, we actually made a profit off the sale. I took my portion and paid off some debt. Shenita got the Stratus and all the furniture. She finally convinced Kelly to move to Houston with her and they got an apartment together. My hard feelings toward my former wife gradually faded away, but I still kept my distance.

I had lived with my pops until moving into my current place. I live upstairs over Lullaby's, my restaurant/supper club. After paying some of my debt off, I found I had enough left over to pursue my dream. I found an old store in Third Ward on Elgin and opened Lullaby's last year to the public. It took some hard work and the location isn't prime, but it's mine and I am finally happy. Some of the food critics from the Chronicle remembered me from Mirage and even gave my new place a mention in the paper. I put that clipping up on the kitchen wall next to my first.

Running a restaurant is so different from being just a chef. I brushed up on my managerial skills with books from the library and have taken risks that have paid off so far. I have a live band that plays every night and managed to get some of my co-workers from Mirage to trust in me. Tookie is waiting tables here and I'm considering making her my hostess.

Me-Me disappointed me and kept her job at Mirage, but she surprised me as well. Our friendship has continued to grow and she sings with the live band every Wednesday night. I predict, from the crowd's reaction, that Mirage may be parting with her soon. In fact, it was on a night she was performing that I saw Reggie.

I didn't recognize him at first from across the club. He was in the shadows and his hair had some sprinkles of gray in it now, which threw me off. In between watching Me-Me blow, as she was finally comfortable doing, I would look back at Reggie's table. It was an awkward moment, as I hadn't confronted all my feelings toward my boy. Eventually, I had a complimentary drink sent over. Absolut on the rocks, his favorite. As he took a sip, he gave me a nod, which I returned with a nod back. I couldn't see his face clearly, but I could swear I saw a smile.

When Me-Me finished her number to a round of applause, I waited for her to walk over. I knew she would want to see Reg. I never told her about the exact reasons behind my break-up with Shenita, as I didn't want to smudge her image of Reggie at all. They had something special and it wasn't my place to ruin it, no matter how jealous I may or may not have been. I looked back toward the table Reggie had been sitting at to point him out to Me-Me…but he was gone. He had disappeared like a ghost in the night. As I ran through the crowd toward the now-empty table, I began wondering if I had been mistaken. My doubts were gone when I got to the table.

On the small two-person table was a folded napkin with the words written on it, "I'm sorry. Reg."

I whispered aloud, "I forgive you, dawg."

I don't know why he disappeared the way he did, but he missed the chance to see a little surprise…his son. It turned out Me-Me had gotten pregnant that night she and Reggie had their romp, but she didn't realize it until right around the time Reggie up and left town. Little Joseph Reginald Bonds was one hell of a kid and I was doing my best to be a surrogate father to the two-year-old. Joseph's mom and me were still just friends and that was fine with me. There was always the future and isn't that was what life was about…the future?

Epilogue-Reggie

I pulled into the driveway. It was a cool morning in Dallas and I had to get directions from the mini-mart down the street to find the house. Her familiar red S2000 was parked in the driveway behind her parents' Buick. I had butterflies in the pit of my stomach as I unfastened my seatbelt and slowly got out.

Lila was on her knees in the garden on the side of the white frame house, helping her mother. She looked so beautiful in jeans and her work gloves. I had never seen her like this. Lila's mother saw me walking up and tapped Lila on her shoulder. Lila was startled and almost said something, but changed her mind and stood up instead.

"Hey, Champ."

"Hello, Mrs. Collins," I replied. "Here. These are for you," I said as I handed her the roses.

"You don't quit do ya?" she said as she sniffed the fresh-cut flowers.

"Not when it comes to the woman I love more than anything in this miserable world. Will you?"

"What?" she playfully asked while taking her work gloves off.

"Y'know…marry me."

"Of course, Champ. Why wouldn't I?" she said as shiny snowflakes fell and filled the sky as far as the eye could see. We embraced in a long kiss on the front lawn as I wept openly with tears of joy from the pit of my soul.

And that's how it always ends. I always go over the same scene in my head as I look at the sno-globe after shaking it. Lila's gift takes me away to a place where there is no pain or hurt.

Lila had moved back to Dallas just before I walked away from my job. I had actually taken a trip to Dallas once and had seen Lila in the yard with her mother. Everything up until the part where I pull into the driveway is true. In reality, I just parked on the side of the road and watched her with a smile until she went inside.

I love Lila more than she'll ever know. I love her enough to let her go. Last thing I heard was that she was engaged to somebody she met while visiting in Los Angeles. He's supposed to be a securities broker with Barnes & Greenwood. Probably the son of some prominent figure out there. Whoever he is, he has to be better for her than I ever was. I wish them nothing but the best.

Oh, I almost forgot to tell you. I found my mother. Well...*actually* she found me. She now lives in St. Louis. She saw my name in a newspaper article and tracked me down all the way in Texas. I flew up to meet her once...just to tell her that I forgive her...and that her boy still loves her. I planned on leaving right after that was said, but wound up sticking around for a while and telling her everything about me. *Everything*. She and I then prayed together for God to forgive me for all the wrongs I'd done and mistakes I'd made. I didn't promise anything, but I'm sure I'll be seeing her again.

As for me, I returned to Victoria, Texas where I became a youth counselor. The pay isn't great, but the rewards are worth more than any paycheck. These days, I don't have a special someone in my life, but then I also don't have a bunch of substitutes in my life either...and for the first time in my life, I'm happy just the way I am.

ABOUT THE AUTHOR

Eric E. Pete was born in Seattle, Washington and raised there as well as Lake Charles, Louisiana. He is a graduate of McNeese State University and currently resides with his family in the New Orleans area. He is a member of Delta Sigma Pi Professional Business Fraternity, the Black Writer's Alliance and the Young Leadership Council of Greater New Orleans. *Someone's In the Kitchen* is his second novel and he is currently working on his fourth novel.

If you have any comments or wish to reach Eric, he can be contacted at: heyeric@att.net.

Eric's website can visited at: www.ericpete.com.